by

Frost Kay

DEDICATION

To the man in my life that showed me what real love is. It's hard, it's gritty, but it's everything. Loving and creating a family with you has been one of my greatest accomplishments. This story is for you. You're the hero of mine.

THE KINGDOMS OF AERMIA

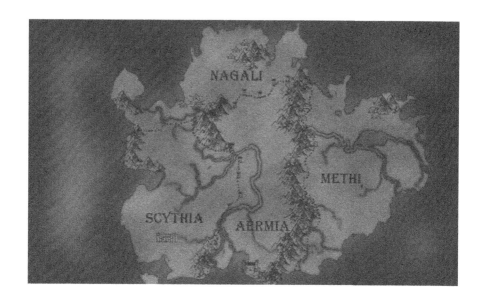

Fear is a powerful thing.

It can slap you in the face or sneak up on you, and then slowly drag you into the suffocating darkness that always seems to linger right out of sight.

It's crippling to know that it could strike at any moment, and steal the very breath from your body, the thoughts from your mind.

But there are worse things than fear.

Haunting memories. Pretty monsters. Self-destruction.

But they aren't all powerful. They can be conquered. Broken does not mean ruined.

There's strength in healing.

In love.

Sage thought she knew love.

She didn't.

Until Tehl.

CHAPTER ONE

Tehl

Stars above. She was here. In his arms.

Tehl buried his nose in his wife's hair, trembling. Sage was home.

He'd always been realistic, and, deep down, he'd felt like he'd never see her again—that he'd find her dead body somewhere. A tear dripped down his face, mingling with the dirt and sweat on his skin. Only now, as he held her in his arms, alive and breathing, could he accept that, deep down, he'd never really expected to bring her back for more than a proper burial.

"You're home," he murmured, his lips brushing the top of her damp head. His mind raced with questions, but he dismissed them, oblivious to anything but the woman in his arms.

"Home," Sage whispered into his vest, her voice weak as her body slumped against his.

He tightened his grip as she sank into him. "I'll take you home."

Her family would be beside themselves when they saw her. "Let's go home."

But Sage didn't reply. Alarmed, Tehl craned his neck and peered down at her. Face slack, lips blue, she lay heavy in his arms, her parted lips releasing small unsteady puffs of breath.

"Sage?" he asked, shaking her. His own breath caught in his chest when she didn't stir. Something wasn't right. He hoisted her and shivered as the chill from her body seeped through his clothing.

"Zachael! I need you. She's too cold." Tehl turned on his heel and then froze at the menacing snarl that ripped through the air. He slowly turned back to the leren, making eye contact with the man-eater.

"Steady, boy," the weapons master breathed from somewhere behind him. "The beast is concerned for its mistress. Speak slowly and calmly to it."

Tehl's arms trembled as he held Sage away from his body like an offering, forcing his movements to be precise. "Easy. I'm not going to hurt your mistress, but she needs to be warmed or she'll die."

Sage shivered as he spoke, her whole body trembling, punctuating his statement. The beast's ears flattened, but it remained where it was. Tehl nodded; likely, that was all he was going to get from the creature, and he didn't have time to wait for more. Ignoring every instinct that commanded him to do otherwise, he slowly turned his back to the animal, his heart thudding in his chest. Zachael detached himself from his men and warily approached, his gaze pinned over Tehl's shoulder. The weapons master pulled his attention from the leren and motioned to Tehl.

"We need to get her dry as soon as possible," Zachael murmured. He laid a hand against Sage's chest, his face grave. "Her body is dangerously cold. There's no time to lose." The weapons master yanked his cloak from his shoulders and placed it on the ground.

Tehl dropped to his knees and gently laid Sage across the cloak. She looked so fragile and blue, as though she was already dead. His breath caught at the grim thought, and he steeled himself. Life was never certain, but surely it couldn't be so cruel as to give him a few moments with her and then let her die?

He shook his head, dismissing the idea as he began to unbutton her heavy, sodden vest. It did her no good for him to sit in fear. All that mattered was here and now. He hesitated when her shirt opened beneath his fingers, revealing creamy skin pebbled with goosebumps. He glanced at his men. Warmth and gratitude filled him despite the circumstances; his men had turned their backs and formed a protective barrier around him and his wife, respecting her privacy.

"Hurry up, son," Zachael admonished. "We don't have time to dally."

Tehl's numb fingers fumbled as he yanked off his cloak and dumped it unceremoniously on the ground. With care, he lifted Sage's torso, pulling the sodden top from her body before hastily covering her bust with his own cloak.

His jaw ticked when he caught sight of the monstrosity still wrapped around her neck, partially hidden by her hair. The collar's thorns had embedded themselves into her delicate skin, causing an angry red. It made him want to puke. The warlord had collared his wife like an animal. A rage unlike anything he'd ever known ignited inside him. A hard haze descended over his vision;

the only sound he heard was the beating of his own heart.

The warlord would pay.

That *monster* would pay.

Tehl reached for the collar just as Zachael placed a hand on top of his.

The weapons master shook his head, sorrow in his eyes. "Not now. It's deeply embedded in her flesh. We'll need a healer to remove it. If you try now, you will cause more harm."

The collar glinted in the light, as though taunting him. How could he leave that *thing* on his wife?

"Think about your wife, what she needs most." Zachael seemed to read his thoughts.

His friend was right. His fury wouldn't serve Sage.

Tehl swallowed hard and nodded jerkily, scrubbing her damp hair with the corner of his cloak while Zachael yanked her boots and socks off.

Someone paused by his side. "For your princess, and my sister."

He glanced at Sam who averted his gaze from Sage, a bundle of cloaks over his arm.

Emotion clogged Tehl's throat as he handed his wet cloak to his brother and wrapped one of the dry ones around Sage's shivering form. He settled her on the ground and eyed the leather encasing her legs. There was no way he could get her out of wet leathers. Zachael pulled a blade from his sheath as another growl brought them both up short.

"Listen here, beast," Zachael said sternly. "I understand you're worried about her. We all are. But if you don't stop threatening and scaring everyone around us, you'll make it that much harder for us to help Sage. You're welcome to watch over her, just stop growling. It will all be okay." His tone brooked no argument.

Tehl stiffened as the beast chuffed, onyx fur teasing the edge of his vision. A tail brushed his back, causing his pulse to jump and his brother to curse. He blew out a breath as the feline settled beside him, surveying the scene.

"We need to cut her out," the weapons master said, dismissing the man-eater at their side. "Do I have your permission?" His blade hovered above her leather-clad hip.

"Do what you must."

Zachael eyed the beast and slowly began cutting the leather. The feline's body tensed beside them, but she didn't make any moves toward Zachael. His progress was slow, so Tehl drew his own blade, earning a hiss from the leren. Tehl held out his weapon on a flat palm so the beast could sniff it, praying it didn't bite his hand off. His fingers twitched as the feline locked eyes with him and sniffed. Its lips curled back slightly, but it didn't attack. He pulled his hand back gently.

"I'm going to help."

Grimly, Tehl set to the task of cutting the sodden leather, anxiety rising as Sage's shivers ceased. A bad sign, he knew.

"How far to the camp?" he asked as, at last, the stiff leather was pulled away. He set about working the cloak around her frozen toes.

"Not far, but it will be hard regardless..." Sam railed in response. Tehl nodded, tucking Sage's fingers underneath her arms and wrapping her up tightly.

"Let's ride." Immediately, his men mobilized.

"Blast." Sam frowned.

Tehl followed his gaze to Jasmine, who'd sunk to the ground and now listed back and forth, her eyelids heavy, skin ashen.

"Why hasn't she been taken care of?" Sam barked.

"We've done the best we could. She wouldn't let us near her, and she's clearly not well enough to redress herself on her own," James growled, glaring at the stubborn woman.

"I don't care what you have to do, but you get her warm and ready to travel," Tehl said before moving toward the copse of trees.

"I can handle this," Sam muttered, storming over to Jasmine. "Are you bloody stupid?"

"Ma-a-ay-be-e-e, bu-ut at least I-I-I am no-t-t-t ugly," she stuttered.

Sam yanked a blade from his waist and squatted. "Ugly is better than dead."

Tehl kept walking as stuttered curses burst from behind him. He ignored them. The bloody woman was too proud. She had to know she couldn't possibly do more on her own.

Tehl's men fanned out around him as they pushed through the last of the trees, their horses coming into view. They suddenly reared back and shied away; he stumbled and nearly fell. What in the blazes?

His gaze dropped to Sage's furry protector who licked her lips. Oh, hell no.

He stopped and met the feline's golden gaze squarely. "Our horseflesh is not for you to eat." It felt silly speaking to an animal, but, so far, she seemed to understand him. His mind flashed to the camp full of his men. "I'm taking your mistress to camp where we can heal her properly. None of my people are food. *None.* You hunt outside of my camp. If you hunt inside my camp, we will hunt *you.*"

The feline growled at his tone, but with a flick of her tail and a chuff, she seemed to acknowledge his demands.

Tehl walked faster and handed Sage off to Zachael as he swung

7

up onto his own mount's back. The dark warhorse shied away from the feline lurking close by, but he didn't bolt.

"That's a good boy," Tehl murmured, stroking Wraith's silky neck. He took Sage from Zachael, who adjusted the cloak once more.

Just then, Sam stormed into the grove, carrying a now-unconscious Jasmine. Despite the anger and frustration on his face, he held Jasmine with the utmost care and deposited her gently into the weapon master's arms before mounting. Once he'd secured himself, he reclaimed Jasmine from Zachael. Settling her in his arms, he nudged his mount toward Tehl.

"Ride on!" Tehl shouted, nudging Wraith into a canter. The wind bit at his skin, blowing right through his damp clothing. He ought to have changed himself, or at least donned a dry cloak, but his mind had been on other things. He tightened his grip on Sage and ignored the chill.

The ride was miserable, as one emotion after another washed over him. Joy that Sage was alive. Anger at the state she was in. Fear that she might still not survive. It was miserable to be in his head.

Once or twice, he caught sight of flashes of black. He'd no idea how fast or far a man-eater could run. He doubted she could match the stamina of a horse, but then, he'd never had to find out before. He swallowed hard and prayed the creature wouldn't cause them any trouble.

When at last the tan peaks of his camp came into view, the anxiety inside Tehl loosened. The three-hour ride had seemed to drag on. Sage had survived the ride; she'd survive the healing.

A cry pierced the air at the approach of their party, and Tehl made out Hayjen as he stepped to the front of the awaiting group.

Tehl nodded, meeting the man's anxious gaze, and slowed Wraith to a stop as Sage's uncle halted at their side and held out his arms.

"I have her," Tehl said, swinging his leg over the horse and sliding down. As soon as his boots touched the ground, he was moving, Sage's weight surprisingly light in his arms. There wasn't any time to lose.

"Lilja stoked the fire in your tent and had men bring water. It's heating now."

"Thank you."

"How is she?"

Tehl eyed Hayjen. "Not good. But she's alive."

A nod, as if he had already expected the news. "Rafe found Blaise. She's in rough shape herself."

"Then we have all three women."

"All worse for the wear." A pause. "He will pay."

The fury Tehl had been burying suddenly flared to life again. "That he will."

Hayjen moved ahead of him and held open the tent flap. A wave of hot air slammed into him as he stepped into the dim tent. Sweat beaded on his forehead and on the back of his neck. "I've got her, Lilja."

A small cry of alarm escaped from the usually-composed Sirenidae as she rushed toward them, her own skin covered in a sheen of sweat. "Sage?"

"She's alive, but her core is dangerously cold."

Lilja's expression hardened. "Lay her on the center cot." Her gaze flicked behind him. "Make sure to keep the tent flaps closed. We can't afford to lose the heat."

Tehl squeezed around cots piled with furs and blankets and did what he was told. It was hard letting go of Sage. His hands opened and closed as Lilja bustled around him, barking orders at Hayjen. He gazed down at Sage's pale face and knelt by her side.

"What can I do?" he asked.

"Grab that rock heating by the fire. Wrap it in a horse blanket so you don't burn yourself or Sage, and place it underneath her feet. If we don't get her toes and fingers heated up, she'll be in worse trouble."

Tehl moved to the fireplace, his breath coming in heavy pants. The air was stifling. He'd just plucked a stone from the fire when the sound of loud cries and startled shouting rent through the air.

"What the bloody hell is that?" Hayjen demanded, drawing his sword.

But there was only one thing that would make Tehl's men react like that.

"Prepare yourself, and don't make any sudden movements," Tehl said.

A shadow burst through the tent flap and skidded to a stop, hackles raised.

"Stars above," Lilja breathed, freezing, her hand pressed against Sage's chest.

The leren hissed and slunk toward Sage, her movements liquid. The beast leapt onto one of the tables, eyeing Lilja. Ever so slowly, Lilja removed her fingers from Sage and held out her hand, palm up.

"I mean you no harm, nor your mistress. She is my kin, and I offer you my friendship as well."

Tehl watched the exchange with wide eyes as the feline dropped from the table and silently padded toward Lilja.

"Love, that's a very large man-eater," Hayjen said softly, his tone holding a warning.

"She's just protecting her bonded. She won't hurt me, will you, darling?" she cooed.

Tehl sucked in a breath as the beast sniffed the Sirenidae's hand, bumping it with her nose.

Lilja smiled and brushed a hand along the feline's velvet head. "Hello to you, too." She turned from the beast and began to resume her work as the beast nudged Sage's face, giving her a gentle lick. Tehl gaped.

The Sirenidae glanced up and jerked her chin at him. "The stone."

He blinked a moment before hastily obeying.

Lilja tugged Sage to one side and patted the cot. "Wild one, she needs you."

The large beast nimbly climbed onto the cot and curled around Sage.

"Help me, Tehl. I need you to lift her. I'm going to pull this off. It's too damp to do her any favors." She motioned to the cloak.

Tehl averted his eyes and shivered as Sage's chilly flesh touched his own fiery skin. When requested, he let her back down, still staring in awe as the big cat accommodated Lilja, who tucked a fur around Sage.

"We need help!" Sam yelled, his voice drawing closer. His tone was oddly panicked. Sam rarely panicked.

Tehl pulled his gaze from his wife's pale face and glanced at the tent entrance as his brother burst in. His lips thinned as he got a good look at the source of Sam's distress. Jasmine's body hung limp in his arms. A pale leg escaped the confinement of the cloak, adorned with bruises, ugly red welts, and deep lacerations. Tehl's jaw clenched as the anger burning in his gut grew hotter. One brutality after another appeared in the warlord's wake, it seemed.

"Place her right here," Lilja commanded, sparing her niece a final look before rushing to Sam's side.

Tehl stood and tugged needlessly at the fur warming Sage, helplessness overtaking his features as he took in the dark smudges marring the skin beneath her eyes. She looked all but dead. He swallowed hard. "Lilja, what do I do?"

"Nothing," a husky voice rasped.

He hid his flinch as his gaze slid to what he had thought was a pile of furs. Swollen brown eyes peeked out at him from underneath a blanket. Blaise. She licked her cracked lips and slowly closed her eyes again, shivers shaking the furs around her. "She'll be fine."

"How do you know?" he barked.

A wry smile twisted the Scythian woman's battered face. "Do you really think the warlord would allow his prize to die so easily?"

Hatred washed over him like ice water along his skin. It was not a feeling he was accustomed to. "What did he do to her?" he hissed, dreading her answer.

Blaise cracked one puffy eye. "I'm sure he's given her an elixir to protect her from real harm. Her body will fight off the sickness and then heal itself."

A cough seized her, and Tehl quickly filled a cup with water and held it to her lips. Blaise drank weakly, water dribbling down her cheeks.

"Thank you," she whispered, her words garbled.

Tehl set the cup on the little wooden table and stared down at Blaise. "There's no cause to worry?"

"There's every cause to worry." Blaise chuckled and then winced, her hand clutching at her ribs. "But not about her body.

She'll fall into a deep sleep and wake up in a few days." Her gaze slid behind him. "You should be concerned for Jasmine."

"Thank you," he said, nodding and pulling the fur up higher over Blaise. Her eyelids slid closed, and her breathing evened out.

There wasn't anything he could do for his wife or Blaise, if what she had spoken was truth. He rolled up his sleeves, the fabric sticking to his damp skin, and turned to Lilja.

"What can I do?" he pleaded once more. Stars above, he needed something to keep himself occupied or he'd run mad.

Her worried magenta gaze met his. "Stoke the fire and pray."

CHAPTER TWO

The Warlord

She'd stabbed him.

The vixen had stabbed *him*. There was nothing Zane hated more than a traitor, and yet... he'd *liked* it. Reveled in it even.

Bubbles escaped his mouth, the river pulling him deeper and deeper into its watery clutches. Sage kept surprising him. He both loved and loathed it. Every time he thought he had her figured out, she surprised him, and not always in a good way. But that's what kept him coming back. She was a drug he craved, he needed—and he hated it. The dependency. The addiction to her goodness.

An emotion that he didn't want to acknowledge worked its way through him: worry. Not for himself. He'd survive. He always did. The river wouldn't kill him, but the death of his consort might.

He'd lived hundreds of years, and this was how he would lose the last person he'd ever cared for. It had been a mistake to keep her, but he couldn't help himself, much like the sun couldn't help but rise each morning.

His back slammed into a rock, but he welcomed the pain as it drowned out the voices inside him, howling in rage that his consort was dying and he was doing nothing. Even now, his limbs seemed heavier, dragging him deeper into darkness, his lungs screaming for air.

In freeing herself, Sage had killed herself. He'd seen others drown. It wasn't clean. It was brutal. Violent. He closed his eyes to the frigid swirling darkness around him. There was poetic justice in that. Their relationship had been brutal and violent in the best way. Only his queen would try to kill him and kiss him in the same breath. That was love. True love.

His lips curled back, the freezing water flooding his mouth. Love. The twisted emotion always managed to burn all his hard efforts to the ground. The darker part of him railed at the betrayal, but logically, it was bound to happen. Humans hurt the ones they loved the most. It was the reality of life. When you lived as long as he had, you saw it time after time.

Dark satisfaction filled him. At least his love didn't do it by halves. She'd dove in headfirst, and that's what had drawn him to her. If she was still alive when he found her, he'd never make the mistake of underestimating her again.

His black heart squeezed in his chest at the *if*. He grappled with emotions he'd long thought he was immune to: loss, sorrow; despair. He'd always been a master at power plays and manipulation. He never compromised. She made him softer, and he hated that, but not enough for him to let her go. She changed everything.

At first, he'd wanted to collect her fire and break her down and forge her into his own creation, but she'd fascinated him. She wouldn't break. By standing up to him, she'd fueled his obsession that he could only call love.

A love that she had for him, too. The voices quieted for a moment and seemed to purr. They knew the truth.

Sage loved him, too.

Though she tried to hide it, he'd seen it.

The moment the river tore her from his grasp, he'd seen it in her eyes. If she survived, she wouldn't be able to erase him from her soul. They were bound in ways that no one could imagine or understand. He was imprinted on her skin, just as she was imprinted on his.

Hands wrapped around his arms and lifted his body as his lungs began to burn. His men were just in time. For their sake, they'd better have found his consort.

Light filtered through his eyelids as they broke the surface. He sputtered and gasped for air, but didn't open his eyes as his warriors towed him to shore. Rock and sand scratched his bare back as they laid him down. He had never worried he would drown. His genetics made it almost impossible for him to die, and his warriors were the best of the best.

"My consort..." he rasped, his arms and legs numb.

"The river pulled her under, and we haven't been able to find her, my lord."

No, the voices inside him snarled. The river couldn't take her from him. She was *his*. His fingers curled into the sand beside his hips, rocks jabbing into his palms. Nothing would stand in his way. Not even death could take her from him. He wrestled his rage back. He could *not* lose it here.

"Blair?" he called, something thick lodging in his throat.

"He's still searching, my lord," a deep voice answered.

Ever-dutiful Blair. The man had proven to be beyond useful for all of these years. But Zane knew that his service wasn't given out of gratitude and loyalty. Fear was a funny thing. It motivated people in the most spectacular ways. Blair was the prime example of that. All it took was a casual inquiry after the man's family and he straightened up. But he didn't blame the man. Women had a way of enchanting the best of them.

"Find her," he rasped. His warriors nodded and melted into the surrounding forest.

His breath fogged around him as he slowed his breathing. He rolled his neck to the side, small pins of pain lodging behind his eyes as he stared at the deceptively calm river. How long could Sage survive the water? How long could she hold her breath? Cold dread settled in his stomach as his mind flashed back to her stabbing him. Her lips were already blue by the time he'd reached her.

One of the knots loosened in his chest. At least sickness wasn't an issue. He'd made sure sickness wouldn't take her from him. A small smile tugged at his lips. After her bout in the dungeon, he'd experienced how delicate she was beneath the fire. He'd forgotten how easily people died when they weren't protected. He'd given her the protection she needed. Sickness would never claim her, but accidents and suicide could.

Deep in his gut, unease pooled. He'd allowed himself to be ensnared by her, and now he was paying the price.

She was ours the moment she entered our throne room. The choice was not yours; it was ours. She belongs to us.

The voices never went away. But they went silent or calmed when she was around. Control was easier to accomplish. Her presence soothed all the chaos inside.

He smirked as feeling slowly crept back into his extremities. He wanted her with a fierceness he didn't know he possessed. He *needed* to claim her, but each time the voices urged him to *take*, he held himself in check. He wouldn't take that from her. She'd give it to him.

The temptation had been there every time he'd crawled into bed with her and wrapped his arms around her. At first, she'd been stiff, but at the end, her body molded to his and she sought him out in her sleep. He'd spent hours watching her sleep, caressing her body, relishing the cinnamon scent that drifted from her skin in intoxicating waves.

He'd always known he needed to produce heirs, but the women of his court always lacked something. However, in the stillness of the night with Sage asleep in his arms, he'd allowed himself to entertain the idea of heirs. Once the idea was planted, he could never free himself from it.

Sage, heavy with his child, was the reward. His future.

A future someone had tried to rob him of.

The warlord slowly sat up and placed a hand against the ground to steady himself. His consort was a brilliant woman, but she didn't have all the necessary skills to avoid detection so well.

She'd had help.

He rubbed the back of his neck, feeling the small wound. A toxin that could paralyze him for more than ten minutes was a rare thing. Whoever had given that to her possessed a dangerous weapon, and more so, they possessed dangerous knowledge. Someone had betrayed him.

He carefully pushed to his feet and strode toward his boots. There was a traitor in his midst. His gaze narrowed on his boots as his mind jumped to several options. He'd keep silent until the right moment, then strike.

You'll not hurt her.

No, he wouldn't hurt Sage. He'd punish her, for sure, and she'd beg him, but he wouldn't hurt her. Nothing would mar her skin.

He bared his teeth at the river, thinking about the state she'd been in when he'd finally caught up: cuts, bruises, scratches had covered every inch of her body. He'd hated that. Even though hunting her had been the most engaging event he'd participated in for years, it angered him that she'd abuse herself after all the effort he'd taken to heal her.

"Report," he commanded, his words sharp.

Blair appeared by his side and knelt. "She lives."

Just two words, but they calmed the voices inside. "Where is she?"

"She escaped."

He'd expect nothing less from his consort. "And are you tracking her?" he asked with a smile. The hunt was on.

"Yes."

"Very good."

"She's been retrieved."

The warlord stilled. That was not what he wanted to hear. "By whom?"

"By the crown prince of Aermia and his party."

The rage he'd been barely suppressing threatened to overwhelm him. The filthy cur had put his hands on *his* consort. The princeling would rue the day he stole what was his. No one took what was his.

Kill. Kill. Kill.

Tremors worked down his arms as he tried to get control of himself. He was dangerously close to losing control. Even when

19

Sage had scorned him the first time, he'd not been this bad. He needed to calm himself. The stakes were much higher now. If he let emotion rule, he'd make a mistake, and he didn't have time for mistakes.

He blew out a breath and uncurled his hands. The Aermian boy was playing a game he couldn't win. A cruel smile tipped the corners of Zane's mouth. He'd relish taking everything from the pup of a prince as he claimed his consort once and for all. Aermia was as good as his.

The prince's actions accelerated his plans more than he liked, but it would be all the more satisfying to take Aermia and his consort as the prize in the end.

He turned to Blair, who still knelt at his feet, staring at the ground. If he were a lesser man, he'd kill him, but men like Blair were rare. His warrior didn't hesitate when telling him the news of his woman's disappearance. That was bravery.

"They're being followed?" he asked.

"Yes."

"Then leave them."

It was almost painful to say the words. The voices demanded he give chase and hunt Sage down, but he knew better. Recklessness always ended in failure. He'd plot and maneuver, and in the end, he'd be the victor. If he wanted her, he had to be patient.

In time, Sage would come to him, beg him to take her back.

And he would.

For a price.

CHAPTER THREE

Tehl

Neither worked.

All three women worsened through the night and the next day.

Tehl rubbed his bleary eyes and scanned the cramped room. Hayjen snored quietly in the right corner, his chin resting on his chest. Sam sat near Jasmine, bloodshot eyes staring blankly into space, while Rafe sat between Sage and Blaise, his face betraying his anxiety. His gaze flickered to Lilja, who buzzed around the room, humming a haunting tune. She'd worked tirelessly since the women arrived. Tehl didn't think he'd seen her sit down once.

He pushed to his feet and edged around the cot toward the Sirenidae. She paced to and fro in the tent, her brow furrowed, lips pursed. Something was on her mind, that much was obvious.

"You'll wear a hole in the floor," he said softly.

"It's better than sitting still while they die."

His spine snapped straight, and Rafe growled from his spot.

Lilja immediately halted and took Tehl's hand, an apology in her eyes. "I'm sorry. That was thoughtless of me. I shouldn't have said that."

Tehl squeezed her hand once and pulled back. He swallowed hard, choking down his fear before stating the thought he knew he shared with the other two men. "So...you believe she may die after all?"

She sighed and hung her head, her silvery white hair hanging limply over her shoulders. "I've done everything I can for them, but they need more care than I, alone, can give, and I'm running out of supplies." Lilja glanced at him from beneath her lashes. "I'm afraid we only have one option, and it has risks."

"We need to move them," Rafe guessed.

Lilja cast a look his way. "Yes." Her tone was resolute.

Tehl had been thinking the same thing, but there were so many factors he couldn't control.

"Of course, they may not be strong enough for the journey." She hesitated before continuing. "But if we don't get them the help they need, they'll die anyway." Lilja pressed her palms to her eyes and rubbed. "They will have a chance if we get them back to the palace, but if we stay here for too long, they will die." He glanced at Sage's still form, pensive.

"There's a storm brewing," Rafe added softly.

Tehl looked to the Methian with a raised brow. How did he know? The man stayed silent. Tehl glanced down to Sage and ran a thumb along her cheekbone. At this point, he didn't care how the man knew or what secrets he kept. Tehl was too damn tired for any more revelations, anyway.

"I sense it, too," Lilja said. "We must leave now, before it strikes."

"And how do you expect us to get them there alive?" Sam's voice whipped through the air. "They almost didn't survive the journey from the river to our camp. Do you really think they'll make it to the castle? It would be a death sentence."

Lilja placed a hand on Sam's shoulder. "She'll die without help. Can you hear her breathing? You know I'm speaking the truth."

Sam shrugged off her hand and pushed to his feet. He ran a hand through his disheveled blond curls and down his face, his gaze snagging on Tehl. "Will you risk Sage?"

No, Tehl wasn't *willing* to risk Sage, but he trusted Lilja. "We can't stay here. There's a frost every morning. We have to go." It was the only choice.

Sam scoffed. "But you're willing to risk Jasmine?"

He frowned. "What?"

His brother laughed bitterly. "Look at her!" Her wet cough punctuated his words. Sam frowned and tugged the fur higher on the girl. "The others might stand a chance, but Jasmine...it could be the end of her. She's too weak."

"We need to leave *for* her, brother. Her odds are no better if she stays. Think about it."

Sam shook his head, scorn heavy on his face. "And you know this, do you? Speak truthfully. We all know you aren't thinking about *her*. You care only for yourself and your own."

Tehl blinked, startled. Where was this coming from? Sam's words were filled with venom. He took another breath before answering, studying the color in Sam's cheeks, the dark lines at the corners of his eyes. All of them were anxious. All of them were tired. He couldn't remember the last time he'd slept a full night.

Tehl looked closely at his younger brother, noting the same ragged signs of exhaustion that surely marked his own face. When was the last time Sam had had a full night of sleep?

"Sam, you know that's not true," he said gently. "You know how much I appreciate everything Jasmine did for Sage. I owe her a debt for her sacrifice. Have I ever ignored such a debt?"

The fire popped and crackled in the silence as Sam stared at him. His brother's shoulders slumped, and he hung his head. "No, you haven't."

"And I'm not starting now. I have a duty to Jasmine as much as to Sage."

"You're right." Sam rolled his neck and straightened. "So, when do we leave?"

"Now," Rafe rumbled. "Or the storm will catch us."

***

Chills ran down Tehl's spine as the wind blew his hood from his face and rain dripped down the back of his shirt. He pressed his heels into Wraith's sides and urged his mount to move faster. The temperature had dropped steadily as they drew closer to Sanee. He cast a worried glance down at Sage. Her skin seemed almost translucent now. "Please don't die," he whispered, his voice lost to the howling winds and rain. She couldn't die now.

He leaned forward in his saddle and kept his gaze ahead as familiar landmarks began to appear, his heart beating in tandem with every stride Wraith took. They were so close. Just a little further and they'd be home. When the spires of the castle rose in the distance like ragged teeth from the cliff, some of the worry in his chest loosened. Just a little further.

His surroundings blurred around him as he thundered forward, closing the distance between him and his goal. The only thing to rouse him was the guard's cry that pierced the air when he neared the gates.

Tehl pulled hard on the reins, steamed breath pouring from Wraith's nostrils. His men surrounded him and Zachael held his hands out. Tehl let the weapons master take Sage from his arms. He swung his leg over his mount and slid to the ground. The impact reverberated through his stiff legs, nearly bringing him to his knees. He gritted his teeth, ignoring the pain and questions others barked around him, and took his wife back from Zachael. He brushed past his men and rushed toward the castle, the rain pelting him the entire time as if to mock him. To tell him he was too late.

He burst through the castle doors near the sparring ring and startled a few maids. Brusquely, he charged forward, tuning out their squeals and gasps. His wet boots squelched against the lush deep-blue carpets, water dripping from his cloak in a constant pattern as he forced his tired legs forward with each step. Heat suffused his side, and he spared a quick glance toward the beast following close by him. Ah, so it was not his own presence that had startled the servants after all. Absently, he smiled. By noon, there'd be all sorts of monster stories floating around the castle.

Gavriel materialized next to him, followed by Sam, Rafe, Lilja, and Hayjen.

"I've sent a messenger ahead to alert Jacob and Mira of our arrival and to make ready."

"Thank you."

His cousin nodded and then stared at the beast. "Are you sure it was the best idea to bring the cat with us?" he asked, an eyebrow raised.

"There was no 'letting her come,' she just did. Be my guest to stop her."

Gav shook his head. "Let's hope she doesn't eat anyone before morning." A curse. "I'll need to warn Isa. There's no way I'll be able to keep her from the man-eater once she spots her."

"Maybe she'll eat some of the bastards around here," Sam said, adjusting Jasmine in his arms. "It would save us from ever having to deal with their idiocy again."

A small smile curled Tehl's lips upward. It was hardly the time to joke, but at least his brother was behaving a bit more like himself.

They cut through a room or two and used the servants' darkened corridors to reach the infirmary. Tehl led the way, the others trailing close behind him. Mira hustled around the cots, tying her blond hair onto the top of her head. Tears dripped down her cheeks as she rushed toward him.

"How is she?" She pulled up short when the beast growled. Her eyes widened, seeming to take up her entire face. "Is that what I think it is?" she squeaked.

"Yes."

Jacob took a careful step forward. The Healer showed more bravery than most men.

"She won't hurt Sage," Lilja murmured to the animal, daring to place a hand on the man-eater's head. "Jacob and Mira are friends. The Healer will help her."

Mira tore her gaze away from the feline and moved closer to pull back the cloak. She gasped. Tehl knew what she'd see. A woman pale and death-like, but more than that, a woman changed in a way not thought possible.

Mira grimaced, her eyes flitting once between his face and Sage's unfamiliar one. In that one look, he saw many questions, but she kept them to herself. She placed her hand on his wife's

26

forehead and then immediately went to work. "Leave them on the cots and get out." She pulled away and gestured toward the cots near the fire.

All three men moved into action, depositing their charges onto the designated cots. Jacob bustled around his herbs, placing pastes, tinctures, and tonics on a table with wheels. He eyed them over the rims of his round glasses, his copper eyes pausing briefly on Rafe and Blaise before settling on Tehl.

"You brought her back."

Tehl brushed a wet strand of hair from Sage's face. "Have I really?" It was too early to tell.

Jacob pulled back the cloak and scanned Sage, his expression giving nothing away. "She's a strong girl. She'll make it."

"Can I assist in any way?" Lilja asked, stepping closer.

Jacob nodded. "I'd be pleased if you did, my lady." He turned his attention back to Tehl. "You need to leave."

Everything inside Tehl rebelled at the command. "I'm not leaving her."

"We need to keep this room free of all contaminants. That means all of you." Jacob scanned all the men glaring at him. "You're a hazard to their health. If the stars are willing, we'll save all of them, but I'm not taking the chance of you making them worse. Not to mention, only the princess is married. You are not anything to these young women. You'll ruin their reputations. Unless you plan to marry them all?"

"We've already seen them," Sam argued.

"But it wasn't *here*," the Healer reminded. "Appearances in the palace are different."

"Wise," Rafe murmured. He dipped his head and retreated, followed by Gav, and reluctantly Sam.

Tehl was Sage's husband. He wasn't going anywhere. She didn't deserve to be alone after everything she'd gone through. Tehl crossed his arms and stared down the Healer. "I'm not leaving her side."

The old man adjusted his spectacles, eyes gleaming. "You're wasting our time. I'm not saying you cannot come back, but you cannot be here now."

Tehl fumed. He was the damn crown prince. He had the authority to do whatever he pleased. How dare Jacob give him a command?

"How dare you—"

"Tehl," Mira said softly.

He glared at the blond healer. "What?"

She didn't flinch at his sharp tone. "You will do more harm than good right now. Do you want to help?"

"Yes," he gritted out.

"Then bring her mother."

He stilled. Her family. The last time she was sick, she had asked for her mother. Tehl pulled a surprised Mira into a hug. "Thank you." He released her and sketched a bow. "I'll fetch her, myself."

He placed a swift kiss on Sage's feverish forehead and spun on his heel. If he hurried, he could have her mother at the palace in an hour. He spared one last glance over his shoulder at the unlikely group and then shut the door behind him.

Four pairs of eyes latched onto him. Gav, Sam, Rafe, and Hayjen all stood just outside the infirmary in various states of agitation.

"I need to collect Sage's family."

Hayjen held a hand out. "I'll take care of that."

"I should be the one who goes," Tehl said, moving through the men. "It's my duty."

A large hand settled on his shoulder. "Your place is here, with your wife. I'll retrieve my sister."

Silence. Then, "You're Sage's uncle?" Sam asked. "I'll be damned."

Tehl ignored his brother and smiled at Hayjen. "Thank you." He didn't want to leave Sage alone when she was so vulnerable. He glanced to Sam as Hayjen disappeared around the corner. "Does Jasmine have any more family?"

Sam snapped his mouth closed and held up a finger. "We're revisiting this revelation that you kept from us." His brother gave him a dirty look. "No, just the children."

Right. Jasmine's niece and nephew.

"Where are they now?" Tehl asked.

"Here," Sam said, leaning one shoulder against the wall. "They're in the care of Isa's nursemaid."

"Wait a moment." Gav held up a hand. "As the only father among us, I advise against making the children aware of Jasmine's presence until she's well."

"You don't want the children to have to mourn her again?" Tehl asked. That was logical.

"Yes. They've only just begun speaking again. They've had enough sorrow in their lives." Gav shook his head. "They deserve peace, not upheaval."

"But do you really want her niece's last memory to be of the death of her aunt?" Rafe asked. "Speaking from losing someone as a child, the memory warps, but the guilt stays. You should give them a chance to say goodbye, or that little girl will blame herself for the rest of her life."

Tehl dropped his head, thinking over the situation. Either choice could harm the children, but he would do anything to have one last moment with his own mother. "We'll leave them be for now. But if things turn bad for Jasmine... They deserve a chance to say goodbye."

Gav pursed his lips, looking like he wanted to argue, but dipped his head in acknowledgment. "Speaking of children, I'm going to go find Isa and hold her for a while. I'll return in a few hours. Do you need anything?"

"Nothing but the good health of those women," Tehl answered.

Gav hugged him and slapped him on the back. "She'll pull through. Believe in her."

His cousin released him and slipped away into the darkness. Tehl stared after him, long after Gav disappeared, unspoken fears swirling through his mind. He blinked when his eyes grew dry and the darkness shifted.

"You need to sit down, son."

His father's voice disrupted his reverie, the king's face slowly taking shape in the shadows before him. His father hugged him tightly, but Tehl's body stayed frozen as emotion battered against him like the sea against the cliff face.

"You retrieved her?" Marq asked.

"We did," he choked out.

His father pulled back and stared him in the eye. "In what condition?"

"I'm not sure," he whispered. He snapped his mouth shut when a gurgle escaped the back of his throat, sounding suspiciously like a sob.

Marq clapped him on the shoulder and sank down to the floor; patting the space beside him, he held out a bottle of spirits. "The waiting is the worst. Tell me what's happened to my daughter."

Emotion lodged in Tehl's throat as he collapsed to the floor and took his father's offering. The liquor burned, but it gave him time to collect himself. "That's the problem. I don't know what's happened to her, only that she's different."

His father took the bottle and had a healthy swig before passing it to Rafe with a nod. "The experiences in our life tend to change us."

That wasn't what he meant. "She *looks* different."

His father stilled and released a shuddering breath. "All women change. It's part of nature."

"Not this change." The words tasted like ash on Tehl's tongue. Her change was partly due to his failure. His wife still looked like herself, but part of her was now alien, otherworldly, too perfect. "Everything has changed."

Marq stared at the back of his hands. "You're right. You're at a crossroads. This is where you decide your future."

"My future?"

His father speared him with his serious blue eyes. "Everyone's future."

Chapter Four

Mira

It was like being inside a nightmare.

She scrubbed her hands vigorously in the basin until her skin turned red from the abuse.

"Mira, are you ready?" her papa called.

She ducked her head and panted, nausea swirling in her belly. For the most part, blood and disease didn't bother her. She could look past it, but she couldn't look past the hideous contraption wrapped around her friend's neck or the way it dug into her tender flesh.

Mira gagged and grabbed the edge of the table to steady herself. She needed to pull herself together. Her papa's hands weren't as steady as hers these days, so she had to remove the collar. There was no one else to take her place; no one she'd trust with her friend.

Swallowing hard, she straightened and wiped her hands on her apron. She had a duty to do. She spun around and strode to Sage's side. She'd changed so much in Scythia. It was almost like looking at a stranger.

Lilja placed a shallow bowl with warm water on the cot and pressed into her space, making Mira's teeth snap together. She understood that Sage's aunt wanted to help, but her hovering was making Mira feel more on edge.

"How do you plan on doing this?" Jacob asked, lying clean tools across a linen-covered table.

"Originally, I planned on placing a small piece of wood underneath the collar to keep it from her neck and then slowly breaking pieces off." She leaned closer and pointed to where Sage's skin was attached to the metal. "But the longer I examine her neck, the more I think it will cause more damage. If I pry at the metal at all, it'll press the wood into her neck. That's a concern for infection."

"What about a towel?" Gwen offered, brushing a strand of hair from Sage's pale face.

She shook her head. "It's not strong enough. The metal will just rip through it and will offer no protection to her neck."

"What about someone's hand?" Lilja said.

"The chance of breaking someone's hand, due to the pressure, would be high." And extremely painful.

Lilja rolled her neck. "I'll do it."

"Can you handle the pain?"

A dark look crossed the woman's face. "I was bred for pain."

Mira blinked and narrowed her eyes. "I can't abide a martyr here. Can you keep calm if I happen to break one of your fingers?"

Magenta eyes met hers with absolute certainty lurking in them. "This will be a cakewalk."

It was unorthodox, but they didn't have much choice. The crown prince had made it abundantly clear that he wanted the monstrosity taken off her as soon as possible. Gwen shifted the bowl out of the way so Lilja could sit on the cot and wedge her fingers between the thorny collar and Sage's skin. Mira hissed out a breath when blood dripped down Sage's neck, slowly soaking the white linen beneath her head.

It was painful to watch. Mira plucked a file from her toolkit and began to delicately file at the collar. She winced as each of her movements caused Sage to bleed, but she dared not speed up her work. One wrong move and the file could slip, slashing open her friend's neck.

"You're doing great, love," Gwen breathed softly.

Mira bit her lip as she cut through one section of the collar. She wiped her forehead with the back of her hand, then moved onto the next strand.

It was slow going and her hands began to ache, but she soldiered on, keeping a close eye on Sage's blood loss. When she reached the last strand, she straightened and handed the file to her papa and shook out her hands. Only one last strand. It was the thickest one of all, and proved the most difficult to cut.

She held out her hand once the tingles had left her fingers, and Jacob laid the file back onto her palm with an encouraging smile. Mira focused on the last strand and began to saw. It was stubborn, but it, too, eventually gave up to her insistence. She dropped the file into the bowl of warm water and glanced at her papa.

"I need you to start to pull the collar away from her neck where it overlaps. It should break where I've been sawing."

Her papa shuffled to her side and began to delicately pry the shackle away from Sage's throat. Lilja's lips pursed, the only sign

34

the metal was pressing uncomfortably into her fingers.

"That's it," Mira encouraged as the metal began to groan. "Just a little further, steady now."

No sooner had the words come from her mouth when the collar snapped, and one side gouged into Sage's neck.

"Damn it." Jacob pulled the offending metal from her neck.

Mira snatched a towel from the table and pressed it against the heavily-bleeding wound. "We need a poultice to pack it." She lifted the edge of the towel and peeked at the cut. "It's bleeding too much to stitch it now."

Her papa dropped the thorny chunk into Gwen's hands and swiftly moved to his herbs. For some reason, she couldn't pull her gaze from the collar lying on Gwen's palms. What kind of human being did that to another?

"He's not human," Lilja murmured.

Mira blinked, and then realized she had said that out loud. "On that, we can agree," she growled, glancing down to the crimson soaking through her towel. She frowned. That seemed like too much blood for the wound.

She lifted the edge of the towel and cursed. Not only had the metal cut Sage, but it had sliced Lilja across her fingers. She glanced up at the woman next to her. Lilja looked like she could be having tea, her expression was so calm. She stared at Sage's aunt, and a random thought passed through her mind: she'd never play cards with the woman.

"Papa," she called. "Make some for Lilja. She's been cut, too."

Lilja shook her head. "Don't worry about me. I'll heal."

Jacob moved to her side with a poultice. "Ready?"

"Yes."

"On the count of three. One, two, three!"

Mira pulled the towel out of the way and switched places with her father as he pressed the poultice to Sage's wound. He glanced at her and jerked his chin toward the tweezers. "Why don't you start on the other side? We won't be able to do the same thing. It's much more embedded on her right side."

She nodded, feeling sick. Gwen shuffled out of her way but never looked away from what she held in her hands. It seemed Mira wasn't the only one morbidly fascinated with the crown. She plucked her tool from the table and sucked in a deep breath to fortify herself. She could do this. It wasn't anything she hadn't done before.

Mira's stomach lurched painfully as she pulled the skin from around the metal. Gwen choked beside her.

"Gwen, I know you want to be here for Sage, but if you can't keep it together, you need to leave," Jacob said softly.

"I can do it," Gwen panted. "I'm not leaving my little girl."

"Then, take a deep breath, and, good hell, destroy that piece of trash."

Mira also inhaled deeply as she carefully worked on Sage's neck. She gritted her teeth as blood coated her fingers, causing the tweezers to move around in her hand. Quickly, she wiped her bloody hand on her apron and began her work anew.

From strictly a healing point of view, she was interested in how clean the damaged skin was. Normally, there would have been pus and infection, but there was nothing. What had they used to keep her neck clean?

She bit the inside of her cheek to keep herself calm. They had kept the collar clean but allowed her skin to grow around it. It was disgusting and inhuman.

A sigh of relief escaped her when she'd finally detached the last piece of skin. "I'm done," she whispered.

"Good," her papa said, glancing at her over his spectacles. "You grab your side, and I'll pull on this end, near Lilja's fingers."

She did what he asked and bile burned her throat as the thorny collar pulled away, somewhat stubbornly. Jacob cursed when it refused to budge in the very middle. He tugged lightly, causing the skin to stretch but hold. "We'll have to cut it away."

"Gwen, could you hand me the short dagger?" Mira asked, her voice hollow.

Sage's mum plucked the dagger from the table and placed it in her hand. She swallowed and held the collar from Sage's neck to cut away the attached flesh. Mira choked on bile as she cut away the metal. Jacob pulled away the collar, and she had to fight to not cast up the contents of her stomach.

Her friend's neck was a bloody mess, but that's not what bothered her. She dabbed at the blood, her stomach curling on itself. It was the impressions of thorns and roses carved into Sage's neck.

"Dear God," Gwen whispered. "My poor baby."

Lilja said curse words that normally would have had Mira scowling, but they somehow felt insignificant for what she was feeling. Woodenly, Mira placed the bloody dagger into the bowl of warm water and stood on numb legs.

Her papa bustled her out of the way and began to treat and dress Sage's wound. As if in a trance, she dressed Lilja's hand. All the while, Lilja watched her, but it didn't bother her. She couldn't feel anything.

Mira spun and forced herself to the wash basin. She dipped her scarlet-covered hands into the water and watched, detached, as the clear water battled with the blood and eventually lost, turning to a crimson pool of cruelty. For that's what it was. Mira was washing cruelty and depravity from her skin.

Rage unlike she'd ever known flooded her. This was not what the world was supposed to be like. Sure, she'd seen horrific things happen over the years as she trained to be a healer, but none of them had been this sadistic.

Something ugly formed in her heart. She'd never been one to take revenge, but there would be an accounting for what her friend had suffered. She wasn't a warrior in the truest sense, but make no mistake, when the time came to yank that bastard from the Scythian throne and destroy him, Mira would be there to witness him gasping his last breath, all the while laughing. And she'd make sure his lifeless body was left on the godforsaken battleground.

Monsters deserved to die like animals. Alone. Forgotten. Desecrated.

CHAPTER FIVE

Sage

Everything hurt.

She was bloody tired of waking to everything hurting, but, this time, a smile touched her mouth. Pain meant she was alive—battered and bruised, but alive.

For how long? a hideous voice whispered in her head.

Her breath hitched as she battled the fear that threatened to swallow her whole. She was out of the warlord's grip. He couldn't get her now.

Sage shifted, her fingertips grazing soft fur on her right. Carefully, she cracked one eyelid and then pressed her face into Nali's silky fur. "Nali," she croaked.

A purr greeted her, rumbling through her body.

A voice cried out behind her, and a hand brushed along her arm.

"Sage?"

Tears sprang to her eyes. She'd know that voice anywhere.

"Mum?" she replied, her voice catching on the word.

Slowly, she turned to the left, praying she wasn't dreaming. Words failed her as her mum's beautiful hazel eyes locked on hers. Surely it wasn't possible to create an illusion so beautiful?

It seemed impossible that her mum was here with her, but she couldn't help the hope that unfurled inside her chest like a flower in the sun. "Please, tell me you're real?" she said.

"Oh, baby girl!" her mum cried, tears tracking down her face. "I'm real. I'm here, love." Her mum brushed her hair from her face and peppered her forehead with kisses.

"I'm home?" It didn't seem real.

"You're home," a deep voice echoed.

Sage pried her eyes from her mum's dear face and glanced behind her. Pain washed over her at the little movement, but it was worth it.

Her papa's green eyes, so like her own, crinkled at the corners as he smiled down at her and ran a hand down her hair.

"Hello, baby girl."

It was too much. Sage squeezed her eyes shut, losing the battle with her emotions as sobs tore from her throat. It hurt just to look at them.

Large arms curled around her shoulders and pulled her into a tight embrace. Her lungs protested at the treatment, and pain ran up and down her arms and legs, yet she celebrated. She lived.

"It's okay, love. Papa has you," he crooned, his voice thick as he rocked her from side to side.

Sage clung to him like a little girl and wept. She'd made it home. Finally. Home. Tears dropped onto her face like rain, but she didn't care. Her pain was shared by her family.

"I love you," she said.

Her parents' murmurs of love became a chant in her mind as she let go and surrendered to the tears. When at last they abated, her papa didn't let her go. He whispered words of nonsense and love as her mum sang little songs quietly in the background. As Sage's eyes drooped and fatigue hit her, terror set in. What if this was in her mind? Would they still be here when she woke up?

"I don't want to go to sleep," she whispered into her papa's wet shirt.

"It's okay. You need to let your body rest," her mum answered, running a hand down the back of her head. "We'll watch over you. Protect you."

"Will you still be here when I wake up?" The words were small and vulnerable, born of suffering, fear, and uncertainty. Speaking them aloud sickened her, but she needed assurance, even if it was all in her mind.

A finger crooked underneath her chin and lifted. "Open your eyes, love."

She steeled herself and opened them to gaze up at her parents. Her mum leaned her head against her papa's shoulder and caressed Sage's face tenderly. "Nothing could tear your papa and me from your side. We'll stay."

"Promise?"

"I swear it," her papa said gravely, hugging her more tightly to him.

Her papa never lied to her. She released a deep sigh and rested her head against his chest, his steady heartbeat lulling her toward sleep. A small smile curled the corners of her lips as she breathed in. Fire, iron, and smoke teased her nose, a smell unique to her papa.

No dream could replicate that.

"Love you," she whispered.

"Love you most-est." Her mum's voice followed her into the dark and wrapped around her like the loveliest blanket on a chilly day.

***

Awareness slapped her in the face.

She jerked, her eyes snapping open. Her heart pounded as she scanned her surroundings. Nothing made sense. Everything was white, and it was bloody hot. Where was she?

Wait.

White walls.

Gleaming white walls.

The room blurred around her. How had he gotten to her? Had she never left the Scythian palace in the first place? A whimper escaped her. When would this torture end?

"Love?"

Her head snapped to the side. For a moment, she couldn't process what she saw.

A pair of worried green eyes stared back at her. "Baby girl?"

Recognition filled her mind. "Papa?"

His smile was full of relief. "Yes, it's me, baby. You're safe."

Safe? She was never safe. Safety was an illusion for the naive.

"What are you doing here?" she asked.

His brows furrowed. "Here?"

"In my mind."

Tears gathered in his eyes as he grabbed her hand. "I'm real, love. See the truth."

She forced herself to examine the white walls. Her stomach rolled, but the longer she stared, the more imperfections she

42

noticed. The color of the walls wasn't white, but cream. Sage blinked and scanned the room. She recognized it. The infirmary. The Aermian palace. How did she get here?

She blew out a breath, ruffling the hair hanging in her face, and tried to sort through the fragments of her mind. Her brows slanted together when she tried to move her arm. It didn't move. She glanced to the left, and tenderness flooded her. Her mum slept, her cheek resting on the back of Sage's hand. The poor thing looked exhausted. Surely, her imagination couldn't conjure pain like this?

Her skin prickled, and she glanced back to her papa. "I'm here?"

Her papa stared at her, his eyes bloodshot. "You don't remember?"

Rain, crying, her mum singing. Her mind snagged on the last blurry memory. "Some."

He nodded, his face creased with worry. "The mind is a tricky thing."

That it was.

"I'm sure you'll have your memories back before you know it."

She already had her memories, ones she wished to lose. Ones that haunted her dreams. Her hand crept to her throat and she froze as her fingertips grazed gauze not metal. Gauze, *not* metal. The room spun, and she clung to consciousness with everything she had.

"Did you sleep okay?"

No, but she wouldn't tell him that. Her papa didn't need to know about the warlord's presence overtaking her nightmares. "Like a rock." She shifted carefully, pulling her arm out from underneath her mama. Tingles ran up her arm as she wiggled her fingers.

A chuff ruffled her hair, causing her to smile. Nali. If Nali was here, this had to be real. Tears pricked her eyes. She'd made it. Truly made it. "I love you," she said. Right then and there, she vowed to say that to anyone she cared for at any time she desired. Life was too short not to let the ones you cared for know you love them.

"I love you, too." She shared a smile with her papa before he glanced over her head, his smile hitching up one side of his face and making him look years younger. "She's magnificent."

That wasn't the response Nali usually gained. Most shied away from the massive feline. Sage combed her right hand through Nali's fur, earning a rumble of pleasure from the beast. "She's the best." The leren had protected Sage with her life. They had forged a bond that wouldn't ever be broken.

Sage scanned the room. The infirmary was exactly as she remembered it. White-washed stone walls were adorned with shelves full of plants and herbs, and the roaring fire Jacob was so fond of keeping crackled, bringing comfort to her mind. A wet cough sounded to her right, alerting her to others in the room.

Shame washed over her. She hadn't even thought about the others. "Blaise and Jasmine? Are they okay?"

The last time she had seen the both of them was at the river. Had they both made it?

"Both girls made it to Aermia. Blaise was allowed to leave today. As for Jasmine..." Jacob trailed off, his lips pressing into a thin line. "She's not well."

Her heart sank. Jasmine had been injured, and the water was beyond cold. Who knew how much damage that had done to her? The warlord's face flashed through her mind, how he prowled toward her, his wet body caging hers. Her stomach lurched, and she panted as she tried to push the memory away. They'd escaped, but at what cost?

"Sage?"

"Help me up, please." Her tone roused her mum, who shot up with wide eyes.

Gwen glanced around the room before her gaze settled on Sage. "You're awake."

Panic seized her lungs; everything was too confining, too small. All she could feel was the warlord's skin pressed against her. "I need to get up." Spots danced across her vision as hands levered her up. The room spun, and she clung to the cot, her nails digging into the canvas. He wasn't here. He couldn't touch her.

But for how long...

"Breathe, love," her mum soothed, her hand running up and down Sage's spine.

She would if the fist around her lungs would let go, if the monster would let her go.

"Look at me," Mira's calm voice commanded.

Sage's head snapped up, and her green eyes clashed with beautiful blue ones. Her friend knelt before her and reached for her hand.

"Breathe when I do." Mira pulled in a slow breath and released it just as slowly while Sage's papa wrung his hands beside her.

She tried, she really did, but she kept feeling the warlord's hand on her skin, his heated breath on her neck, his lips gliding across her cheek.

Mira pinched her chin between two fingers. "You're not there, Sage. Focus on me. You're in the castle. Leave that place. It has no hold on you."

Her eyes focused on her blond friend, Mira's words

45

penetrating the fog in her mind. *He* wasn't here. Her breath came slowly, and the panic receded.

Sage squeezed Mira's hand, hardly believing her friend knelt before her. "I never thought I'd see you again."

Tears flooded the healer's eyes. "I always knew I'd see you again. We have too much mischief yet to cause."

Tears pooled in Sage's own eyes. "Stars above, I've missed you." With a choked sob, she threw herself at Mira. Her friend's arms wrapped around her tightly.

"I've missed you, too," Mira whispered into her hair.

"It's so good to see your face," Sage cried.

Mira pulled back and laughed, wiping her tears from her cheeks with her dress sleeve. "I'm such an ugly crier. Shame on you for making me cry in the presence of others."

"I won't tell anyone," her papa remarked. A pause. "Gwen is worse."

Sage smiled when her mum smacked her papa's arm and grinned up at him with adoration.

She glanced to the right, and her smile faded as she got a good look at the patient in the cot next to her. Jasmine's face was impossibly pale. Her honey-brown hair was soaked with sweat and clung to her head in clumps of Medusa-like strands. Black hollows marred the skin beneath her closed eyes, and harsh, struggling breaths passed her chapped, parted lips.

"Oh, Jasmine," she whispered. "How bad is she?"

"She's not well," Mira replied.

"That's not a real answer." Sage turned back to the healer. "The truth."

"Her injuries were serious, but it's the sickness that's settled in her lungs. There's too much fluid in them. Every breath is a painful labor for her."

"What can be done?"

"We're doing everything we can. Lilja has brought me special herbs I've been using to ease her breathing, but now we have to wait."

Sage swallowed. "Wait for her to live or die?"

"That depends on the fever and if Jasmine is a fighter," Mira said grimly.

A halfhearted laugh escaped Sage as she glanced back at Jasmine. "Fighter would be an understatement. She'll survive." She had to.

"I dearly hope so," Mira said, squeezing her hand and standing.

"She has to," she whispered, staring at the girl who had dared to help her—and at a greater cost to herself. "She has little ones who need her. Jasmine wouldn't let anything take her from them."

Jasmine's niece and nephew meant the world to her. There's no way her feisty friend would die from something as common as a fever. She couldn't. It wouldn't be right. Sage's mind turned to the twins. Where were they?

"I need to speak to Tehl." She turned back to her parents. "Better yet, take me to him."

"You've just awoken." Mira placed her hands on Sage's linen-clad hips, causing her to pause. "You're not well enough for that. I refuse to nurse you back to health again because of your bullheadedness."

Sage recognized her friend's stubborn stance from prior times. There would be no changing Mira's mind. Her gaze narrowed on the Healer, Mira's attire dawning on her. She wore only a shift. "Are you warming her?" Mira had done something similar for Sage when she was sick with fever.

"Yes," Mira replied. "Her fever is causing wretched shivers. I've had to place a thin cloth between her teeth, so she doesn't break them."

The heat at her back shifted as Nali repositioned herself behind Sage. Her gaze moved to the feline who eyed her through the slits of her eyes. "Maybe she won't need you anymore. I have something better."

Mira arched a blond brow. "You need your leren to keep yourself warm."

"I am in better health than Jasmine. Nali can help her more than myself."

"No."

The command in Mira's tone gave Sage pause. She peeked at the healer through her lashes. "You presume to give me commands?"

Mira raised a brow at her haughty tone. "I'm your healer and your friend. I will not let you jeopardize yourself because you feel guilty for the other girl. You are my priority."

Sage gaped at her friend. "I am healed."

Her friend snorted. "You're not healed. I bet you can't even stand by yourself."

She narrowed her eyes on the blond at the challenge, hating that she was right.

"What about a compromise?" her mum offered. "Nali can be split between the two of you."

"I think we're ignoring the most important being in this problem," her papa murmured. He lifted his chin toward Nali. "It's her decision. She hasn't done a damn thing except for what she wanted to for the last few days."

That was true. Nali only did what she wanted.

"Nali," Sage murmured, stroking her head and left ear. "Would you help Jasmine?"

The feline's eyes slid toward Jas. It still amazed her how intelligent leren were. It was almost as if she understood every word she said.

Nali's golden gaze moved back toward her, and she chuffed before lazily stretching and arching her back. She hopped down from Sage's cot, causing it to rock with her weight, and slunk around Jasmine's cot. The leren sniffed Jasmine's hair and sat staring straight at Mira.

"I think that's my cue to make room for her," Mira muttered. She rushed to Jasmine's cot and scooted the girl to the left side to make room for the massive feline.

With care, Nali climbed onto the cot, dwarfing it, and settled. Immediately, Jas moaned and turned toward the leren. Nali nuzzled the girl and then laid her head on her paws, her eyes shut.

"Well that settles that," Mira said, placing a hand on Jasmine's forehead. Her lips pursed as she pulled her hand away and tugged the blanket up over Jas.

"Any improvement?" Sage asked, already knowing the answer.

"None, but with Nali's help, that will soon change," Mira said brightly. Too brightly.

Sage glanced away from Jas to stare at her hands in her lap. How many times would she put Jasmine in danger? Would this time kill her? Her hands curled into fists, her nails biting into her palm. She couldn't break down now. Mira knew what she was doing. If it was within the Healer's power, she would do it. As much as it killed her, now was not the time to worry about Jas. The warlord would have plans already in motion. No doubt Zane would—

Her body stiffened, and her breath froze in her lungs.

Zane. She'd used his name. Stars above, she was going to be sick.

"Love?" Her mum's voice echoed around her, distorted.

"I'm going to be sick," she mumbled through numb lips.

She'd used his name, like a friend, like a lover. A bowl appeared in front of her right before she retched. Tears dripped down her face, her shame and disgust threatening to swallow her whole. After everything he'd done, she'd used his name? Maybe she was as depraved as he was.

Sage panted and her lips quivered as small sobs escaped her. Large arms wrapped around her, and she gagged. "Don't touch me," she whispered.

The arms immediately disappeared. "I'm sorry, baby girl." Her papa's voice was deep and near her ear, pain evident in his tone.

She squeezed her eyes closed as more bile flooded her mouth. Poison. She was tainted by poison. Even now, poison was leaking from her, tainting everything around her, hurting those she loved.

Her gasping breaths came harder, and stars danced across her vision.

"Sage?"

She shuddered and squeezed her eyes tighter. Why wouldn't Tehl go away? Why did he always come back when she was at her worst?

"Look at me, Sage," Tehl said more firmly.

No, she wouldn't. She couldn't. He was just a figment of her imagination.

"If you won't look at me, then breathe with me."

She dropped her chin to her chest and tried to slow her breathing to match his slow, deep ones. Each breath felt like she was suffocating. Her lungs burned, and her heart raced.

"I can't," she gasped out.

"You can, and you will."

His comment cut through all the vile emotions rolling inside of her. He was right. She wouldn't die right now. She had to calm down.

Sage started counting down from one hundred to calm herself. Painfully, she sucked in deep breath after deep breath, her inhales and exhales lasting five counts each. By the time she reached twenty, her heart had slowed, and her breath came in steady gusts.

Fingers brushed her knuckles in a fleeting touch, and she jerked backward, rocking the cot. She curled her hands around the edge of the cot to steady herself. She wouldn't risk anyone else by letting them touch her. Just being near her was dangerous enough.

"I'm sorry," Tehl said softly, his deep voice curling around her. "You need to open your eyes."

"Are you real?" she muttered.

"I'm as real as your family and that giant man-eater eyeing me."

His comment caused her lips to twitch. Tehl always told her the truth and protected her. If he said he was real, he was. If he said she should open her eyes, she needed to do it.

One at a time, she opened each eye and stared at the bowl in her lap, the scent of her vomit reaching her. She swallowed thickly as a masculine hand pulled it from her lap. Her eyes snapped shut. The last time they'd shared eye contact, she was being paraded around as the warlord's conquest. Guilt and shame weighed heavily on her.

"Come, now. Look at me."

Her mind flashed to the fuzzy memory of him reaching his hand out toward her while Nali stood between them. If he could face a leren for her, she could face her family and her fear for him. There wasn't room to be a coward. There was no place for it in her life.

Sage lifted her chin and forced her eyes open. He stared back at her, a black lock of hair dangling in front of his face. He watched her, but made no move toward her. She glanced to the side, her family observing her with worry. Slowly, she turned back to Tehl. What if this was all a dream?

One by one, she uncurled the fingers of her right hand from the cot and reached out. She expected him to move forward, but he held still. Her hand hovered in the air for a moment before she steeled herself and brushed the wayward lock of hair from his face.

Her breath stuttered out of her lungs as the silk of his hair slipped through her fingers. He was real. He was here. With her. His smile bloomed across his face, making him so beautiful her eyes hurt. Her gaze moved from his deep blue eyes to her scratched pale hand resting against his cheek.

He was beautiful, and she was beastly.

She snatched her hand back and held it against her chest and then held it out in front of her. Even though the skin was damaged, she knew it would heal into flawless smooth pale skin like her injuries had never happened.

Sage curled her hand into a fist. She was defiled, sullied, rotten, no matter how flawless she appeared. No one could remove the stain on her soul. The wounds that bled freely inside her soul would turn into ugly scars. Her eyes flickered to Tehl. She shouldn't be allowed to mar him by touching him. She wasn't fit to be in anyone's company.

His smile dimmed and the sadness that entered his gaze made

her want to slap his face. She didn't want his sadness, his pity. She wanted his hate, his revulsion. That would make this whole situation easier. She could handle those emotions.

"Don't let him win," Tehl breathed.

His words were barely audible, but she heard them nonetheless.

Sage closed her eyes and dropped her head, sucking in a deep breath. He was right. What was important was the monster coming for them. They didn't have a second to lose. Each moment she let pass by, floundering in despair, was another life potentially lost.

Her brows furrowed as she pictured each horror that taunted her, each pain that she felt, as a single light in her mind. One by one, she extinguished them, a cool, disconnected feeling coming over her. As long as she kept herself numb, they *might* be able to get through this.

She slowly registered the overwhelming heat licking at her clammy skin, and the intense silence that hovered in the room like low clouds before a storm.

Sage waited patiently until all of the lights were firmly gone before she opened her eyes to meet Tehl's concerned gaze. Throwing her shoulders back and lifting her chin, she stared him down, uttering the words that threatened to lodge themselves in her throat.

"He comes. We need to prepare for battle."

CHAPTER SIX

Sage

Tehl just stared at her, with no reaction to her words. Did he not understand the significance of what she said?

"Did you hear me?" she asked softly.

Tehl blinked. "I heard you."

"And?"

"It's being taken care of."

One sentence. One measly line of information. "How?" she bit out.

An emotion flickered in his eyes before he shifted his gaze to the floor. "I have men working on this as we speak." He looked at her through his dark lashes. "Don't concern yourself about it. All you have to do is make sure you heal."

He had spoken the right words, and yet her gut rolled. He was shutting her out. Hiding things.

Sage slowly stood on wobbly legs, anger igniting in her belly.

Her mum reached out for her, but she brushed her hand away and stared at the man kneeling before her. "You will not keep me in the dark," she said. "Stop hiding things from me."

Tehl blew out a breath. "I'm not hiding things from you." He rocked back on his heels and stood, towering above her. "Please get back into bed."

It was a reasonable request, yet everything inside her chafed at his words. "No," she said. "You will not tell me what to do!" The venom she heard in her own voice shocked her. "I refuse to be left in the dark," she said again. "If I had not been left in the dark about Rhys's disappearance, things might have been very different."

Tehl's face fell. She winced but didn't take back her words. It was plain that the words pierced her husband. They were ugly, but true.

"Love," her mum murmured, brushing a hand down her arm. "Tehl wants what's best for you, as do we all. Everything will be taken care of. Why don't you lie down and calm yourself?"

She flicked a glance to her mum. "I am calm." And she was. "You haven't seen me upset."

"What do you want to know?" Tehl asked, his voice soft.

She faced him and lifted her chin. "Everything."

A small smile tugged at his lips. "That's a very long list. Start with a smaller request, for my sake."

Her mind raced. What did she really want to know? "Has the border been protected?"

A nod. "Reinforcements have been stationed along the entire wall. No one will get through without someone seeing."

That was doubtful. If the Scythians didn't want to be seen, they wouldn't be. She'd experienced it firsthand. But something was better than nothing.

Sage glance at Jas sleeping fitfully. Where was her other friend? "Where's Blaise?"

"With Sam."

How nonspecific. *Again.* Her eyes narrowed on her husband. "She's not in the prison, is she?"

"No."

"*Where* is she?" Words were tricky things. You could make one believe the complete opposite of what your words actually meant with a flick of the tongue. Everything was in the details.

"She's in the war room with Sam. She's giving him information on Scythia."

Sage arched a brow at him. "Willingly?"

"Last time I checked," he said with humor.

Her breath caught, and some emotion leaked through. Stars above, he was handsome when he smiled. Her lips thinned at that thought. Smiles couldn't be trusted. Smiles hid a numerous amount of falsehoods, even if it was Tehl.

"I want to see her."

He dipped his chin. "I'll fetch her at once," he acquiesced. "Is there anything else you need?"

"Many things, but nothing you can give me."

His smiled slipped as a steely glint entered his blue eyes. "I'll only bring her on one condition."

Her jaw clenched. *Here it was, the bargaining tool.*

"You need to rest and stay here."

"You cannot cage me," she growled. She'd go wherever she pleased.

He held up his hands. "I would never cage you."

"You already have." Sage snapped her mouth shut, hating the biting words she'd thrown at him like daggers. Why was she acting this way? They'd moved past all of this.

Tehl winced. "I wish I could erase our past, but I can't. I can give you my oath that I will do whatever is in my power to make sure you never feel caged again, if only you would let me."

"Why are you keeping me here?"

"Because you're not healthy," Tehl muttered. "And I made a promise before all of this I'd see you healthy and whole." A pause. "And I need you."

That was unexpected. She blinked. "Why?"

"Because you are the key to helping us win the war."

Everyone always wanted something from her.

Skepticism must have shown in her expression, because he continued. "And because you balance me."

"How?" All she did was bring chaos into his life.

Tehl shifted on his feet as if uncomfortable, but never looked away. "I see the world a certain way, and the way you see it is completely different. Having you rule by my side will make Aermia better. *You* make me better." Her traitorous heart tripped at his self-deprecating smile. "I've been told I'm too blunt."

"I prefer blunt," she blurted. And she did. She'd had enough secrets and betrayal for several lifetimes.

"And that's why I'll tell you the truth, even when I think it will hurt you. We both are brutally honest. It's a blessing and a curse."

Honesty. What a strange word. When was the last time she'd experienced something honest? Pure? Bitterness flooded her. She wasn't even sure she knew what purity was anymore. "Are you sure you know what honesty is?" They'd had their fair share of deceit between them.

"Sage," her mum chastised.

Tehl held a hand up. "It's okay. She's allowed to speak her

mind." He moved closer, causing her pulse to spike. "My mum taught me of honesty, and you know how much I loved her. Would I besmirch her memory?"

She knew the answer. "No."

"No. If I make a promise to you, I will keep it." He scanned her face. "Now, will you compromise with me? I need your help for what is ahead of us, but we can't do that if you're sick. Promise me you'll get back into bed?"

Part of her didn't want to compromise, hated that she had to bow to his wishes, but her logical side understood he was right. Her legs shook beneath her, and, soon, they would collapse from her weight. As much as she wanted to jump into the thick of things, she wasn't at her best. Sage crossed her arms. "I will get back into bed if you bring Blaise to me."

"It will be done."

"Now." Specifics mattered.

"Now," he repeated. He slowly held his hand out, palm up.

Sage stared at it. It should've been an easy thing to take his hand, but it wasn't. *You're not worthy of touching him.* She'd made too many mistakes.

"It's just a hand."

If only he knew. It was so much more. She wasn't good anymore. She was poison.

"I won't leave until you take it."

She studied the stubborn slant of his jaw and bit her lip. He was as stubborn as she was. If she didn't take his hand, he'd stand there for the rest of the day. Her left leg buckled, and she locked her knees to keep standing. Sage puffed out a breath and steeled herself. Holding his hand wasn't as bad as possibly collapsing in front of him and allowing him to see how weak she really was.

Sage pulled her right hand from her chest and lightly placed her hand in his. She forced herself to stay still as his calloused thumb brushed over hers in a gentle caress, and then he leaned closer and placed a feather-light kiss on the back of each of her hands.

Tears pricked the back of her eyes. Each touch was tender and careful, like he was worried she'd run away. But really, it was the complete opposite. It made her want to jump into his arms and never leave. He was her safety, but she was his death. She'd hurt him if she allowed herself to get too close.

She pulled her hand from his and avoided his gaze, focusing on the blanket hanging over the edge of her cot. "Blaise?"

"I'll bring her to you."

"Thank you," she said.

"You're welcome, love."

The floor blurred as Tehl left the room. *Love.* He'd called her love. A fat tear escaped her left eye. Love was what started this whole mess. Love twisted people. Love was death.

CHAPTER SEVEN

Tehl

He strode down the hallway, relief and anger warring inside him.

When he'd walked in and she was awake with color in her cheeks, a knot had loosened in his chest. Blaise had spoken the truth. Sage had healed at a remarkable rate. He was both grateful and disgusted. Grateful that she hadn't died, but disgusted that the warlord still had an effect on her even though she was far from him.

His teeth ground together as he thought of how she'd panicked and then completely blanked out. It was like her light had gone out. All feelings and warmth just disappeared in a breath.

Tehl nodded to a servant who bobbed a quick curtsey before scurrying along. His brows furrowed as he glanced over his shoulder, and the servant disappeared around the corner. He'd been in such a black mood since Sage had been taken that hardly any of the servants looked him in the eye anymore. Another one of his sins to atone for. They didn't deserve his anger.

He tucked his thoughts away as he strode into the war room and skirted around the table, ignoring the heated argument and the bows that followed in his wake. There wasn't anything he could do to change his past actions, but, from today on, he could be better.

He caught his father's attention as their advisors began to argue again. The king rolled his eyes as Tehl sat down and clapped him on the shoulder.

"Son."

"Father."

It was odd having his father here after his prolonged absence. Odd, but not unwelcome. If they were to survive the upcoming war, they needed every man, especially their king.

Tehl focused on their advisors. Jeren was red in the face, but that wasn't new; the man was perpetually angry.

"What's going on? What's Jeren angry about this time?"

"Jeren is arguing for throwing the Scythian woman in the prison."

Tehl straightened and zeroed in on Blaise, who sat five seats down from him on his left. Her fingers clenched around the arms of the chair as Jeren said something particularly rude. Surprise flickered through him, though, when Rafe slid a hand over the top of her left curled fist. Her head whipped to the side, and she hissed at him quietly, pulling her hand from his. Interesting. What was that about?

"You can't expect us to believe that you'd help your enemy," Jeren accused, "and become a traitor for nothing. Why have you come here? To spy?"

"How long has this been going on?" Tehl whispered out of the

61

corner of his mouth.

"Going on twenty minutes," his father answered.

"And why have you let it go on for so long?" The whole thing seemed a bit ridiculous. Blaise had already proven her loyalty.

"Because our advisers had a valid point that needs to be argued. *We* both know she's not here to harm us, but they don't. They deserve to have their say, and I'm curious how much it will take to crack her," his father murmured. "She seems most unflappable, but there's an undercurrent of rage flowing just below the surface."

"She won't crack," Tehl muttered, watching the drama unfold as the voices rose. "She was in our prison for months." They'd tried everything, and nothing had worked.

"But you didn't have him with you," his father remarked, glancing in Rafe's direction. "He seems...very protective of her."

Tehl studied the rebellion leader, noting how close he sat to Blaise. Rafe shifted in his seat, causing Blaise to glare at him and scoot closer to Sam. That in itself was interesting, but what intrigued Tehl even more was the dangerous expression Rafe was aiming at Jeren.

"He's angry," Tehl commented. That was an understatement. He looked like he wanted to rip the advisor's head off.

"Indeed," his father said softly. "Why do you think that is?"

His gaze slid to Blaise who sat so still she looked to be carved from stone, completely ignoring the giant of a man by her side. "She's rebuffed his help."

"Every man hates when a woman won't let him protect her," his father commented. "Especially when he considers her *his*."

Tehl's brows rose. Now, that was an interesting turn of events. Blaise and Rafe? Well, more like just Rafe. Blaise was doing everything in her power to ignore the rebellion leader.

"Who knows how much we can trust you?" Lelbiel commented, interrupting Tehl's thoughts. "We don't know you. How can we be sure you weren't part of the plot to hurt the princess?"

Blaise slapped her hands against the table and stood from her chair, her body vibrating with anger. "How dare you?" she hissed.

His advisor wrinkled his nose. "It was a valid question, my lady."

She leaned forward, her gaze locked on Lelbiel. "I would never, *never* hurt Sage. That woman has been through more horrors than all of you put together, but not by my hand." She scanned the table. "Some of you were even a part of those horrors," she accused. "I refuse to be lumped in with that sick monster on Scythia's throne. We may share the same bloodline, but he is *not* my family."

William steepled his finger and met Blaise's penetrating gaze. "We're not blaming you, my lady."

"It sounds like it," Rafe growled.

Blaise glared at the rebellion leader, and then focused back on William.

"I understand your frustration. We know what you've done for our princess." He held his hands out. "Please understand our position, though. How would you react if an enemy found their way into your inner circle? Not only that, but they were from the royal line and claimed to renounce their kingdom? It sounds a little far-fetched, doesn't it?"

Blaise chuckled and straightened, crossing her arms. "As much as an immortal king creating a perfect race of enhanced people?"

Silence met her statement.

Her gaze swept the table, and she paused on Tehl. "I am here because it is right to be. My people live in fear. Death and cruelty occur all too often." She pushed back her heavy, braided black hair and bowed at the waist. "I am here to help and serve Aermia in the dangerous time ahead. If the warlord continues to rule, both our peoples will cease to exist. His tyranny cannot continue."

"Agreed," Tehl said. "Are you prepared to fight against your own people? You will be branded a traitor. Think carefully. Words are easily said. Action is much more difficult."

She straightened, her lips thinning. "I have already been branded a traitor. The decision's already been made. The moment I cross into Scythia will mean my death." Her expression hardened. "And anyone who stands with that monster are not my people."

A quiet descended over the room at her declaration.

Tehl's father slowly stood and stepped down from his seat. Blaise warily watched him as he approached her. She crossed her arms over her chest and sketched a bow. "Your highness," she murmured.

"There's no need for that," his father rumbled, taking her hand. "You're as much a royal as I am, my lady."

Tehl hid a smile as Blaise blinked, clearly not expecting his gracious words. That was the thing about his father, he could charm almost anyone.

"I thank you," she said, still gaping at the king.

His father patted her on the hand. "You've made an immense sacrifice for my family. It will not be forgotten any time soon. Aermia will gladly accept your help, and, what's more, we'll support you after we rid the world of the warlord. Scythia could stand to have a leader like you on the throne."

Her eyes widened at the oath, and she glanced over his father's shoulder at Tehl for confirmation.

"It will be done." It was only fair they do what they could for her after the sacrifice she'd made and would still make. Logically, it was brilliant. If Blaise took the throne, they'd have an ally in Scythia for the first time in hundreds of years.

"Thank you," she said to his father. "I accept your offer."

Chills erupted on his arms. In that moment, they'd made history. Aermia had formed an alliance with Scythia. Never in his lifetime had Tehl guessed such a thing was possible. It was surreal.

His father released her hand and turned to the table. "Lelbiel, draft up an alliance. I'd like it in my office by tomorrow morning." He paused and scanned the table of men. "We've changed the course of history today. Now we have to prepare for it."

The men nodded around the table.

"We'll meet again tomorrow to discuss and sign the treaty." The king turned back to Blaise. "As long as that's acceptable to you?"

She looked startled at his attention to her. "It is."

The king smiled at Blaise. "It's settled then. Until tomorrow."

The Scythian woman blinked, and an answering smile adorned her face. It was all Tehl could do not to gape. He snapped his jaw closed and blinked several times. She was usually so stoic and grave. When Blaise really smiled, it transformed her into a completely different woman, and he wasn't the only one to notice. Rafe openly stared, his entire being homed in on her. But she seemed oblivious, smiling prettily at the king.

"I look forward to it, your highness," she murmured.

His father grinned down at Blaise and waved a hand at the table. "The rest of you are dismissed."

The men around the table reluctantly stood and filed toward the doors. Zachael stretched in his chair and stood, making his way toward Tehl. "Any change in Sage?" he asked, leaning a hip against the table.

"She's awake." That was the best news he had.

The weapons master clapped his hands together and smiled. "That's wonderful news. I knew she'd pull through. Our girl would never let sickness take her from us."

Tehl swallowed hard, loathing the way he felt thankful that the warlord had given Sage a draught and yet hating it at the same time.

Zachael eyed him and placed a hand on his shoulder. "Focus on your gratefulness, so your anger doesn't tear you apart."

He blew out a breath. "How do you always know what I'm thinking? It's uncanny."

"I've had a hand in raising you, my lord."

"That's the truth if I ever heard it," Garreth said, limping closer. "We basically lived in the training ring for years."

Tehl forced himself not to focus on his friend's shuffling gait. It hurt to watch each painful movement. No matter how much Garreth tried to hide it, the pain still showed through. "Brothers in arms." He held his forearm out.

"Absolutely," Garreth said, clasping forearms. "How is our princess?"

"Awake." He glanced over to Blaise, who had turned in their direction.

"She's awake?" she asked, concern plainly on her face.

"Yes, and she's asking for you."

"Then I better go to her." She turned on her heel.

He pushed from his chair and strode after her. "I'll escort you. I promised I'd bring you to her." This was not a promise he'd break.

Blaise glanced over her shoulder, a black brow arched. "In

exchange for what? What deal did you strike with her to keep her in bed?"

Tehl scowled, holding his arm out for her. "Why must everything be an exchange?"

"Because you're both much too stubborn, from what I hear."

"Rumors," he muttered as she waved away his arm and followed him to the door.

"I'm sure," she replied sarcastically.

Their journey back to the infirmary lapsed into silence, but it wasn't uncomfortable. Tehl always cherished a companion who didn't need to fill the silence with chatter. Blaise seemed to be of the same mind.

"How is she really?" she asked when they neared the infirmary.

He wouldn't sugarcoat it. "Disoriented. Cold. Anxious."

Blaise opened and closed her mouth before staying silent.

Clearly, she wanted to speak.

"Just tell me," he sighed. "I prefer the truth, even if it is blunt and harsh."

"She won't be the same person as before," she cautioned.

He already knew that. "I know."

"The girl you married is dead. My uncle will have made sure of that. He—" She paused in the quiet hallway, squeezing her eyes closed. "He is an expert in breaking people and reshaping them into what he desires them to be."

"Sage is strong."

"She is, but he is old, calculating, and vicious. I'm amazed she was able to function at all when we escaped." Blaise hung her head.

A rock sunk in his gut. "What are you saying?"

She exhaled heavily. "I'm saying that every step you make

needs to be a calculation, it needs to be for her benefit. If she gets in too deep, you have to pull her from the water. Your burden might be too much for her to bear now."

Understanding dawned. "You don't think she can rule."

"I don't know," she whispered, her dark eyes sad. "Maybe she will be able to. I only understand the warlord. What he's capable of." She sighed. "Nothing will be all right for a long time, if ever. Prepare yourself for that or let her go."

"Let her go? Like a divorce?" he asked, the words tasting like ash on his tongue. He'd never divorce her. She was his wife even if she was changed, suffering damage. They were bound, and he wouldn't abandon her.

"No, not a divorce. I meant you'll have to put her in a country home to live out her life in peace. She deserves that." A shrug. "If she can't handle ruling, that will be the best option for her, instead of letting her waste away in some tower in this castle. She'd be miserable there."

He hated the idea outright. Hated it. He'd grown accustomed to Sage, and, what's more, he loved her family. They'd become part of his own family while she was gone. If she was gone, it would tear another hole in his. He glanced to the side. None of that mattered. No matter how he felt about it, if it was the best thing for Sage, he'd do it. That was what you did for your family, and there was no one who deserved it more.

"If that's what she wants, I will do it. But I won't force anything on her."

Blaise studied him, her head cocked. "I was taught that the princes of Aermia were monsters. In my mind, I found it hard to imagine anything worse than the warlord." A dark smile. "Which is why he always hated me. But, after spending months in your dungeon, I realized one important thing."

"What was that?" he asked, not knowing where the conversation was going.

"That no matter how much the warlord tried to turn himself into the hero, he was always the villain. And no matter how much I tried to turn you into the villain, you were the hero." She held his gaze. "You're not what I expected, Tehl Ramses, and you treated me better than I deserve after what I did to that village." She swallowed hard. "I'm sorry for my part in hurting your people."

An apology. He didn't expect that.

"We have all done things we aren't proud of. It's how we fix those mistakes that is important. And, by my account, you've done everything in your power to atone for those things. You not only have my forgiveness, but my thanks," he said roughly. Sage would still be stuck in that hellhole if it hadn't been for Blaise and Maeve.

"I don't deserve it," she said, shaking her head.

"No one deserves forgiveness. That's what makes it so special." His mother had taught him that.

"I'll keep that in mind." She smiled at him and held her hand out. "Allies?"

He clasped her small hand. "Brothers in arms."

She flashed her teeth in a grin. "Sisters in arms."

Tehl smiled. No wonder Sage liked the fiery Scythian woman. She was a lot like his wife.

Chapter Eight

Sage

She wanted out of the bed and the room.

"Haven't you slept enough?" a familiar voice asked.

Sage glanced to the side, and she smiled. "Blaise."

The Scythian woman grinned at her from her chair. "I thought you were never going to wake up."

Slowly, Sage pushed herself up from her cot and brushed a strand of hair from her face. "It's the only thing I'm allowed to do, apparently," she grumbled.

Blaise stood and sat on the edge of the cot, patting her foot through the thick blanket. "You need to heal. That takes time."

"I know." And she did. Her legs had collapsed out from under her almost the moment Tehl left, and she'd been weak as a kitten since. Sage slid her hand over her friend's and squeezed before releasing it. "I'm so glad you're okay."

A wry smile. "Not much can hurt me."

Red flashed across Sage's vision. "There was so much blood." She shook her head to dispel the memory. "The last time I saw you, I thought you would die. How did you survive such a beating?"

Emotions rippled over Blaise's face. "There's not much I can't survive." A shrug. "I'm Scythian. I was bred to survive, and I've been through worse."

That broke her heart. Blaise caught her expression and shook her head.

"It is what it is."

That bastard had scarred more than just Sage.

Blaise glanced over her shoulder at Jasmine. "How is she?"

Sage glanced at her sleeping friend, frowning. Mira hadn't been able to hide her concern. If Mira was concerned about Jasmine, her condition was dangerous. "She's not well," she admitted. "But, with time, I'm sure she'll get better. Plus, Nali will help."

The feline's ear twitched at her name, but Nali otherwise made no move but to cuddle closer to the shivering Jasmine.

"She doesn't deserve this fate," Blaise growled.

"No, she doesn't," Sage whispered. Who knew how long Jasmine's body could survive such a fever? It had to break. It had to. A wave of sorrow and guilt moved through her. Sage ruthlessly shoved her feelings down. They wouldn't change anything. The best she could do was hope and pray.

Sage exhaled and focused on Blaise. "Have you been taken care of?"

"My care has been excellent."

"I can see with my own two eyes that you're fine physically," Sage said. "I meant, are they being kind to you?" Harsh words could be worse than a beating.

"By 'they,' do you mean the royals?" Blaise asked, picking at her nails.

"By the stars, you know how to skirt an issue," Sage muttered. "Sam would be proud."

"I'm sure after the few months I spent in the dungeon, he understands my gift of avoidance."

Sage rolled her eyes. If they beat around the bush, she'd fall asleep before she got the information she wanted. "Is the Crown forcing you to do anything you don't want to?" she demanded. "If so, I will march from this room and fix it right now." And she would as soon as her legs stopped shaking.

Blaise chuckled. "I'm sure you would, and it would be a sight to see, but don't worry yourself. Your royals can't make me do anything I don't want to."

"You don't have to help us." Sage exhaled and said what she'd been rehearsing in her mind for the last half an hour. "You are Scythian, and you're a wealth of knowledge, but you hold no allegiance to Aermia. I will not force you to help us, nor will I allow the Crown or council to either. You helped me escape that prison," she said thickly. "That I can never repay. You have my everlasting gratitude."

The Scythian woman cocked her head, her dark braids sliding over her shoulder. "You aren't the only one. You could've left me in the jungle."

"No, I couldn't have." No one deserved that fate. She would've killed Blaise before she allowed *him* to take her.

A shrug. "Anyone I know would have."

She scowled. "Then you've surrounded yourself with the wrong people."

"That matters not," Blaise said. "I am thankful nonetheless. You risked yourself for me. If the warlord had caught me, my fate would've been worse than death."

Sage breathed heavily, and bile flooded her mouth. She understood better than anyone what he would've done. Blaise would've suffered in an inhuman way.

"For that reason," Blaise soldiered on, "I give you my friendship and fealty."

Sage swallowed and shook her head. "You don't owe me anything. As far as I'm concerned, we are equal."

"I want to help. That monster needs to be destroyed."

The room spun, but Sage held on, gritting her teeth. "This is a serious decision. You'll have to fight your own people."

"So be it. The sacrifice will be worth the reward."

"It will be a thankless job." Sage's people would be suspicious of her. In their minds, Scythians were the monsters underneath the bed. Overcoming prejudice and deep-seated fear was no easy task.

"Indeed." Blaise grinned. "Your council wasn't too happy with me today."

Sage's brows rose. "You were at a war meeting today?"

"It was more of a trial."

"Surely someone stood up for you?" Sage gritted her teeth. Someone better have.

"A few, but the majority watched me with contempt and suspicion." Blaise waved off Sage when she opened her mouth to retort. "I'm the enemy who ended up in their inner circle. I would've been suspicious as well. I will win them over. It's only a matter of time. Despite their prejudice and wariness, they know how useful I will be to them." She flashed Sage a smile that looked so much like Maeve.

Maeve. Was the older woman okay? What kind of horrors

would the warlord unleash on her? Shame washed over Sage for not thinking about her sooner. "Do you think your mother is all right?" she asked softly.

Blaise sucked in her cheeks and nodded. "My mother is wise and clever. I doubt he has figured out who helped you, but the entire court will be under scrutiny from now on. It will be very dangerous at court."

Sage shivered and rubbed her arms. Even thinking about Scythia caused her skin to crawl. Her brows furrowed as she glanced around the room, realizing it was quite empty. "Where are my parents?" They promised they wouldn't leave. It was unlike them to break such an oath.

"Your mum needed a bath, your father is waiting outside of the infirmary, and the healer is fetching Lilja."

Some tension drained from her body. "Oh."

Blaise shuffled to a stand and hugged her. "Colm seemed to think we needed privacy. I'll be back soon."

"You'll keep me apprised of what's going on?"

Her Scythian friend grinned wickedly. "Why, princess, are you asking me to spy for you?"

"It's not spying if you should be there in the first place," Sage called as Blaise moved toward the door.

"True," her friend said. "I'll let your father in."

"Thank you, Blaise."

She paused in the doorway and bowed her head. "My pleasure, my friend," she said before disappearing out the door.

A moment later, the door creaked open and her papa peeked in, his gray-streaked, brown hair tousled. "Hey, love, you have company." He pushed open the door, and Mira bustled in, followed by Lilja and Hayjen.

There was no stopping the tears that always seemed to be lurking in the corners of her eyes. "Lilja," she cried.

The Sirenidae rushed to her side and threw her arms wide, wrapping them around her. A citrus aroma surrounded her as Sage pressed her face into Lilja's silvery white hair. "Stars above, I missed you."

"I missed you, too, ma fleur," Lilja whispered, her words rough.

Huge arms circled both herself and Lilja, and her eyes sprung open. She lifted her head and smiled at Hayjen whose ice-blue eyes were surprisingly wet.

"It's so good to see you Sage," her burly friend rasped.

Lilja pulled back and pressed her long, graceful fingers against either side of Sage's face. "My heart is so happy to see those beautiful green eyes." She wiped her tracks of tears from her face only to have new ones appear. "Ma fleur, I dare say it's the most beautiful thing I've ever seen."

"I didn't think I'd ever see you again." The words hurt coming out, but they were the ugly truth.

Sage stared at Lilja's face, and, to her horror, another face imposed over hers. Her breath hitched when Lilja blurred into Ezra. Her heart began to race, and she couldn't tear her eyes away from the apparition before her.

"I'm sorry," she whispered. "I'm so sorry."

Ezra smiled, blood trickling from his mouth.

"Sage?" a distorted voice asked.

She tried to blink to dispel the nightmare, but she was frozen in place. He gurgled something that she didn't understand. If only she could help him.

"I'm so sorry," she sobbed, wishing the memory would release her.

Fingers dug into her shoulders and shook her roughly. She blinked hard and tore her eyes from Ezra, staring up into Hayjen's very-worried face.

"Can you hear me?" he asked softly.

Her bottom lip trembled as she nodded her head, *yes*. More tears flooded her eyes as she stared at her friend, not daring to look in Lilja's direction. She'd gone crazy. Specters of people haunted her everywhere she turned. There was no escape.

"Your eyes blanked, and we couldn't reach you. I'm sorry I shook you." Hayjen touched her cheek and knelt on the side of her cot, rubbing Sage's left hand between his. "Your hands are so cold."

Like her soul. Everything inside her was cold. If only it would numb the pain that plagued her. The guilt. The shame.

"Ma fleur?"

Sage slammed her eyes closed and held her right hand out to Lilja. The Sirenidae clasped her trembling fingers between her own. Maybe if she didn't look at her, it wouldn't happen again. She couldn't handle seeing Ezra again, reliving that moment. Each minute was a struggle to hold on. Memories crashed into her, one after another, threatening to drown her.

"I'm fine," she whispered. It was a pretty lie.

Lilja squeezed her hand. "What happened?"

Death. Her past sins and demons were catching up with her. "Memories," she choked out.

"Oh, Sage," Lilja said, her voice breaking.

Sage turned back to Hayjen and opened her eyes to stare into his sad face. If she was her normal self, she would've hated the pity and sorrow in his eyes, but, at that point, she was too tired to even care. He could pity her if he kept holding her hand and kept the monsters at bay. Pathetic, really.

Mira stepped next to Hayjen's right side and leaned close to place a bottle of warmed water underneath the blankets.

"Thank you," Sage said, grateful for the heat now suffusing her body.

"Anything for you, sis," Mira said with a smile.

Emotion clogged her throat for what felt like the umpteenth time. True friends were one in a million. They stuck around when things got bad, and, somehow, she'd managed to surround herself with so many wonderful people just like that.

"Look at all the visitors," a chipper voice exclaimed.

Sage peeked at the door, staring past Lilja's face at her mum, who bustled forward, her cheeks flushed, dark hair shiny and wet. She must have come straight from her bath without even drying her hair. Love and affection filled Sage. There was no one like her mum. She was the best.

Her mum pecked her papa on the cheek and then pushed in between Lilja and Hayjen. She cupped Sage's cheek and pressed a quick kiss to her forehead. "How's my favorite daughter?"

"I'm your only daughter," Sage said sarcastically, not missing a beat. Her mum had always said that since she and her brothers were children. She had her favorite daughter, favorite youngest son, and favorite oldest son.

It was nice to play at something normal, even if she felt far from it.

Her mum pulled back and cocked her head, frowning as she scanned Sage's face. "What's wrong?"

Everything. "Nothing." She forced a smile on to her lips.

"You can't lie to me, Sage Blackwell." Her mum stopped and grinned. "Sage *Ramses*." Her smile dimmed. "You never have been able to. I can see it on your face. It's like you've seen a ghost."

Sage shivered. "Just memories."

Lilja's jaw clenched, her papa's fingers curled into fists, Hayjen stroked the back of her hand softly, and her mum hummed. Then Mira outright cursed.

"That bastard," Mira seethed. "If your family doesn't get to him first, I will."

Sage blinked. She didn't think she'd ever heard the blond healer curse.

"Get in line," Lilja whispered. The hard edge riding her voice caused Sage to shiver.

Mira scanned the group. "You're lucky to have such an amazing family."

"I am," Sage said.

Mira handed her a cup of tea. "I admit, I'm a little jealous. I never got to meet any of my aunts and uncles. They had died before I was born."

Sage slowly blinked. *Aunt and uncle?* What in the bloody hell? She glanced between her mum, papa, Lilja, and Hayjen.

Lilja stiffened and Hayjen stopped warming her hand, but no one corrected Mira. They just watched Sage as she processed the healer's words.

Lilja and Hayjen were really her family? How many more surprises could she take?

She sighed and settled on one simple word. "Why?"

Why had they kept this from her?

CHAPTER NINE

Sage

"I'm so sorry," Mira mumbled miserably. "No one told me it was a secret."

Sage sat up straighter, swung her legs over the cot to face the group, and patted the healer's hand. "It's not your fault. You didn't know, and you're not the one who lied to me." Stars above, she hated secrets.

Mira's stricken face crumpled further, but she nodded and bustled toward her herbs, leaving the group in an awkward silence.

Sage eyed her family, reeling from the news. Why did they think they had to keep it a secret?

"Why?" she asked again, staring her mum down.

Her mum pursed her lips, but answered, "For protection."

What an opaque answer. "Protection from what?"

Her mum glanced to Hayjen but kept silent.

Sage's attention slid to her burly friend, and she scrutinized the person she thought she knew.

Lilja was clearly not her blood relation, so that left Hayjen. Her papa didn't have any siblings, and her mama's older brother died before Sage was born. Her eyes narrowed as she studied Hayjen. He looked close to her age, but she knew him to be much older, thanks to Lilja's special seaweed. He didn't exactly look like her mama, but the shape of his eyes, and the point of his nose hinted at...

Hayjen held her gaze, not looking away as she worked through each piece of the puzzle.

"So, you're my mother's brother?" she said softly.

He smiled and nodded. "I am. Older brother."

"By several years," her mum piped in with a smile.

Even though she knew what Lilja's herbs could do, her brain was having a hard time fathoming it. Hayjen looked like her mum's younger brother, maybe even her son, and yet he was older than she was. He looked like Seb. "Do my brothers know?"

"No," her papa said. "It's been too dangerous."

How long did they plan on keep the truth from her? "Were you going to tell me?" Was it just a happy circumstance that Mira said something she shouldn't?

"Of course," her mum replied. "We've always planned on telling you when the time was right."

"When the time was right?" Sage repeated. How convenient. "I would have said the time was right when you sent me to Lilja in the first place. Don't you think?"

"I asked her to keep silent," Lilja confessed.

Sage forced herself to look at the Sirenidae. Magenta eyes so foreign from her own gazed at her with affection. "Go on."

Her aunt patted her leg. "You understand why I hide myself, right?"

"You'd be hunted if others knew Sirenidae still existed." And they would. People were relentless when their anger and greed got a hold of them.

"Yes. People are greedy and desperate to live as long as they can and make the most out of the world they live in without consequence to others. But that's not the only reason we kept silent. It was to protect your family."

"Your family would've been outcasts," Hayjen said. "The old stories had a way of painting the Sirenidae people as monsters. No one would've come to the forge for anything. You'd have been forced out, and that's the best-case scenario."

Sage nodded. That made sense. It felt like years ago that she'd met Lilja, but hadn't that been her same response? Fear? "So, you lied."

Her mum nodded. "To protect those we love. It was a danger to them if we associated, and a danger to us." She leaned close and cupped Sage's cheek. "I was pregnant with you when they left the first time. We had more than just ourselves to worry about."

Hayjen squeezed Sage's right hand. "We didn't have another choice. The community knew your mum and me. I couldn't hide. It was too dangerous to stay when I didn't age any longer. So, I died."

"So, you died," she whispered, turning to her mum. "I saw you cry for him. You told me you missed your brother."

"And I did. He was my only family. He practically raised me."

"Couldn't you meet in secret?" Sage asked. Lilja's ship was perfect to hide people.

"We did for a while," Gwen explained. "But it became more

dangerous after you and your brothers were born. We couldn't risk you remembering them. So," she sighed, "we wrote letters."

"Every couple of years I'd sneak to the forge and visit just long enough to see your mum and leave gifts," Hayjen said with a smile.

Her mind immediately went to the trunk that always sat at the end of her bed growing up, filled with trinkets and exotic gifts. So, that's how they afforded some of the things. Sage had always figured her parents squirreled gold away.

She glanced around the group. It still hurt that they hadn't told her the truth. They had lost so much time together. And if there was one thing she understood, it was that time was most precious. You never knew how much of it you'd have with someone.

"I would've kept quiet, you know," Sage said.

"Ma fleur, I know you would've," Lilja said, a tear sneaking out of the corner of her eye. "But, again, it was too dangerous. If anyone suspected a thing, your whole family would've been in jeopardy." Her aunt leveled her with a serious look. "You know, as well as I do, that information can be extracted."

Sage swallowed hard. She did. Everyone had a breaking point.

"Do you forgive us?" her mum asked.

"There's nothing to forgive. You were just doing what you thought was best. I don't necessarily agree with everything you did, but—" She shrugged. "I don't know what I would've done in that situation. The only thing I'm upset about is all the lost time." She smiled at her family. "I would've loved growing up around the Sirenidae."

Lilja wiped her face and pulled her into a hug. "You're always welcome in my home."

"And what of the sea?" She'd love to go for another swim.

Her aunt pulled back with a grin. "As soon as you're well

enough, I'll take you for a swim. The Leviathans are getting ready to have their pups."

If anyone else said that to Sage, she'd pass out from fear, but not Lilja. She had a wonderfully strange effect on the sea monsters. They acted almost as pets, and it was something to behold. She'd never forget swimming with the majestic creatures, or the peace of being in the embrace of the sea. Peace was something she severely lacked.

Her brows furrowed as a thought occurred to her. "Were any of the stories you told me of how you met true?"

"Some," Hayjen said. "If you have any questions, all you need to do is ask."

Her gaze dropped to his scarred wrists. "Were you a slave?"

"I was," he said gruffly. "Lilja saved me, though."

A chest-rattling cough interrupted them. She glanced over her shoulder at Jas. Even in the short period of time since this morning, she looked worse.

"Is there nothing you can do for her?" she asked Lilja.

"I've done everything I can. Her body is so weak."

Sage hung her head. "Will she die?"

"I don't know. Jacob, Mira, and myself are doing everything we can to undo what those animals did."

Jasmine being stabbed flashed through Sage's mind, momentarily blinding her. Dots moved across her vision and metal bit into her wrist while she screamed for her friend.

"Just breathe, ma fleur. The memories are just that, memories. They're not happening right now. They're not real."

"They're *very* real," Sage growled, her fingers clenching the sheet beneath her.

"They'll fade in time. I promise."

"How do you know?" None of hers had. Demons plagued her everywhere she looked, every time she closed her eyes.

"Because I've been there. I know what goes on and I *promise* you, it will fade. You'll heal."

A buzzing filled her ears as she blinked away the dots and focused on Lilja's sensual features. She couldn't have heard that right. "What do you mean you've 'been there'?"

"I was also held captive in Scythia, so I understand your pain."

Lilja said it so plainly. Like she was speaking about the weather, not the hell that Scythia was. Not like she'd just broken what was left of Sage's heart.

"When?" she rasped.

"At least thirty years ago."

Thirty years. Sage blinked. Lilja had known what was happening for thirty years and she'd done nothing. A blind rage filled her vision, and, before she knew what was happening, she'd slapped Lilja across the face. Her family gaped at her in shock, and she stared at her hand, wondering how it moved on its own.

Lilja touched her cheek and turned back to Sage, completely unruffled. "Anger is okay," she soothed. "It's okay to be angry."

It wasn't about anger. It was about betrayal. Her body began to tremble as she stared at Lilja. The creature in front of her had played human all these years and not stopped the monstrosities across the border. "You knew this entire time they were taking women? Hurting them? Using them as breeders?"

"Yes."

Bile burned her throat. She was just as guilty as the Scythians by doing nothing. "And yet you've done nothing?"

"That's not true," Hayjen spoke. "I was a slave headed to Scythia. My ship was full of women, and Lilja saved us all. We've been destroying their suppliers at sea for years, rescuing girls."

But they didn't save *her*. Her eyes slid to Jasmine. Or Jas. "This has been going on for years, and you've told no one?"

"Who would've believed them, love?" her mum asked gently. "They're pirates."

"The king would have," she spat. Marq never judged someone based on their appearance or their lot in life.

"Many went forward, but they were considered only rumors. They weren't important enough to garner attention," her uncle explained. "They needed proof. Solid witnesses."

"You're telling me that Poseidon's daughter wouldn't be received well by the king?" She shook her head at her family's startled looks. "Come now, don't be coy. I've done my studies and put the pieces of the puzzle together. Lilja could only come from the royal line. You had the power to make a change and you didn't." Sage stabbed a finger at Lilja. "You told me it was my responsibility to help if I was in the position to. You are a coward and a hypocrite." She cleared her throat to keep it from cracking, and gestured to her face. "If you had done as you asked me to months ago, this would not have happened."

"We can't change the past, love," her papa admonished.

"That I understand well." Her eyes began to well up. "But Lilja protected herself and the Sirenidae people, and, because of that, thousands have been tortured in..." Her breath hitched. "In unspeakable ways. Thousands more will die in the upcoming war."

"I'm so sorry you've been hurt." Lilja's voice cracked. "It kills me that you were hurt."

"Hurt?" she scoffed. "He didn't hurt me. He burnt me down to the ground and then formed me in the way that pleased him the

85

most." She gagged while tears ran down her face. "How did you get out?" she found herself demanding. How had Lilja escaped that hell?

"I was given to a warrior and his men. One of them helped me escape."

A warrior helped her?

"Who?" What were the odds it was someone she knew?

"His name was Blair."

The nausea hit her, and she bent over the side of the cot, emptying the contents of her stomach. Blair, the man who'd tried to protect—but also hurt—her. The one with a pregnant slave at his side. She heaved again.

Mira slid a pot underneath her and held back her hair as she continued to retch.

"This is too much for her," Mira said sternly. "You need to leave."

Sage wiped the corners of her mouth and straightened, her bitterness and rage threatening to drown her. "He helped you escape?"

"Yes. Did you know him?" Lilja asked.

She cackled. "Oh, I knew him. He beat me regularly on our journey to Scythia. Even stripped me in front of his men."

Her mum gasped and began to cry, but Lilja didn't look away. Sage wanted her to, to be ashamed. To understand the pain and suffering she caused because of her inaction. "I can't abide to look at you," she said heatedly. "You are not my family, nor my friend. Get out, and don't come back."

"I will come back when you need me," Lilja said softly.

"Oh, you will," Sage said darkly. "War is coming, and I'll need your people to step up. They've hidden all these years, and it's time they faced the monster they've been hiding from and fight alongside the rest of us. You will aid me in that."

"Sage," Hayjen began, but she pulled her hand out of his.

"Get out."

He studied her, his lips pinched, and then stood. She ignored him as he placed a kiss on her forehead.

"Everything will turn out all right," he whispered. "We'll always be here for you."

Except they weren't. Where had they been when she was taken? How could she trust the words of cowards and liars?

Lilja stood slowly, not looking away from her. "I know what this is. I've done it myself. I will *never* abandon you, ma fleur. Never. I love you. When the time comes, I will come when you call."

What an ideal notion. "Lies."

"Sage," her papa said softly.

She turned to her parents. Even though she wanted them to stay and not leave her, she couldn't handle looking at them. They didn't deserve her anger and poison. "Please leave."

"Love, I'm not leaving you." Her mum's face hardened. "I'm your mother."

Sage turned to Mira, who stood by her side like a quiet sentinel. "They need to leave."

Mira stared down at her, searching her face before turning to her family. "You all need to leave. Your presence is upsetting her. I only agreed to allow you in here as long as you didn't disturb her."

"No," her mum argued.

"Yes," Mira said with a steely edge. "If you do not leave, I'll have you escorted out."

Her mum glanced at Sage for help.

"Please leave, Mum. I need—" She hiccupped. "I need to be alone."

Her mum tossed a nasty glare Mira's way and wrapped Sage in a huge hug. "I'll be right outside the door if you need me. I love you."

"Love you," she whispered back.

She watched as her family filed out of the infirmary, and she felt nothing, even though they all looked as if they'd lost. That was her fault. She knew it, and yet she couldn't stop herself from lashing out.

The old saying was true.

You always hurt the ones you love.

CHAPTER TEN

Sage

"Please, wake up, please," Sage whispered, brushing a strand of sweaty hair from Jasmine's gaunt face. She winced as another wet cough wracked Jasmine's fragile body. In the three days since she'd awoken, Jasmine had only worsened. Each breath she took was a struggle. Sage clutched her friend's limp hand and kissed her knuckles.

"You have to wake up, Jas. You have to."

"You need to go back to your own cot," Mira said softly. "I don't want you to get sick. You've only just recovered yourself."

It wasn't possible to obey Mira's request even if she wanted to. Her legs had long since gone numb while kneeling next to her friend's bed.

"How can I leave her when I've done this to her?" she whispered.

Mira knelt next to her, her hand resting on Sage's right

shoulder. "This isn't your fault. She's here because you saved her."

"Have I really?"

No. In her heart, she knew Jasmine would die. Only instead of a quick death, it would be long and painful. She'd drown from the fluid in her lungs. An awful, brutal way to die.

"You need to rest."

"All I've done is rest." Sage swiped at her wet eyes. Or attempted to, at least. Sleep evaded her.

"No. I've hardly seen you sleep."

Sage slid her gaze toward the healer. "Except for when you drug me." That was the worst. It trapped her in the nightmares.

Mira's lips thinned. "I wouldn't have to drug you if you slept. You can't go on without sleep."

She turned back to Jas, ignoring Mira. She couldn't sleep. Every time she closed her eyes, *he* was waiting for her. No sleep was better than the nightmares she couldn't escape from.

She swallowed hard. The sick part of it was that she missed someone holding her at night. A curse tumbled from her lips as a tear slipped down her cheek. Maybe this was penance for her sins.

"This isn't your fault."

"Someone should pay."

"Yes, but not the innocent," her friend said. "You blame yourself for everything. Even the things you can't control. Sometimes, things happen that we can't control. That's just life."

"I'm no innocent. If you knew the things I've done..." She bowed her head. "I deserve to pay for my sins."

"Pay for your sins? Oh, Sage." Mira sighed. "My God would not punish you this way. He's known for love, not suffering. Why would he take someone you loved? Or punish Jasmine when she's helped you? That makes no sense. It would hurt the innocent. Only someone cruel would do that."

When Sage didn't respond, Mira muttered under her breath, "I think you need to leave the infirmary."

"What?" Sage whipped around.

"I agree with that," Jacob said, shuffling into the room.

"I'm not leaving," Sage said, holding Jasmine's hand a little tighter. Her place was at Jasmine's side. "Plus, you have all been telling me I can't leave for days."

"Three days," Mira remarked. "And you've caused mischief the entire time."

Sage ignored her as Jacob edged around the cot and leaned over Nali to rest a hand upon Jasmine's forehead. The leren cracked an eye and then ignored him, much like Sage wished to after his last comment.

"Her fever hasn't increased, but it hasn't lessened, either." His peculiar bronze eyes narrowed on her through his round spectacles. "You're making yourself ill by staying here."

"How can I leave her?" Sage asked, wiping a damp cloth against Jasmine's temple. "She deserves to have family at her side to watch over her." To protect her.

Jacob laid a wrinkly hand over hers and pulled the cloth from her hand. "And no one should have to watch someone they love die."

She glared at Jacob. "She's not going to die." Sage wouldn't allow it. Jas had too much ahead of her to die.

His eyes softened into something sad, yet knowing. "She's not well, Sage. I don't know how much longer she'll remain."

A sob caught in her throat. She hated lies, but, now, all she wanted was for him to lie to her. "Is there nothing we can do?"

"We've done everything we possibly can for her."

"Fix her, damn it!" she cried.

Nali's ears laid back, and she hissed at the Healer as Sage's tears blurred Jacob into a collage of color.

"I've done all I can. But you can help her, Sage," he said, frowning at the feline.

"How?" she croaked.

"By leaving," he pleaded. "Despair clings to you like a cloak. That will not help her. She needs peace and quiet. If you love her, you'll leave."

A bark of laughter burst out of Sage. What a clever way to get rid of her. "I see through your games, old man," she growled.

He was manipulating her, but she wouldn't challenge him and stay if she would hinder Jasmine's recovery.

She leaned close to Jasmine's ear. "Listen here, Jas. There are two precious children in this castle waiting for you. You will not abandon them a second time. You must get better. Don't let the monsters win. Don't let them take your family from you."

Sage pressed a kiss to her pale cheek and then stood on shaking legs. She pushed back her shoulders and stared down her nose at the Healer. "I'll go, but you'll keep me apprised of her health."

"Yes, my lady." He bowed. "There's an escort waiting for you outside the door."

She nodded and turned on her heel to leave.

A rumble stopped her in her tracks. Sage walked around the cot and placed a hand on either side of Nali's face. As much as she didn't want to part with her companion, Jasmine needed her more. "I need you to stay here and help her."

The feline's alert, golden eyes blinked as she stared at Sage.

"Stay, please."

Nali whined and bumped her nose against Sage's cheek. "I'll

come back for you, but I need you to keep helping Jas. And no eating anyone," she added.

The leren gave her a good lick with her rough tongue and snuggled back down beside Jasmine. It was decided then. Sage scratched Nali behind the ear, receiving a contented purr before she moved toward the door, dread sitting in her belly like a lump of lead.

Sage hesitated, her hand hovering over the doorknob. This was what she'd been begging for over the last three days, and yet…a thrill of fear went through her. Once she stepped out of this door, she wasn't safe—or, rather, she left the illusion of safety behind.

Sage closed her eyes and prepared herself, pulling open the door. Her eyes snapped open, and she froze. Her papa and mum stood to the side speaking between themselves, but it was the big man grinning at her that caused her lungs to seize.

"Garreth," she breathed, not daring to move lest she disturbed the apparition. "I'm so sorry." Another senseless death on her hands. At least she could apologize for her stupidity.

"Nothing to be sorry about, love. Now, let's get you up to your room."

She still remembered the first time he had carried her to her room. She couldn't even walk and was so scared of what they'd do to her. It felt like a thousand years ago, not months.

"Love?" her mum asked.

Sage opened her eyes, not realizing she'd closed them. "Are you here to help me to my room?" she asked, ignoring another one of the ghosts haunting her.

Her mum's brow wrinkled. "We're coming with you, but," she said, gesturing to Garreth, "this nice gentleman will be the one helping you."

She gurgled and glanced between her mum and Garreth. "You can see him, too?" *Please say yes.*

Gwen's fingers tightened on her own. "Yes, love."

A cry gurgled in her throat, and she threw herself against Garreth. "You're okay?"

Big arms wrapped around her. "No one told you?" he rasped.

She shook her head *no*, his leather breastplate rubbing against her face. "I thought you died," she cried. "He told me you died."

"I'm okay, love. I'm okay," he soothed, running his hand over her tangled hair. "It's all right. I'm just fine." He pulled back and grinned at her. "See? Nothing wrong." He hoisted her up into his arms and smiled. "No man can keep me down."

She smiled wobbly and wrapped her arms around his neck as he began walking through the hall. Once again, the world had turned on itself. After being away from the castle, it felt foreign, not like her home. She turned her thoughts from the things around her and stared at the side of Garreth's face. New scars adorned his countenance, and his nose was slightly crooked.

"If you keep staring at me like that, I think the crown prince might take exception to it."

"Did Rhys give you these?" she asked as more warriors added to their ranks. Her fingers dug into the cloak that hung off his shoulders as she avoided the glances cast her way. Garreth glanced at her and moved faster, accentuating the limp she didn't bother asking about. It was the sick kind of thing Rhys would have done.

"He gave them to me." A smile. "Don't worry, princess, they add to my beauty, do they not?"

"They certainly do," she whispered. In truth, the scars were jagged and ugly, but, to her, they were a badge of honor, of survival. They'd both survived that monster. "My guess is that women fall all over themselves for you."

A snort. "They can't keep their hands off of me."

"Garreth," her mum chastised.

"Forgive me, my lady," he said, looking anything but apologetic.

"I see how you and Sam are such good friends," her papa remarked with a smile. "I'm sure you would've gotten along with our boys as well."

"Indeed," her mum grumbled, causing Sage to smile as they ascended the servants' stairs. "What's one more mischievous boy?"

"Thank you," Sage whispered.

"For what?" Garreth asked, his eyes on the stairs.

"For taking this route." She didn't think she could bear all the stares and whispers.

A slight smile. "You've never been one for fanfare."

"No, I have not."

"Although, I have to say I don't care for stairwells any longer."

That she understood. "Me, neither."

They reached the last stair and entered the royal wing. Some of the tension in Garreth drained as they moved down the corridor.

Her brows furrowed as they passed Tehl's room and moved toward her old room.

Garreth caught her look and answered her unspoken question. "The prince thought you'd be more comfortable in your own room."

Disappointment poked her. Of course, he wouldn't want her near him after everything she'd done.

He paused outside her old room. "Are you ready?"

"Yes." A lie, but what was one more?

CHAPTER ELEVEN

Tehl

"Good hell," Tehl cursed as Sam was thrown across the ring. The Scythian woman's strength was incredible.

His brother hit the ground and rolled with the fall, popping back up. He staggered and shook his head before narrowing his eyes at his opponent. "That was cheap," Sam accused with a dangerous smile.

"War *is* cheap." Blaise sauntered up to the fence that encircled the training ring, her back to Sam. "If you see an opening, you take it, or you die." She wiped her face while Sam snuck up on her. "Scythians are stronger and faster than you."

Tehl leaned against the post, eyeing the woman. "You should never turn your back on the enemy."

"True, but he's not really my enemy now, is he?" she asked before spinning and meeting Sam's lunge head on.

The ring of swords echoed around them as the two locked in

battle. Sam bared his teeth at her and pulled a dagger from his belt. Blaise kicked his leg out from underneath him as he slashed at her right leg, just missing her as she danced out of range, dagger and sword in hand.

It was a thing to behold. He'd never seen someone so fluid with a dagger and sword. She held the sword in one hand like it weighed nothing at all—for her, it probably did. What had started out as a training session between himself and his brother escalated when Blaise showed up in all her heathen glory.

His brother's schemes knew no bounds. It was brilliant, really, to invite her to spar with them each day. His men were already becoming accustomed to her presence. Tehl eyed the training yard, now surrounded with so many Elite he couldn't see past them. They, as well as he, couldn't pass up watching Blaise trounce his brother in fantastic fashion. It was amusing, to say the least.

"Kneeling before a woman, brother?" Tehl called. "Here, I thought I'd never see the day."

Sam spat blood on the ground and grinned at him. "If you've never knelt before a woman, then you've never lived. I'll gladly kneel before one."

Blaise snorted. "I doubt you'd know what to do with a woman."

Sniggers surrounded them as his men enjoyed the show.

Sam staggered to his feet. "I could show you better than I could tell you."

"Mmmhmm..." she hummed, eyeing him. Blaise strolled toward him, lashes fluttering. "You think you can handle me?"

"I know I can." Sam's words were careless, but the way his gaze tracked her wasn't. For every move the Scythian made, his brother countered it. Sam wasn't stupid. The key was staying out of her range. If she got a hold on him, he was done for.

She smiled and feigned to the right, but Sam was prepared. He blocked her, once, twice, and then, in a blink of an eye, he was on his knees with her sword held to his throat.

Tehl blinked. How in the stars had she done that?

The men around him stilled, each reaching for their own blades. Blaise scanned the ring, noting the hostile change in the men. Her expression blanked, but she didn't remove her sword from his brother's neck.

Tehl kept his pose casual. He knew she wouldn't harm his brother, and he wanted to show his men he trusted her. They needed to trust her if they wanted to survive in the upcoming battle.

Sam had concocted the idea three days before. The fastest way to integrate Blaise with his men was for her to train with them. Training was a dangerous thing. Accidents happened all the time, but if she trained with them, they'd begin to trust her. You had to have a measure of trust in your partner.

Blaise slowly lifted her left hand and ruffled Sam's wavy hair. "Do you yield?"

Sam grinned and lifted his chin to stare up into her face, exposing his neck even further to her. "What will you give me if I do?"

"Your life."

"That puts things into perspective." He flashed her a dimpled grin that knocked most women on their asses. "I concede to you, beautiful lady."

She shook her head at his antics and released him. Sam rolled his neck and grinned as she held her arm out to him as a gesture of goodwill.

That was a smart move. Sportsmanship was important to his men and she'd just honored Sam, even though they were born enemies.

Sam accepted her arm and stood, brushing himself off. "I didn't even see that last move."

"I'm faster than you. You have to be smarter," she said, sheathing her sword.

"Surely, you're not only going to challenge him?" a deep voice asked.

Tehl hid his smile as Rafe pushed through the Elite and leaned against the post. The rebellion leader couldn't keep away. Tehl had noticed a pattern in the last few days. Anywhere Blaise showed up, so did Rafe. It was an interesting turn of events.

She stiffened and glared at Rafe. "Surely you have something better to occupy your time, Methian?"

Rafe jumped over the fence, landing in a crouch. "Nothing would please me more than to spar with you."

"Do you really think it would be a fair fight?" she asked, cocking her hip. "I've been sparring for the last hour, and you're refreshed."

Rafe unclasped his cloak and laid it over a post. "By all means then, refresh yourself. I was led to believe you had much more stamina."

Tehl whistled as his brother clambered over the fence and dropped next to him. Rafe was playing with fire, but Tehl wanted Rafe to keep pushing her just so he could watch her grind him into the dirt.

"He's baiting her, the nutter," Sam panted, wiping the sweat from the back of his head. "I don't think I've ever been beaten this badly before."

"Indeed."

"Thanks," Sam said sarcastically. "I can always rely on you telling me the truth."

"True."

Sam shook his head. "She'll tear him to pieces."

"Why do you say that?" he asked, eyeing the two warriors in the ring like one might a pit of snakes. One wrong move, and the enemy would strike.

"She was holding back."

He'd noticed that himself. She'd pulled her punches a few times. "That was probably wise. I didn't wish you to be murdered."

"How touching," Sam deadpanned. "It was all I could do to keep up as long as I did. If that had been a real fight, I would've died in the first fifteen seconds. The warlord really did breed them for war."

"Bastard," Tehl cursed. Everywhere he turned, that monster was the cause of something that gave him trouble.

Rafe held his forearm out.

"I accept." Blaise slapped her hand against his and stalked back to his side of the fence.

She locked gazes with Tehl as she snatched a cloth from the fence.

"Insufferable dog," she growled. "He won't like what happens when he forces my hand. This was supposed to be a training, not full-out war."

"You can say no," he pointed out, handing her a ladle full of water from the bucket.

"And walk away after he challenged me?" she scoffed. "I don't think so."

"He challenged you?" Tehl frowned. He didn't remember that.

Blaise rolled her dark brown eyes. "Men."

Sam scoffed. "I will not be lumped in with him, thank you very much. He's as dense as a rock sometimes."

Tehl didn't bother defending himself. It was the truth.

She patted Sam on the cheek. "You, my pretty friend, should be in a class all of your own."

His brother beamed. "Thank you."

Her expression blanked. "It wasn't a compliment."

Sam pouted. "I'm hurt."

"I'm sure," she retorted, rolling her neck. She threw her shoulders back and straightened, a feral grin on her face. "I'm going to smear him across the dirt of the earth." With those parting words, she turned her back on them and moved to the center ring.

"She's going to slaughter him," Sam said with glee as Rafe prowled toward the center, his entire focus on the Scythian woman.

Tehl studied him and shook his head. "No, she won't."

Sam arched his brows. "She has every advantage over him."

"It's something in the way he moves, the way he carries himself. I believe they're evenly matched."

Sam narrowed his eyes on Rafe. "Perhaps you're right."

Zachael lifted his hands and nodded at Blaise. "Are you sure?"

"Yes." She secured her braids and sank into her fighting stance.

The weapons master dropped his hands, signaling the beginning of the match.

Neither lunged. They circled each other like one might a leren. Tehl's mind flashed to the beast who had attached herself to his wife. It was an apt description.

Rafe glided forward and lunged. Blaise danced out of his way and darted in, only to be blocked by the rebellion leader. Tehl sucked in a sharp breath when Rafe countered in a flurry of movements he couldn't keep track of, movements that flowed into another set.

Again, they circled before coming together in a series of clashes of steel and fists. Rafe hissed, and some of the Elite whooped as Blaise struck the first blood.

The rebellion leader held up one finger. "That's your one time." He smiled, but it wasn't nice. "You're fast, I'll give you that."

Blaise didn't respond. Her expression didn't even change.

In a wickedly quick move, Rafe attacked. Tehl's jaw clenched as steel scraped against steel in a teeth-rattling attack.

"Damn, he's not messing about," Sam said. "It hurts my arms just to watch her block those blows."

Blaise gritted her teeth and shifted forward, pushing the huge man back.

"Stars above," Tehl said, shaking his head. "How strong is she? He's double her size." It didn't bode well for Aermia if Scythia's army was made up of warriors like Blaise. They were way out of their league. His men needed more training.

He continued to watch the bout and winced as Blaise took a heavy blow to the chest. She staggered but recovered and slid under Rafe's guard to slap his stomach with the broadside of her sword as he wrapped a hand around her throat. They froze that way, face to face, both breathing hard.

No one cheered or spoke a word. It was almost a reverent silence for what they'd just witnessed. Sparring was an art, and Blaise and Rafe had taken it to another level.

"Yield," Blaise said, blushing.

Rafe smiled. "We're at a standstill, little leren. Concede."

"I will not," she said. "I will never bow to you."

"Never say never."

Blaise scanned his face and did something Tehl didn't expect—and neither did Rafe. She smiled. The rebellion leader didn't stand a chance. His mouth slackened, and his hands loosened. Poor sucker. Women were always tricksters like that. They never made much sense and were always surprising.

That was all the opening she needed.

Blaise slammed the butt of her dagger into the muscle of his thigh and threw her head into his face. Blaise pulled back and skirted out of his reach as he threw a blind jab.

Rafe seemed to swell in size as he pinned her with golden, watering eyes. "That wasn't pleasant," he said softly.

"It wasn't meant to be." She smiled and batted her lashes at him. "Are you ready for more, Methian?"

"Here it comes," Sam said with glee. "He's going to let loose."

A tremble went through Rafe, but he didn't lash out, he threw his head back and released a roaring laugh.

Blaise blinked, and so did Tehl. That was the last thing he expected Rafe to do.

He wiped his watering eyes and held out his forearm. "It's been a long time since I've enjoyed a bout. I thank you."

She stared at his arm, her fingers clenching around her weapons, and shifted, not taking his hand.

Take his hand, Tehl urged. If she couldn't get over her prejudice, how could she expect his men to?

"Take it," Tehl said under his breath.

Blaise cocked her head, her gaze flitting to him like she heard his words.

Rafe raised his brows at her hesitation. "What, little leren?

Afraid to touch a Methian?"

Her jaw clenched, and her nose wrinkled. She exhaled and then approached Rafe. "Well met," she said clasping his forearm.

"Well met," Rafe said.

Tehl pushed from the post and began to clap. A bout like that deserved praise. Moreover, Blaise deserved a round of praise by accepting Rafe's hand when she clearly didn't want to.

She yanked her hand from Rafe's and turned her back to him. However, the rebellion leader never looked away from the woman strolling away from him to be congratulated by the Elite.

"If he stares any harder, her clothing will go up in flames."

Rafe jerked and glanced in their direction like he heard their conversation. Tehl crossed his arms and raised his brows at the rebellion leader.

A shrug was all he received in reply.

He wasn't getting off that easily. Tehl had questions that he wanted answers to.

CHAPTER TWELVE

Sage

It was just as beautiful as she remembered.

"Please, put me down," she said softly, soaking in the room that had changed her life.

The giant four-poster bed crafted from the pale aqua wood of the jardintin tree still dominated the room. White, gauzy curtains, draped from post to post, floated around the bed. Rich, dark blue carpets covered the stone floor, and deep-cushioned chairs were scattered around the spacious room in a sea of colors.

She slowly walked toward the bed and ran her hand over its silky white coverlet. The color bothered her. Before, she loved how crisp and clean it looked. Now, it was a symbol of how sullied she was.

Swallowing hard, she turned from the bed and, once again, took in the room. The large fireplace that occupied the wall adjacent her bed, its mantle comprised of purple shells, shimmering abalone, and the dainty starfish, still made her smile. That could never be taken from her, her love of the ocean.

Next, she looked past the fireplace to the two large doors of pale wood that overlooked the sea. Her heart lurched as she got a glimpse through the glass at the top. The ocean stretched for ages before kissing the setting sun that exploded into color after color. She'd missed the ocean with a fierceness that stole her breath. The sea was home.

"Love?" her mum called.

Sage turned and blinked at her parents. She'd forgotten they were still there. "What is—" She paused and stared at the dressing table and mirror. Distinctly male items were lying all over the surface.

Garreth followed her gaze. "The crown prince has been staying here," he said, answering her unspoken question.

She studied the room once more, noting little changes here and there. Male boots beside the bed. A broadsword on top of the dresser. A huge cloak thrown over the back of one of the chairs near the fireplace. Why had he stayed here? Was this a new development?

"How long?" she asked.

"Since before," Garreth said softly.

She swallowed hard and stared blankly at the room, not knowing how she felt about that. Part of her loved that he'd stayed there, but the other part wasn't sure if she liked him invading her space.

Her gaze was drawn back to the balcony doors. That was her special place. In her bones, she knew if she could just get out there, everything would be okay. The world would make sense again.

Sage rushed to the doors and flung them open, her heart

pounding. A salty sea breeze ruffled her hair, the loose strands lifting in the air. Taking a step, her bare feet moved across the sun-warmed stone to the balcony. Gulls heckled and chased each other playfully. This was freedom.

The cool air kissed her bare arms and left a trail of goosebumps in its wake. She placed her hands on the balcony railing and closed her eyes to soak in the sounds of the crashing sea below. Home. This was home.

She sighed and opened her eyes. Nothing was as beautiful as the sunrise. The cool air brushed over her skin, and a shiver worked through her.

And, on the heels of it, a memory.

The sky painted with rich reds, oranges, and purples. His lopsided smile, while he held her tightly as the sun faded from view. Kisses to the top of her head. Affection.

Sage stared sightlessly at the ocean before her and shuddered. Even now, he was ruining her safe place. "Get out of my head," she whispered.

Still, she could feel the ghost of his arms embracing her. How could she think about such a thing after all he'd done? Her fingers turned white as she squeezed the railing. Part of her missed him, wanted the comfort and connection of his presence.

A soft curse left her lips. She was sick. Sick in the mind and heart. Heat burned behind her eyes, but she wouldn't cry. She'd done enough of that.

She inhaled the salty air and watched the gulls play, darting here and there to outrun their pursuer. If only she had wings to fly away. If she had wings, no one could reach her, nothing could touch her. Wings meant safety.

Her gaze dropped down to the waves below. Swimming was

like flying. Lilja had flown through the water, riding the currents. It had been unlike anything she'd ever experienced. There was peace to be found under the waves, where silence reigned. How she longed for the peace. Her wings were waiting for her, if she only chose to grasp them.

A hand touched her shoulder, causing her to jump. She glanced up into green eyes like her own.

"Are you okay?"

Sage placed a hand over her papa's and forced a smile on to her face, even though the waves sung a siren song to her soul. "I'm tired." More than anything, she wanted to be alone. To think. "Mum?"

"Love?" Her mum stepped onto the balcony.

She glanced between the two of them. "You both look like you haven't slept in days. Go and get some sleep."

Her mum waved her away. "We're okay, love."

Sage reached out and clasped her mum's hand. "I need to bathe, and then I'm going to sleep. Please, please go and take some time. I'll be here when you get back."

"We don't need—"

"Gwen, I think Sage needs a little time." Her papa squeezed her shoulder and threw an arm over her mum's. "Let's go."

"But we promised," her mum argued.

"I have Garreth for company and protection if I wake up and you're not back. Right?"

"I'll be right here the entire time, my lady," he called from the doorway.

Sage smiled at her mum and hugged her. "Take your time."

Her mum brushed Sage's cheek. "You sure?"

"I am."

Her mum squinted at her, and then pecked her on the cheek. "We'll be back before you know it, my love."

Sage held it together as her parents disappeared from the doorway. Then her forced smile fell, and a sense of relief filled her as Garreth stepped into view.

"Do you need anything?"

She laughed. "I need many things, but all are things no one can give me."

Garreth hesitated in the doorway, shifting from foot to foot. "I'll stay in the room until your family or Tehl comes back, if you'd like?"

"No." She waved him away. She needed privacy to think.

"If you need me, I'll be right outside the door."

She nodded, hating his scars. "I'm sorry about what happened," she said, her voice small. "I'll never go anywhere without my escort again."

"Bad things happen. That doesn't mean it's your fault. It means there are horrible people out there."

That was the truth if ever she had heard it.

"I should be the one apologizing to you." Garreth stared at floor. "I didn't protect you like I should have."

"You did your best."

"Did I?" He shook his head. "I'm so very sorry, nonetheless."

"It seems we both like to blame ourselves for circumstances out of our reach," she said, hoping to soothe him. "I don't blame you." She faked a yawn and sat on the bed. "I'll call for you if I need you. Thank you for everything you've done."

"My pleasure, my lady."

Her pulse picked up as the door closed with a thud, leaving her alone. When was the last time she was left alone? "Stop thinking," she whispered to herself. She couldn't go back to that place. It was too easy to fall down the black hole of nothingness.

She stood, turning to the balcony, and moved to the railing. She stared at the ocean below. It was incredible that the waves made so much noise, when underneath the surface it was so still. The sea was the exact opposite of her. Inside was the rushing ocean crashing against the rocks, but on the outside, she kept herself still and placid. At least, she tried.

She lifted her arms out to the side of her body and relished the wind beneath her fingertips. Stars above, what would it feel like to jump? To have the wind rushing past her until the ocean met her and silence reigned supreme?

Sage glanced over her shoulder at the empty room and then to the waves below her. Her hands trembled as she lifted her nightgown up and swung a leg over the balcony. She froze as the thrill of fear went through her, but for the first time since she woke up, it wasn't because of a monster. This fear was within her control.

It would be so easy to slip off the railing and fly...

"Darling, could you come off the railing? It's giving me quite the scare," a deep voice asked.

"No," she whispered, not looking in the direction of her newest guest. Of all the times for him to visit, it had to be now.

"Well then, I guess I'm coming to you."

Large weathered hands clasped the stone railing. Marq swung a long, leathered leg over the stone edging and adopted her stance. She peeked through her fringe at the older man whom she held dear in her heart. Did he want to fly, too?

He didn't look her way but out toward the ocean. "I never tire of this view. Each sunset and sunrise are better than the last, and no two are alike. It gives me a measure of peace to watch it sink into the ocean's embrace."

The king finally turned to her, his steely, dark blue gaze sweeping over her. "I'm happy to see you."

She tried to speak, but the words lodged in her throat, and she trembled, causing alarm to show on Marq's face. She missed him. Missed his visits.

"Darling, I know it's not your intention to scare me, but I don't think you're quite well enough for this adventure. Would you mind getting down with me?"

"I can't," she whispered through her cracked lips. "I want to be free."

"You are free. No one is holding you here."

Lifting her head, she stared at the birds, the wind twisting her hair around her. "I want to fly."

"I know the feeling well. I have a floor to ceiling window in one of my towers that I used to stand in. I always admired the birds from there. I wished I could fly, too."

She met his gaze. "Do you want to fly with me?"

"No, darling, I don't."

Her shoulders slumped. "Why?" How could anyone *not* want to be free?

"I remembered what was important." He held her gaze as he slid off the railing and back onto the balcony floor, and then held his hand to her. "I know it might not feel like it now, but you will fly. Maybe not in this way, but you will fly."

She glanced down at the water. It would be so easy to let go.

"Sage, look at me, darling."

Forcing herself away from the view, she watched him as he edged closer. "I need peace," she murmured. "Every move I make is plagued by monsters and horrors."

Marq smiled at her. It was a sad smile, but it didn't hold pity. "The monsters disappear as you slay them. That is up to you." He inhaled deeply and placed his hand over hers. "There will always be evil in the world, but it's up to people like you and me to protect the others."

"I'm not strong enough," she choked out. If she couldn't protect herself, how could she protect others?

"We can't always protect ourselves from calamity, but we show courage in how we deal with the aftereffects. Those, usually, are more difficult to conquer. I need you to be my warrior. You have it inside yourself, but you need to choose to fight. No one can force you to do that."

"I'm so tired," she said. She didn't have the energy to fight. She needed sleep.

"I know, sweetling. I know. But that is what your friends and family are for. Your fight is not alone. You are not alone, and you're not the first person to feel this way. You are loved." He swallowed hard. "Please take my hand."

She gripped the railing harder as she warred with herself. Flying would be the easy choice, but when had she ever made the easy choice?

"Be my warrior. Take my hand."

Her hand felt heavy as she pried her fingers from the balcony and placed it in the king's. He sighed and pulled her from the railing and into his arms.

Sage shuddered in his arms as he squeezed the air from her, his heart thundering against her ear.

"That's a good girl. You're so brave."

He pressed a kiss to the top of her head and shame crashed into her. Why did she do such a thing? It was beyond dangerous. There was a chance she'd have died if she attempted the jump.

"I'm sorry," she cried. "I'm sorry."

"It's okay, darling. You took my hand like a warrior. That's all that matters."

"I'm just so tired. I want the nightmares to leave me alone."

"I know. It'll get better. We'll fight them together. You'll never have to fight them alone."

With each memory, it was like she lost a little bit more of her sanity.

She leaned back and stared into the king's dear, wet face. "I think I'm broken."

He smiled, flashing his dimples, and cupped her cheek. "You're not broken. Maybe a little bruised and scarred, but whom of us aren't?"

That sounded familiar. Like she'd heard it before, but she couldn't place her finger on it. Exhaustion weighed heavily on her, and she leaned into Marq. If only she could sleep.

"Father?"

Sage pried her eyes open and blinked slowly as Tehl materialized next to her.

"She needs rest."

Marq transferred her to Tehl, his leather and pine scent wrapping around her as he hauled her into his arms and then placed her in the bed. She curled into a ball and snuggled into the covers. Maybe she would sleep. The bed was so soft.

Tehl's weight shifted and her eyes snapped open. Somehow, her fingers were clutching his shirt. His deep blue eyes met hers as he placed a hand over hers.

"Please, don't leave," she said.

"Never. I just need to remove my boots."

Marq leaned over the bed and brushed hair from her face. "Remember, you are my warrior. I'll be here if you need me."

"The king's warrior," she whispered.

He grinned at her. "It has a nice ring to it, doesn't it?"

CHAPTER THIRTEEN

Tehl

In the span of ten breaths, Sage had fallen asleep, clutching his shirt and curled into a tiny ball, her face pinched as if she was trying to hide from her pain. Slowly, he pried her fingers from his shirt and shifted to sit up as his father pulled a blanket up over her.

She shivered in her sleep and burrowed further into the bed, her dark brown hair a striking contrast against the white pillow. It was surreal to have her here. He'd hardly dared to hope they would retrieve her; he knew it was a high possibility she'd never come home. It was a blessing that he was eternally grateful for.

Unable to help himself, he brushed his thumb across her worried forehead. Even in sleep, she looked terrified. His jaw clenched, and he pulled his hand back, meeting his father's gaze. This was the warlord's fault.

He glanced at his father. "How long has she been here?" he

asked, moving to sit in the chair next to the fireplace. His father dropped into the other chair while Tehl pulled his boots off and dug his toes into the carpet. *Stars above, what a long day.*

"Garreth said only about an hour."

Tehl sighed, flexing his toes in his socks. Then he sat back, taking a real look at his father. His stomach dropped at the expression Marq wore. That look never boded well. He didn't want to ask what put that expression on his father's face, but he had to.

"What happened?"

His father dropped his head into his hands. "I had a conversation with Sage today that I never wanted to have with another human being." Each word held a weight. He lifted his head, a sheen of tears in his blue eyes. "I found her straddling the railing of the balcony." His voice cracked.

Chills erupted along Tehl's skin as his body flashed hot then cold, and a dull ringing filled his ears. His father's lips moved, but he couldn't understand them. They didn't make any sense.

"I don't understand," he muttered through numb lips.

His father scooted his chair closer and placed a heavy hand on his shoulder. "Sometimes, the world looks so bleak, a person only wants relief from the pain." He swallowed thickly. "It doesn't mean they want to leave the ones they love."

She didn't love him.

Tehl placed his head in his hands and struggled to breathe. Did she want to escape life that badly? She had so much to live for. So many people who loved her. "How did you get her down?" he managed to ask.

"I asked her to fight. She's always been a warrior, Tehl. She needed to be reminded that there were people who saw her strength, even if she couldn't see it anymore." His father sighed. "I don't think she actually wanted to hurt herself. She wanted peace and quiet. Her memories are haunting her."

Tehl nodded and pinched the bridge of his nose. The nightmares, he understood. The brutality of them haunted his own dreams.

"She's barely slept, and, when she does, it's more of a fight. She thrashes and cries out, but when she's awake, it's worse." Tehl rubbed his eyes. "She's a specter of herself. When a memory crashes into her, emotion cracks through for a few moments before it flickers away, and she curls back into herself." It was like watching the destruction of a beautiful painting.

His father pressed his lips together. "It'll take time for her to heal. Physically, she might be okay, but emotionally and mentally, she's not. It'll take time."

But how much time? He swallowed and glanced at the open balcony doors. "What if she doesn't get a chance to heal?" It was sheer luck that his father had been here. What if it happened again? What if she changed her mind?

"Do you remember when you found me in the tower?" his father asked.

He'd never forget that day. Even though he'd said some terrible things to his father, he hadn't meant them. All he wanted was to shock his father out of his rut. It broke him to watch his father wither each day and clearly long to be away from his family.

"Yes."

His father squeezed his shoulder and sat back in his chair, running a hand through his silvering hair. "That day, all I wanted was peace. When your mother died," he rasped, "a part of me also died. Each day was a struggle to breathe, to live. The pain was indescribable. Everywhere I looked, memories assaulted me. I saw her in everything and everywhere. It was exhausting."

He placed a hand over his mouth, his gaze going distant. "I never wanted to die. I wanted a measure of peace. That's all." His eyes focused back on Tehl. "Sage didn't want to die. I saw it on her face. She wanted an escape from the memories. That's it."

He shook his head. "My memories were of our wonderful life. Hers aren't. They're nightmares. I can't even imagine." A pause. "Has she told anyone what happened there?"

"No, not really." He only was privy to a few things because she screamed them while she slept. Mira had been very tight-lipped about Sage, and her parents didn't have any more information than he did.

"She needs to speak to someone," his father said, glancing over his shoulder at the bed. "She can't keep all of it inside."

Tehl followed his gaze to the precious woman sleeping fitfully in their bed. Lost. He felt lost. He wanted to be the person she confided in. "How do I get her to confide in me? I've never been good with understanding people and emotions. How can I help her?" That's all he wanted. To help her.

"By being there for her. The most important things you can do are support, listen, and love her. She needs all of those things."

He could do that. His father made it sound simple, but Tehl knew it was more difficult than that. He'd rather listen to someone than speak to them, anyway. As for love... He pushed from his chair and tiptoed to the bed, pulling up the blankets she'd shrugged off, so they now reached her chin.

He certainly cared for her. It had killed him while she was gone, but was that love? Or just devotion and caring for a friend? He didn't know, but he'd do his best to love her in the way he knew how. "I'll do my best," he vowed. He wouldn't give up on her.

"You will, son. You're a good man," his father said softly.

High praise that he'd hold close in times ahead.

Tehl turned as his father stood. Then, he pulled the king into a hug.

"Be patient and kind. Nothing will be easy. The time ahead of us will be brutal and bloody, and the only way either of you will survive is by supporting each other."

His father released him and pressed a kiss to Sage's cheek. "Sleep well, my little warrior, for tomorrow you'll have to fight." He straightened and strolled around the bed, pausing at the door. "I'll have Gwen and Colm stay in the room across the hall. Then, if she needs them, all you have to do is holler."

"Thank you," Tehl said, some of his fear dissipating. Neither one of them was alone.

"There's no need for thanks. Just take care of our beautiful girl."

"I intend to."

His father smiled and slipped out the door.

Tehl rolled his neck and glanced around the room. It felt different having her here. Everything looked the same, but there was a contentment to having Sage home.

A cold breeze drifted through the balcony doors, causing him to shiver and taking some of his contentment. He glared at them. They led to death.

He closed the doors and locked them. Then he pulled the royal blue draperies closed for good measure. They were a reminder of what could have happened today, and it was one more thing he didn't want to ponder.

The hearth was cool, and that needed to be taken care of given the way Sage was shivering. Tehl crossed to the door and cracked it. "Garreth."

His friend turned to him. "Yes, my lord?"

"Turn all servants away tonight. I don't want anyone to disturb Sage."

"It will be done."

"Thank you," he said, closing the door.

Tehl rubbed his hand together and began his ritual for bed. He started a fire, pleased that it lit so quickly, and fed kindling into it until it could support a few logs that would get them through the night. He then moved around the room, organizing his things.

His eyes drooped as he washed his face and loosened the ties at his throat. He'd hardly slept in the last few weeks and it had caught up to him. He brushed his fingertips along the stubble on his cheeks and jaw. He should shave it, but he didn't have the energy. His body was demanding sleep. It was a damn miracle he hadn't fallen asleep standing up.

He turned from the wash basin and glanced between the large chair and the foot of their bed. He longed to sleep in a regular bed, but it wasn't worth scaring Sage.

Tehl lugged the chair around the bed and sat by his wife's side, staring at her pale face. It was odd watching someone sleep, but it brought him a measure of peace. She was close and safe.

Even with the dark bruising beneath her eyes from lack of sleep, she was a beauty. It was like she'd popped out of a fairytale. A fairy princess. He smiled at the thought. How would she react if she heard him comparing her to a helpless princess?

His smile dimmed. Sage needed his help, but she wasn't a helpless princess. She was a king's warrior.

He brushed his thumb across the top of her hand, an unexpected swell of emotion rocking him. He could have lost her today.

An uncomfortable heat filled his eyes. "I don't know what he did to you," he whispered, "but understand I'll protect you with my dying breath. I'll protect you from yourself and from your nightmares. But, to do these things, I need you to fight. You're one of the most stubborn women I've ever met." He smiled and swiped at his eyes. "Don't let someone take what you love the most from you. He may have taken some of your time, but don't let him steal your future, because I'll fight for that, too. I'll fight for us."

CHAPTER FOURTEEN

Tehl

In the middle of the night, three things happened: the room lit up with a flash of lightning, followed by a tremendous crash of thunder, and then Sage screamed.

He had lurched up from a full sleep as if slapped across the face, grabbing the dagger at his waist, heart threatening to beat right out of his chest. What in the hell?

For a second, he sat panting, his eyes wildly searching the darkened room for danger. Had someone gotten inside?

Another round of lightning and thunder brought another scream and lit the room in a ghostly light for one blinding moment. Their door thudded open, light pouring into the room. Tehl blinked furiously, his fingers tightening around the dagger in his hand.

"Are you and the princess all right?" Garreth asked, his body a silhouette in the doorway.

Tehl shook his head, trying to clear the spots from his vision, and glanced at Sage. She trembled in the bed, her eyes wide, gaze unseeing. A nightmare.

"She's dreaming," he whispered, horror pricking his skin at the utter terror on her face. "I need to wake her up."

"Do it gently, or you'll make it worse," Garreth admonished. "Do you need any help?"

"No." He didn't want anyone to see Sage at her worst. She'd hate that. She deserved her dignity and privacy. "Thank you."

"It's nothing, my lord." Garreth stepped into the hallway and closed the door, casting the room into darkness once again.

Tehl sheathed his dagger and smoothed a hand over Sage's arm. "Sage? You need to wake up."

She jerked, her eyes wild, more cries pouring from her throat. She rocked away from him and struggled against the covers wrapped around her legs.

"Let go," she whimpered.

He eased from his chair and circled the bed, avoiding pieces of furniture, the hairs standing up on his body as she cried out again. The sound unhinged him, cut him to the heart. No one should experience that kind of fear. What had the warlord done to her? What caused this sort of fear? He pushed aside his thoughts and focused on the terrified creature in his bed.

"Sage? You need to wake up, love," he crooned, barely making out her terrified features in the dark, only illuminated by the dying embers of the hearth and flashes of lightning. "No one will hurt you. You're okay."

But she didn't hear him. Didn't see him. No recognition registered on her face.

"Trapped," she cried, wrenching the blankets from her body

and then tearing at her nightgown.

"Love." He reached out and paused, remembering the last time he touched her during a nightmare.

She'd attacked him with a ferocity that bespoke of an unfathomable pain and rage, but that's when they barely knew each other. Maybe she'd react differently this time. He'd have to move carefully.

He reached a hand out and brushed her cheek. "It's only a dream, love. Look at me."

Sage slapped his hand away. "Hot, so hot," she moaned, her sweaty hair whipping around her face.

Momentary shock rendered him motionless as she yanked her gown over her head. He jerked and glanced away from her as heat rushed through him.

So much skin.

Stars above, how was he supposed to wake her now?

Tehl glanced at her from the corner of his eye as she wrapped her arms around her legs and rocked side to side giving him a peek of what she hid behind her billowing shirts and tight leather vests.

He whipped around and stared at the wall, cursing his body. The circumstances were terrible for him to feel anything for his pretty wife. One flash of creamy skin, and his mind had blanked. Was he so weak? No, he wasn't. It was just a physical reaction. It didn't mean he was a bad person. If he acted on it... Disgust curdled in his belly. He couldn't even finish the thought.

He pinched the bridge of his nose and forced his mind to the problem at hand. How could he soothe her when she was so wild and naked? A memory surfaced of his mother singing to him when he was a child. That had always calmed him when he'd been scared. If only he could remember the words. If he couldn't, he'd just have to make up his own. Tehl exhaled heavily. Singing was not his talent, but he'd exhaust all options before trying to hold her down again.

Clearing his throat, he began to hum gently, still not looking in her direction. Hopefully his rusty voice wouldn't make it worse. He inhaled and began to sing softly.

Darling, darling, there's nothing to fear.
The sun is rising, so there's no need for tears.
I'll hold you and protect you in the dark of night.
The shadows can't touch you, so there's no need for fright.

Darling, darling, there's nothing to fear.
The dawn is approaching, and the sky is clear.
I'll fight your demons and all of your foes,
I love and adore you more than you'll ever know.

Darling, darling, there's nothing to fear.
The night gives way, for the new day is near.
I'll tell you my secrets to keep you awake,
Nothing can hurt you, so there's no need to quake.

Darling, darling, there's nothing to fear.
The sun is rising, so there's no need for tears.

He sang the verses over and over for what could have been minutes or hours. His throat was hoarse when a hiccupping sob, different from the feral cries, came from behind him.

"Sage, love?" he called, his voice rusty.

"Tehl?" she whispered.

He glanced over his shoulder, keeping his gaze on his wife's face. Her haunted eyes met his, tears slipping from the corners of them. She looked wrecked.

"You were having a bad dream," he explained.

She slapped her hands over her eyes and sobbed anew. "I'm sorry," she cried. "I'm so sorry."

Tehl shifted around and averted his eyes as he pulled a sheet up over Sage's body. She may not be concerned over her modesty, but he was.

"There's nothing to be sorry about." He reached out again to comfort her, but hesitated. She hated comfort after a nightmare. His jaw popped as he clenched his teeth and pulled back. Time to give her space.

He moved to stand when her hand touched his arm.

"Please, don't leave me."

He glanced at her in surprise. "I'm not leaving you. I'm moving to my chair."

She shuddered, tears still slipping free, and held up the covers. A clear invitation.

He tried not to gape. That had never happened before. She'd always clammed up and pretended he wasn't there. She'd regret this in the morning. Sage hated others seeing her at her weakest.

Tehl patted her hand. "You don't need to worry. I'll be right next to you in the chair."

"Please," she begged, her voice breaking.

Only one word, but it broke something inside him. He could give her this. She might resent him tomorrow, but he'd be damned if he turned away from her when she needed him the most and her plea was well within his power to grant.

Tehl placed his hand over hers and lowered the blanket. He crawled over the bed and lay beside her, brushing her tears from her damp face. "It's okay," he murmured, even though nothing was okay. "I've got you."

Her deep emerald gaze mapped his face slowly, as if she

searched for something, and another sob burst free as she snuggled into his arms. He stiffened and held absolutely still as she burrowed into him, her face now pressed to his chest, sobs bursting from her in a rough, tortured way.

He slowly slid his arms around her and hugged her to him as she shook in his arms. He kissed the top of her head and whispered comforting words while staring out of the balcony door windows.

This was the first time he'd ever held a woman like this. It should have been a wonderful moment, but a hollowness filled him. The warlord had taken this from them. He trembled, trying to keep his emotions in check. This was not how it was supposed to happen. It was unfair.

Sage hiccupped, her fingers knotting in his shirt as her body shuddered. He'd kill the warlord for what he'd done. He'd suffer.

His wife whimpered, pulling him away from his morbid thoughts. Blinking, he loosened his grasp, knowing he'd been holding her a little too tight. The leader of Scythia would experience justice, but not tonight.

Tonight, Tehl focused on Sage. She needed him.

He began humming the lullaby while brushing his nose along the crown of her head, her cinnamon scent filling his nose. That brought him a measure of comfort. Everything was different, but at least she smelled the same. That was a constant, and it somehow grounded him.

Tehl rubbed one hand up and down her back, continuing to hum. Her tremors slowed, and, soon, she fell quiet. He wondered if she'd pull back, but she didn't—if anything she pressed closer. The storm quieted except for the patter of rain against the windows.

His arm began to ache, and he shifted to his back, trying not to disturb her. He expected her to stay where she was, but Sage cuddled up to his side. Tehl slowly lifted his arm, and she pressed her cheek against his shoulder, her hand laying on his chest.

He swallowed and stared down at the small hand over his heart. Was it wrong to enjoy the sensation of skin pressed to his? He hated the circumstances. Hated it. But he'd always wanted companionship.

Carefully, he lifted his right hand and placed it over hers. He sucked in a breath when she laced their fingers together and sighed, her breath ghosting over his neck.

"Thank you."

Her words were so soft, he almost didn't hear them.

"It's nothing."

"No, it's everything," she murmured. "You've helped me and gained nothing in return."

It didn't feel that way. He had his wife in his arms for the first time, willingly. That felt like a great boon when, only months ago, he thought she'd stab him before sharing a bed with him.

"It's my duty." What a fib. It wasn't his duty. It was his privilege.

She hummed and scooted closer. "Don't let them get me."

His throat tightened at her words. "Never."

***

His arm hurt.

Tehl shifted to relieve the pain and scooted closer to the blazing warmth. His hands caressed silky skin, and he smiled, completely content. When was the last time he woke up so relaxed?

Blinking his eyes open, all his lethargy evaporated. Green eyes watched him from underneath dark lashes. He glanced to his hand, which played along Sage's spine.

Her very naked spine.

He started to pull his hand back when Sage halted him, her hand grasping his bicep.

"It's okay," she murmured. "It was nice."

He swallowed, out of his depth. Who was the creature in his bed? He didn't understand this Sage. His Sage would've yelled and threatened to stab him for taking such liberty without her express permission.

His mouth bobbed when she pressed closer, a contented sigh brushing across his neck hotly. He shifted, not knowing where to put his hands as little details began to filter in the longer he was awake.

His eyes dipped, and he jerked, his gaze moving over her head, not daring to glance down at the beautiful naked body pressed against him. The sheet had slid down at some point in the night to expose her upper half.

Tehl took a shallow breath through his mouth as heat rushed through his veins and her scent swirled around him. This was not happening. He'd be the biggest cad in the world to react to her after the god-awful night she'd had. It was wrong, and yet his body had other ideas that had him scowling.

"It's okay, Tehl. We're married," she whispered.

He stilled. It felt like a trick. A dirty, dirty trick. What did she really want?

Tehl kept his gaze averted but still stroked her skin. He couldn't help it. She was so soft, and he never thought he'd get the chance.

"You've been through hell," he rasped. "I won't take advantage of you, even if you wished it."

The words were easy to say, controlling himself was infinitely harder. He placed a kiss on the crown of her head and ran his fingers through her hair. There. Those were safe touches, weren't they?

He cleared his throat while concentrating on the storm outside. "Are you hungry?" he asked. She had to be hungry. She'd hardly eaten anything in the last couple of days.

Her body grew rigid in his arms, and yet he didn't dare to look down. There was too much to tempt him. Too much to look at that he didn't have a right to. Yet.

His breath hissed out as she pulled away from him and abruptly sat up, flashing him the side of one breast and her entire bare back before he snapped his eyes closed and sat up with his back to her.

That wasn't an image he'd ever forget. He shuddered as the sheets rustled and he placed his head in his hands. What was wrong with him? He'd slept with her before. Why was he having such a hard time now?

"I'm famished," she said, her voice wooden, nothing like it had been a minute ago.

His brows furrowed as he dragged a hand across his mouth. Did he offend her? Had she noticed his reaction? "I'll ring, so we can break our fast," he said brightly, even though he was worn out and confused.

"Appreciated," her hollow voice answered.

"You're welcome."

Brilliant. Now she was down to one-word sentences. He'd done something wrong.

He stared at the pale plastered wall across from the bed, feeling very lost and young. Somehow, he always managed to muck everything up. It was one mistake after another.

Unbidden, the image of her bare body flashed through his

mind, causing his teeth to snap together.

What was that all about? Sage never let him see a scrap of her skin before she disappeared. The only time he saw her tempting curves were when she dressed in one of Lilja's dresses for dinner, a dress that appeared to have been poured over her body.

Again, he asked himself, who was the strange creature in his bed? Sage was here with him, but not *his* Sage. It was like he didn't know her at all.

His heart sank.

They were back to the beginning. They were two strangers.

He knew her return wouldn't be without its difficulties. He understood she wouldn't come back as the same person, but it still hurt. They hadn't been the best of friends, but at least they knew where the other person stood, who they were.

But now he hadn't a clue.

Tehl rubbed a hand across his heart where their hands had rested all night.

Despite all the negatives, maybe there was some good as well.

Sage had never initiated physical contact unless it was needed. Today, she wanted affection from him just because she enjoyed it.

Some of his concern melted away.

That was a step in the right direction.

It would take time to get to know each other, but they'd gone through it once already. They wouldn't make the same mistakes this time.

For better or worse, she was his, and he was hers.

Sage

He didn't want her, that much was clear.

She gazed out the windows at the turbulent ocean, white frothy tips capping the stormy waves. That's exactly how she felt inside. Everything crashed against each other in a raging mess. The wind howled, and Sage wanted to rush onto the balcony and howl, too, if only it would relieve some of the rejection trapped inside her.

Her fingers brushed along the thin, fine linen covering her lap, worrying at the material.

Last night hadn't been what she'd expected. She knew the nightmares would come for her. They always did. The worst of it all was waking up and searching for *him*. Wanting the warmth and comfort he'd provided her even though the warlord was the reason she fought terrors each waking moment.

And yet...she wanted him.

Her fingers knotted in the fabric as shame and revulsion

churned in her belly. What kind of sick person missed their torturer?

She breathed through the nausea and peeked over her shoulder at Tehl. She'd done him a disservice last night. He'd done everything in his power to care and comfort her while she'd been pining for another. No wonder he wouldn't look at her this morning. She was a whore. She was even dressed as a wanton woman.

It wasn't clear to her where her clothing disappeared to in the night, but she was sure it wasn't Tehl's doing. That was apparent by his stiff demeanor and how he held himself back from her. She'd been naked—and in his arms—and yet, he'd done nothing, said nothing.

Did she say something last night to turn him away? All she remembered was his voice and her being so hot and not wanting to be alone. She stared at his back with more shame washing over her. Months ago, she'd have been outraged he'd come to bed without a shirt, but it was she who'd stripped and just about thrown herself at him.

Pathetic. Disgraceful. Desperate.

She turned back to the balcony doors, her toes skimming the cold stone floor. A chill ran along her exposed skin, but she didn't move to cover herself. It was just skin.

She chuckled, the sound hollow and haunting even to her. She'd been a prude before she'd been taken. If there was one thing she'd learned in Scythia, it was that modesty was subjective.

"What's so funny?" Tehl's deep voice washed over her.

"Life," she replied.

"It has a way of surprising us."

More like stabbing her in the back.

She stood and clutched the sheet tighter around her and moved to the balcony doors, resting her palm against the cool glass dotted with condensation and rain. "That it does."

"I love rain."

That was personal. Why was he offering an olive branch? He hadn't done anything wrong.

Sage blinked and spun, the sheet flaring around her legs. Tehl still stared at the wall, but there was less tension in his body. "What do you love about it?"

He leaned back, placing his palms on the bed, and squinted at the ceiling. "It's clean. It washes away filth and rubbish, leaving behind beauty."

"And here I thought you liked it because it was dark and glum, like your personality." Her eyes widened as she realized what had popped out of her mouth. In that moment, she wished she could snatch her words from the air and cram them back into her mouth. He was making conversation, and she was acting like a cornered viper.

Tehl's body began to shake and a roar of laughter escaped him. Her jaw dropped. When had she heard such laughter like that? It was the sound of freedom and joy.

She ached for that joy, that freedom, but she'd settle for being near someone capable of such emotion.

He wiped at his eyes and shook his messy, inky hair, glancing in her direction before pinning his gaze on the far wall, his back to her again.

She made him uncomfortable. Sage cinched the sheet tighter along her body, and her toes dug into the rug beneath her feet. "I'm covered, and I'm sorry."

Slowly, he turned, his brows furrowing. "Why are you sorry?"

"I was rude." She waved a hand, heat filling her cheeks.

His confusion melted into a heart-stopping grin as he flashed two dimples that had her heart in her throat. "Don't be sorry. I've always enjoyed your feistiness. You seem more like yourself when you are..."

"Ornery?" she quipped with an arched brow.

"Fiery. You've always been full of life."

She swallowed. As opposed to the darkness that slowly ate at her now. "I see."

His hands curled into fists, and his smile disappeared as he studied her face. "Can I be honest with you?"

"Yes. I prefer it." She was so tired of deception. Lies.

"As do I." He inhaled deeply and met her gaze squarely. "I'm awkward. I'll always be awkward, but I'll always tell you the truth. I don't know where we go from here. I don't know how to help or be what you need."

There was no help for her. But how could she explain that to him?

"But I'll do my best, and, for that, I need you to tell me what you need, what's on your mind."

She clutched the sheet tighter. Could he handle her monsters? It was a burden she didn't want to level onto anyone.

"Can you handle the truth?" Because she couldn't. She wanted to hide from it. From the things she'd done.

"Sometimes, the truth is ugly, and it hurts, but we have to deal with it."

"We?" she whispered, hardly daring to hope.

Tehl stood and moved around the bed, halting a handbreadth away. "You and I. It will always be you and I against the world. I meant my vows."

Her vows. She'd already broken them in a way that couldn't be fixed.

"I've done terrible things," she whispered. The compromises. Ezra. The warlord.

"Mistakes are part of being imperfect. No one is perfect, Sage, no one. If you expect that from yourself or anyone else, you're inviting disappointment and heartache." He held out his hand to her, palm up. "You don't have to tell me what happened, today, tomorrow, or next week, but you can't hide from what's going on, and you can't hide it from me."

"You can't handle the darkness," she whispered, staring at his hand. "It's too great." Painful.

"Nothing is too great when you work together with those that love you."

Her gaze snapped to his face. "I don't deserve it."

"No one really deserves love, but that's what makes it so special. I need you to fight. Fight for yourself, your family, your friends, our kingdom, us, for the children we might have in the future. I need you to fight with everything you have to not let him win." Tehl seemed to swell in size as he squared his shoulders. "I will fight for all of these things with or without you, but it will be easier to have you by my side. You are a champion, a warrior." He looked her straight in the eye. "You are not the victim. You're a survivor."

His words seemed to wrap themselves around her and sink into her skin. She wasn't a victim.

Sage was a survivor.

Her wounds were brutal, ugly, and dark, but she'd survived them.

But she wasn't the only one to survive such horrors. Her mind flashed to all the pregnant women at the feast table. How many women had been used? Were still being used?

Sage hugged herself, shaking as she fought her way back from the image in her mind. She had to fight for them. Live for them. Survive for them.

If she didn't, who would?

CHAPTER SIXTEEN

Sage

Fighting was easier said than done.

Three days had passed quicker than she expected. Breakfast had been quiet affairs before Tehl disappeared for the day. He checked on her several times during the day and left her with news on the world outside their room. Each time he left, she longed to go with him, but even she knew her body lacked the strength that was needed.

Against Mira's wishes, she'd begun to train in her room. She couldn't stay here forever, and there wasn't time to waste. The times were too dangerous.

Sage scowled at her trembling limbs and sank to the floor. The months in Scythia hadn't done her any favors. Her body may have been healed from the drugs they'd given her, but she'd lost so much of her strength.

Sage cursed and plucked her dagger from the floor. She held

her breath and threw the dagger. It sunk into the bedpost with a dull thud. A small smile tipped up her mouth. At least she hadn't lost her aim. There was her silver lining.

"Stop fouling up the furniture." Her mum glared at her from over the top of her embroidery. "You'd have thought I raised you in a barn."

The urge to stick her tongue out at her mum tugged at her, but she managed to curb it. Barely. "Sorry, Mum," she wheezed, brushing a sweaty strand of hair from her face.

Her mum arched a delicate brow. "If you were sorry, you'd stop doing it."

It was only the third time today. The bed would survive. Her restlessness, not so much. It eased some of her panic to have a dagger back in her hand, to control something. It was satisfying to see it hit her mark each time.

She lay on her back, sinking into the plush rug. Even though she was exhausted, it had been great to work her muscles. There was comfort in routine.

"You should get back into bed. You've overdone it today."

Sage waved a hand at her. "I've done nothing today." It was the truth, but her body complained anyway.

"You've visited Jasmine, spoken to Blaise, and trained against my wishes."

In the scheme of things, it wasn't much. "I can't stand staying still. My mind never stops." Every time she stopped, unwanted memories plagued her. She shook her head. It was better to wear herself into the ground.

"I know, love."

"I need to fill the..." She paused. "The void."

"I understand that, but you shouldn't push yourself too hard.

It's only been a few weeks."

Almost three weeks. It felt like a lifetime and a blink of an eye at the same time.

Time was distorted. The world sped by while she struggled after it. But each moment she let slip by was a moment lost to the warlord.

She shivered, the sweat cooling on her skin. She wasn't a betting woman, but she'd bet her sword the warlord would strike soon. He'd lost the element of surprise. That wasn't something he'd take rolling over.

"Sage?"

She blinked and craned her neck to see her mum. "Yes?"

A deep crease wrinkled her mum's forehead as she gazed at Sage. "Where did you go, love? I called your name three times."

"I didn't hear you." Too lost in her worries.

"You didn't answer my question."

Sage gritted her teeth and rolled her head to the right, staring up at the ceiling. "To a place where there's nothing but rage, pain, and darkness."

Her mum laid her embroidery on the floor and then lay beside Sage, her dear face pillowed on her crossed arms. "You're not alone."

"So people keep saying." It was one thing to hear it and another to believe it.

"And you don't believe that?"

"Mum." She sighed. "I don't know how to deal with all of this."

Her mum placed a hand over hers. "Then tell me."

"I can't," she whispered.

To say the words out loud would give them more power to hurt. The warlord had done enough damage. Sage wouldn't let him hurt anyone else.

"Love, you need to let it out."

Probably. Sage met her mum's hazel eyes. "You kept Lilja and Hayjen from me to protect me. I can't speak of these things. It's to protect you."

Her mum cupped her cheek. "It's my job to protect you, not the other way around."

If only they understood that danger that was coming for them. Blaise and Lilja were probably the only two who truly understood the evil that would descend on their world.

Guilt pinched her.

She'd treated Lilja cruelly the last time she'd seen her. True to their word, Lilja and Hayjen hadn't come back. Sage wanted to reach out, but not today. Today, she'd train and plot.

"It's like you're miles away," her mum murmured, a hitch in her voice. "How do I help you?"

"Mum." She swallowed. "You can't help me or save me."

She smiled sadly as tears filled her mum's eyes. Sage reached for her hands and squeezed.

"It's okay, though. I'll be okay. The best you can do is support me. I need your support. I need someone to believe in me." Even though she didn't believe in herself.

"I've always believed in you, and I always will."

"I know. That's what I need the most. The days ahead will be brutal, Mum. The only way we'll survive it is if we stick together as equals. You will always be my mum, and I will always be your daughter, but I need you to support me as a leader of Aermia. I need you to push me when I falter, because it will happen."

"I can do that."

"Thank you," she said. "I need you to contact Lilja."

Gwen wiped her eyes and nodded. "I can do that."

"It isn't to make up," Sage warned. "I need her." Lilja would be a major key in the upcoming war.

"What do you plan on doing with your aunt once you have her?"

"Persuade her to do her duty."

"You want to use her?" Her mum's voice held disapproval.

"No, not use her, utilize her." Sage wouldn't manipulate the Sirenidae. Lilja would choose to help. She'd understand what was at stake.

"She's a person, not a tool."

"That may be the case, but she's necessary." Aermia needed the Sirenidae to defeat Scythia.

"Don't turn into someone you're not."

Sage smiled at her mum. "That's what I have you for."

Her mum didn't crack. "Stay true to who you are."

"I don't know who I am." That was probably the most truthful statement she'd uttered in days.

Sage shied away from her mum's probing gaze and slowly sat up, her head pounding as the room swirled around her for a brief moment. "I need a bath," she muttered as her stench hit her.

Her mum stayed quiet before a ghost of a smile touched her mouth. "I wasn't going to say anything, but you stink." She pushed to her knees and pulled Sage into a hug. "Don't think I don't see your distractions for what they are. When you want to speak, I will be here. Don't hold it in too long. It only makes it worse." Gwen kissed her cheek and stood, shaking her simple skirts out. "I'll start on that bath."

Sage closed her eyes and lay back down on the floor, listening to her mum hum a song as she started the bath. Water splashed, and the scent of cinnamon and mint wafted from the bathing room.

Footsteps padded back into the room along with the quiet swishing of skirts. "The bath will be ready for you in a few minutes. Would you like me to help?"

"No!" Sage swallowed and gentled her voice. "No, I'm all right. I can do it myself." The last thing she wanted to do was expose her body to her mum. The changes still shocked her sometimes. Her body seemed like a foreign entity.

"I'll be in my room just across the hall if you need me."

Translation: if she heard anything abnormal, she'd storm into the room.

"Thank you, Mum."

"Welcome, love."

The tension in her shoulders leaked away as the door closed behind her mum, leaving her alone. Since the king found her a couple days ago, it seemed like everyone watched her more closely. Maybe it was all in her mind.

Her gaze traveled to the balcony doors, and the shame sickened her, causing her hands to clench in the carpets.

What in the blazes had she been thinking? Clearly, she hadn't been using her mental faculties at all. What she'd almost done was unforgivable. She truly hadn't wanted to die; she just wanted to be free from the pain.

Sage rubbed at her chest where the constant pain and rage threatened to choke her. This was her new reality, and she needed to deal with it. If she didn't, it would consume what was left of her, and there were people depending on her.

Forcing herself from the floor, she staggered to her feet. If she let herself dwell on it, she'd only descend deeper into the darkness.

Sage unbuttoned her vest and moved into the bathing room. Steam caused her clothing to once again stick to her skin as heat and herbs enveloped her.

She peeled off her leather vest and glanced up at the huge tub. The vest fell to the floor from her numb fingers as a memory assaulted her, a hexagonal pool imposing itself over her reality.

"That's it. Just relax," he crooned. *"I'll take care of you."*

A warm, sudsy cloth started on her hand and carefully moved up her arm. Sage kept her eyes closed, blocked out everything happening to her, and focused only on the warm water and the comfort it gave her. She checked in when he washed her stomach and the tops of her thighs, but his hands never strayed to her important bits.

His hands moved to her head, and she hummed, soothed by the soft touch of his hands through her hair. His hands stilled.

"You like that?"

"Mmmhmm... My mum used to wash my hair and brush it for me. I love it," she said, *not knowing why she gave a stranger that information.*

"I'll remember that," he rumbled *and began washing her hair again.*

A few times, she hissed as he untangled her matted locks, but, for the most part, it was the best thing that had happened to her in a very long time. It was the last good memory she'd have before she died. "Thank you."

"My pleasure," he hummed.

"Sage?"

She gasped and stumbled away from the huge tub. Her back met the vanity behind her, rattling the glass bottles on top.

Tehl stood in the doorway, his shoulders almost touching

either side. "Are you all right?"

Far from it. His concern made everything worse. Genuine worry pulled his brows together into a frown when he shouldn't be concerned but outraged by her thoughts. She glanced back at the tub, her sins weighing heavily on her. The longer she stared at the bath, the more certain she became that she wouldn't get in it.

"I'm fine," she rasped.

"Are you getting in the bath?" he asked.

"No," she shook her head, her braid whipping side to side. A quick scrub from the water basin was all she needed.

He stepped into the bathing room and stood next to her, staring at the bath. "It seems like you were going to take a bath." Tehl gestured to the oils next to the pool of water and sniffed heavily. "Cinnamon certainly isn't my scent."

She hunched over as another memory slammed into her.

"Cinnamon," he growled. "How is it you haven't bathed in days and yet you still smell like cinnamon?"

A hand brushed over her head as she panted and forced herself to look away from the smooth stone floor beneath her feet to Tehl.

"You're not there." Tehl bracketed her face with his hands, forcing her to look into his eyes. "You're here with me."

Tears of frustration spilled down her cheeks. "He's everywhere." Escape was nowhere to be found and utterly elusive.

"There's no one here but you and I." His gaze darted to the bath. "Would you like help?"

Horror seized her. After the debacle three days ago, she didn't want him anywhere near her when he could glimpse her skin. "No!"

He studied her face and brushed his thumbs along her

145

cheekbones. "You need a bath."

"Are you saying I stink?" she quipped as her stomach rolled.

He flashed his teeth. "I didn't say that."

It was odd to be joking with him while on the verge of a mental breakdown.

"Can you bathe yourself?"

It was on the tip of her tongue to lie and say she could. But they both knew she wouldn't get in the bath. Chances were that she'd run a wet rag over her body as quick as possible and then avoid this room like the plague.

Tehl must have read her face, for he squared his shoulders and pulled her into a hug. She shuddered and reluctantly wrapped her arms around his muscular form.

"It just so happens that I need a bath, too, and it's always hard to scrub my own back. Maybe we could help each other out."

"What?" she gasped as he swung her up into his arms. "No, Tehl." She couldn't do this.

"Hush," he soothed. "Nothing untoward. I want nothing from you."

He stepped into the tub and plopped down, sloshing water over the edge. Her eyes flew to his face as warm water soaked through her clothing, and panic clawed at her throat.

"You don't understand," she whispered.

"Trust me," he said softly before arranging her to sit between his legs.

Her mouth bobbed when he placed a wet hand against her forehead and gently guided her head back against his chest.

It wasn't a matter of trust. Sage trusted him. He was with her the entire time in Scythia.

It was the memories it invoked. As much as she wanted to say each one was torture, they weren't all bad, and that's what she hated the most.

Her mind flashed to right before she'd left the Scythian castle.

The warlord knelt by the bath, watching her with an intensity that made her gut clench. How long had he been watching her? She crossed an arm across her chest and one to the juncture of her thighs. "Wh-what are you doing?"

"Watching my consort bathe, as is my right."

She shrank deep into the tub, wishing to disappear from his heated gaze.

"My lord, you're making my job difficult. No doubt you wanted her to relax during her bath?" Maeve said.

"Indeed," he murmured. He smiled, all seduction, and skated his fingertip across the top of one of her breasts. "So beautiful."

Everything cried out at the violation. There was nothing she wanted more than to slap his hand away, but she didn't. She let him touch her. She had to.

Her breath caught, and her fingers clenched against each of Tehl's knees.

The warlord hadn't forced her to let him watch her.

She'd allowed it.

She'd let him touch her in ways her rightful husband hadn't.

Sage bowed her head and inhaled the scented steam from the water, her mind tearing her apart with guilt.

Tehl's hand brushed over the crown of her head and down her spine as she fought to ground herself in the moment. It was just her and the crown prince.

He said nothing, but his presence completely surrounded her, making her feel sheltered and cherished. That somehow made her feel even dirtier. She didn't deserve to be sheltered and cherished.

She stared at her reflection. He didn't deserve a wife who was unfaithful. Tehl was a good man. He should be married to a good woman as well.

A tear dropped from her cheek, sending a small ripple through the bath water.

Whore. It was an ugly word, but correct in its description.

Scythia whore. That's what she was.

He deserved the truth, and she couldn't keep it from him any longer.

CHAPTER SEVENTEEN

Sage

It had been on her mind since she'd awoken.

Every time she glimpsed Tehl's face, the guilt and shame almost drowned her.

He'd never abandoned her while she was in Scythia. What had she ever done for him? Lied and cheated.

Sage quashed her sorrow and forced the words from her throat that had been suffocating her since the moment she'd found herself in the infirmary.

"I've been unfaithful."

Tehl's hands froze on her back; the only sound was their breathing echoing in the room.

She expected him to push her away, but he surprised her. His arms wrapped around her middle, and he pulled her snug against his chest, burying his face in her hair.

His breath skated along her neck heatedly. "You are not

accountable for his crimes." His tone brooked no argument. "Never forget that."

He didn't understand. She'd made choices. She bit her lip hard and shook her head. "You don't get it."

Tehl lifted his head and placed his chin on top of her head. "Sometimes when a man takes what isn't his," he said hesitantly, "a woman can be made to feel like it's her fault, but it's never her fault. It's his and his alone."

Pain lanced her heart as hot as a blade straight from the forge.

Tehl thought the warlord had raped her. What had happened was worse.

"He didn't rape me."

Tension drained from his body as he hugged her close.

"Thank God," he whispered, just as she said, "I said yes."

His entire body went rigid, his arms turning to bands of steel around her.

The words tasted vile upon her tongue. The truth wasn't always sweet. It was a double-edged sword. Sometimes, it was painful.

"I'm sorry," she rasped, blinking rapidly to keep the tears at bay. If only she'd been stronger, smarter, better.

Silence reigned, so stifling that Sage couldn't breathe.

She longed to rush from the room, but that was the coward's way out. She couldn't run from her problems. Facing what she'd done was part of her punishment.

Just when she thought she couldn't stand the silence any longer, he spoke.

"What did he do to you?" he whispered.

Everything and nothing.

Her lips trembled as he pressed a kiss to the back of her head.

Heat filled her eyes, and the room distorted around her. Why did he touch her like this after she'd betrayed him?

"I don't blame you," Tehl said.

"You should," she said wretchedly.

"I won't, and I don't."

Sage wrenched around to look at him, water splashing over the sides of the tub as she got a good look at his face. He schooled his expression as he met her gaze. Ever calm.

"Why?" she cried, slapping the water with her hands. "I deserve it!" Why couldn't he see that? Why was he being so nice to her?

His brows slashed together as his blue eyes darkened. "What you had to do in that hellhole to survive doesn't matter." He cupped her cheek, his angry expression at odds with his gentle touch. "The only thing that is important is that you're home."

She jerked completely around, kneeling between his legs, her finger curling around the tub edges, the stone pressing sharply into her palms. "How can you say that? You don't even know what I've done."

"What would you have me do?" he asked, holding his hands in the air. "Condemn you for someone else's actions?"

"You deserve a faithful wife."

"Don't I get a say in what I deserve? Do you think either of us deserves to be in this situation?" He pinned her with his narrowed eyes. "Since the beginning, we've fought. Fought against each other, fought our enemies. Now, we're going to fight *for* each other." He stabbed a finger at her. "I know you better than you think. You seem to think the weight of the world rests on your shoulders and that you're responsible for everyone's actions around you. You're not." Tehl ran his wet hands through his inky hair. "I refuse to watch you take responsibility for that monster's actions." He eyed her and blew out a breath. "What did he do to you?" he asked brokenly.

"He made me fall in love with him."

There. The words were out. The ones that haunted her for months.

Part of her wanted the warlord, and it sickened her.

Sage gagged but composed herself.

Her husband didn't shout, curse, or rage. A sort of sorrow rippled over his face, and he glanced away, rubbing a hand over his mouth.

"How did he manage that?" Tehl glanced in her direction. "He hurt you. How is it possible you fell for him?"

Sage swallowed down a sob threatening to burst from her chest. His questions were fair, but it was like being dragged over hot coals to hear the words from his mouth.

"The only thing I can say is that he broke me down until I had nothing left."

Tehl scoffed. "I can't believe that. You're the most stubborn woman I've ever met."

"When I fought," she hiccupped, "he hurt others."

"And that's *love*?"

"I don't know." She dropped her head into her hands. "But no matter what I do, he's always in here." Sage rapped her knuckles against her temple. "I can't escape him. He was right," she gasped. "I'll never escape him."

Tehl scooted forward and pulled her into his chest. "That's not love, Sage. That's control. That's depravity. True love isn't like that. He can't force you to love him. He's playing sick games with your emotions. He can't claim you—you were already claimed."

If only that was the truth.

She shuddered, clutching at his shirt. "Not fully."

"What do you mean?"

"He married me." Nausea caused the room to tilt. The words alone made her ill.

"What?" Tehl said confused, his brows knitting together. "That's not possible. You're already married."

She'd thought so, too. "It is."

"How?"

"He had me examined." Another violation to lay at the warlord's feet. "Then claimed me as his consort. He knew our marriage wasn't consummated."

A nasty curse burst out of Tehl. She flinched back, but he caught her face between his two hands, his eyes darting all over her face. "Did you consummate his claim?"

"No. He didn't, we didn't..."

Sage's mind darkened. What if the warlord *had* taken advantage when she was unconscious? What if there was some truth in her nightmares and it wasn't just her dark imagination?

His shoulders slumped. "Thank God." Tehl placed a hand over his eyes, hiding his emotions from her.

Everything about this moment was wretched.

She couldn't feel smaller or dirtier if she tried. Her lips trembled, but she forced them together and pushed to her feet, sloshing water everywhere. She'd lost another part of herself by revealing the truth, but he needed to know.

"I'll go," she rasped.

Tehl's hand curled around her wrist, stopping her from leaving the tub. Sage stared at him while he stared at their hands, her clothes dripping water in a constant symphony of soft plops.

"Sit down."

"I should go." It was too hard to stare at his beautiful face after everything she confessed.

"Please don't." He tilted his head back and stared up at her through a fringe of dark lashes. "The only place you should be is here." A pause. "With me."

Her heart squeezed, and her corsets seemed extremely tight. How could he mean that?

He gave a little tug on her wrist and she found herself slowly sinking into the water. What did she do to have such a man in her life? How was it possible that someone so noble was real?

Her pulse picked up its pace when he placed his hand on her waist and pulled her close, her thighs bracketing his. Tehl reached out and pulled the leather thong from her hair and began to unwind her braid.

Her stomach flipped. She knew where this led.

"Wh-what are you doing?" she stuttered.

"Taking care of you. *My* job."

He ran his fingers through her hair and then plucked a vial of soap from the stone edge, pouring a generous amount in his large palms before lathering it.

Entranced, Sage watched his slow but precise movements, completely out of sorts.

He paused and gestured to her hair. "May I?"

When was the last time someone had asked what she wanted? She didn't deserve his kindness, but she wanted it all the same.

Selfishly, Sage nodded, unable to speak past all the emotions lodged in her throat.

Tehl ran his hands along her scalp and began to massage. Her eyes slowly closed as he methodically scrubbed her hair, leaving nothing untouched. He pulled her hair over her right shoulder and lathered bubbles to the tips.

Tears prickled behind her lids. There was something so intimate about another person washing your hair. Anger and sadness battled with each other. This was another thing the warlord had stolen from her. Her memory resurfaced.

His hands moved to her head, and she hummed, soothed by the soft touch of his hands through her hair. His hands stilled.

"You like that?"

"Mmmhmm... My mum used to wash my hair and brush it for me. I love it," she said, not knowing why she gave a stranger that information.

"I'll remember that," he rumbled and began washing her hair again.

A few times, she hissed as he untangled her matted locks, but for the most part, it was the best thing that had happened to her in a very long time. It was the last good memory she'd have before she died. "Thank you."

"My pleasure," he hummed.

She breathed through the onslaught of images and forced her eyes open to stare into deep blue eyes, not the obsidian ones of her dreams.

"I can see he haunts you." It was a statement. No judgement.

"He's everywhere."

"Even here?" Tehl gestured to the tub.

Especially here.

She bit her lip and nodded, waiting for his reaction.

His lips pursed, and his jaw clenched, but they were the only signs he was angry.

He slowly released his breath and began lathering her hair again. "Then we'll make new memories. Happy ones."

"You want to make new memories with me?" Hope fluttered in her chest, unbidden and unwanted. Hope destroyed.

"I do."

"After everything?"

He met her gaze squarely. "Yes."

It seemed too good to be true, but Tehl said he'd always be honest with her. She glanced to the side of the tub, his gaze too much to take in, when her attention snagged on the soap. The crown prince had shown over and over that he was worthy of every good thing life had to offer. Since Sage had entered his life, she'd made a right mess of things.

There was one thing she could do for him. It was small and wouldn't make up for all of her sins, but it was something. "Is it all right if..." she hesitated and gestured to the soap.

Tehl cocked his head, studying her. "You don't have to. This was just for you. This moment is not about me."

She wanted to. To give back to him after everything he'd done. Even if it was as small as washing his hair.

"I want to."

It was only three words, but they held a weight that settled between them.

"If you wish." He winced. "I didn't mean I don't wish it. Only that if you *want* to... I mean, I'd like that."

Sage smiled at his rambling.

His awkwardness was still there. That comforted her in a way she hadn't expected. It was normal. Normal was something she'd lacked for a long time.

She leaned forward and wobbled, her knees slipping. Tehl's hands gripped her waist, steadying her. Her pulse jumped, but she avoided his gaze and ran her soapy fingers through his dark locks.

He sighed, his breath ghosting over her cheek.

It was a simple task, but it was somehow more intimate than anything she'd ever experienced. They were two beings caring for each other who expected nothing in return. It was beautiful. She blinked repeatedly to keep the ever-hovering tears at bay.

She worked at the muscle at the base of his head, and Tehl groaned, slumping further into the tub, his eyes fluttering shut. Her nerves disappeared a little more with his attention not focused on her.

Sage tracked how his obsidian hair slid over her pale skin. It was a dichotomy of opposites.

He was the dark to her light, but really it was the opposite.

He was the light to her darkness.

She cupped her hands in the warm water and rinsed his hair, making sure to avoid his eyes, then openly stared at her husband.

The strong line of his square jaw highlighted his sharp cheekbones. She found herself tracing the bridge of his nose and the delicate skin underneath his down-swept lashes. He was so different from her and yet so beautiful.

Her fingertips skimmed his top lip and the dimple in his right cheek. She continued to follow the length of his neck to the hollow at the base of his throat.

Tehl swallowed, and her eyes flew back to his face.

Brilliant blues met her gaze. They snared her, warmth spreading through her as he gazed back unflinchingly.

"It's okay to touch," he said, his voice gravely.

Their breath mingled as they stared at each other.

Her gaze dropped to his lips.

It felt like a lifetime ago since she'd kissed him.

Without really making the decision, she leaned close and

pressed her lips to his. That's all it was, a press of lips, but she felt it to her toes, and it unlocked a torrent of emotion.

His breath deepened like he was struggling to draw in enough air. Her fingers brushed against the length of his neck, his skin hot and damp.

She stopped breathing when his hands traveled from her hips and wrapped around her waist, like bands of steel, his fingers tangling in the wet strands of her hair.

"I wasn't prepared for this," he whispered against her lips.

His lips brushed hers again, soft, gentle. He kissed her like he was trying to memorize the moment, their lips melding and drifting away. Cherishing.

Kissing had ceased to mean anything to her in the prior months. *He* had done that.

Her lips trembled. She wanted to forget all the former kisses. If she could have one wish, it would be to erase every depraved kiss stolen from her.

Sage surged forward and kissed Tehl with an intensity that had her head spinning.

"Sage," he growled, his arms loosening around her waist.

"Make the hurt go away. Help me forget," she whispered, nuzzling his lower lip. She pressed closer for another kiss when his hands cupped each of her cheeks, holding her back.

"Love," he whispered. "Not like this. He has no place here. This is just you and I."

Tears dripped from the corners of her eyes. What was she doing? Who had she become to use someone who cared about her?

"I'm sorry."

"It's okay, Sage."

She shook head. "No, it's not."

Tehl pulled her close and pressed his forehead against hers. "One day, we'll get there. But it won't be because we're trying to forget." Her eyes flew to his, and he gave her a small smile. "You're not the only one who wants to erase those memories."

"Then why?"

He kissed each of her cheeks, her nose, her forehead, and her chin before answering. "Because it won't be because we're in a rush, or because of fear, or the need to forget, or the need to claim."

She shivered at the word 'claim', and he rested his forehead against hers, not looking away.

"It will be because we can't bear to be apart. It will be because we desire to show honor and love to each other. It will be beautiful." His smile became sinful. "And hot and perfect, because it's us." He brushed a droplet of water from her cheek with his thumb. "We will have what our parents had."

In that moment, she believed every word of his fairytale.

It was a beautiful fantasy Sage would cling to, so she could survive reality.

CHAPTER EIGHTEEN

Sam

"Again! You're not fast enough," Sam barked.

Bodies slammed against each other, Maisy, a pale blur as she tried to take Ruth down.

Ruth lost one of her daggers. She spun, ripping from the holster at her hip. A dart.

One that held a serum that burned like the devil.

Maisy's eyes widened and then narrowed, blocking Ruth's blow as she stabbed at her.

Ruth ducked under Maisy's arm, spinning beneath her grip as she drove her knee into the side of her.

"Better," Sam muttered, studying the two girls. Both were fast, but Ruth was scrappy. She had a dangerous edge to her that Maisy didn't.

Ruth attacked. *Chop. Chop. Block. Punch.*

Maisy met every blow, her forearms slapping against the other spy, and he could see she didn't expect the bigger girl to match her for speed.

Even though Ruth was taller, she was just as nimble. She'd been training as a warrior since she was a child. Her trainers had stripped her reaction time from her, so everything was pure reflex. Because they had taught her how to read movements, she was always several steps ahead.

Every time Maisy countered one of her blows, Ruth was ready for her, already disengaging and striking elsewhere.

Maisy grunted as another knee took her high in the thigh.

The dart flashed silver in the light as Ruth held the light high, and Sam could see the choreography of Ruth's final move as she lured Maisy into a combination that would lead to her writhing in pain.

"Halt!" he called, raising his hand.

Both girls froze, breathing heavily.

Sam scanned the familiar faces of his spies. "That is what we're looking for. You need to be speed itself and anticipate your partner's next move. If you don't, then…"

Maisy rolled her right shoulder back and straightened. "Then you'll be dead."

"Precisely," he murmured. "The Scythians are faster and stronger than you. You need to be smarter about your blows." He met the gazes of his trainees, one by one. "We can't afford mistakes. It'll mean your life and others."

It was a sobering thought that kept him up almost every night, that and the very sick brunette wasting away in the infirmary.

"Dismissed."

He turned on his heel and strode toward the back entrance of his makeshift sparring room. He paused and tugged his shirt from a peg on the wall and pulled it over his head, and then tied his laces as his pupils filed out of the room.

At some point, it was probably a food storage area, but it suited his purposes just fine with its high ceiling, many accesses, and being utterly forgotten. No one had stumbled into his little hideout in well over four years.

Maisy caught his eye for a moment before he glanced away. It hurt to look at the girl. Her every mannerism reminded him of her sister. A sister who had disappeared months ago in Scythia. He'd sent the girl's only family away and now she was alone. Not alone, she'd never be alone. His girls were his family. They may not share blood, but they shared a bond many would never experience.

He sighed as she pushed to her feet and marched in his direction, determination in every step.

"Sam?" she asked, shifting from foot to foot.

He smiled at her and pointedly glanced to her feet. Her shuffling stopped, and she stilled. That was the funny thing about Maisy. In the field, she had no tells, but around those she trusted and loved, she was an open book. She couldn't hide a damn thing.

"Any news?" Her dark eyes were hopeful.

Eyes that she shared with her sister. But that was the only thing. Whereas Maisy was fair and willowy, Lissa was swarthy and all curves. That's what made her the perfect insurgent for Scythia. Lissa could pass for their people, but apparently not well enough. She'd gone silent over six months ago.

Sam crossed his arms and pressed his lips together, hating that he had to tell her the truth. He wanted to lie to her, give her a pretty lie that would help her sleep at night. But he didn't. "There's been no news, Maisy."

Maisy's shoulders slumped, and she swallowed a few times. "I expected that answer."

It was the same answer he'd given her week after week. It broke his heart each time he told her the truth, and a little more hope died in her eyes. Honestly, it was admirable that she still asked. Most shut down and mourned their loved ones.

The girl nodded and pushed back her shoulders, her expression hardening. "I want to go in."

Sam nodded and took his time answering. "I know you miss your sister, but it's not safe for you."

"And it was for Lissa?"

"Lissa was in a different situation, and you know it."

"The situation has changed."

Sam leaned a shoulder against the wall. "You couldn't blend in if you tried. You wouldn't fit in."

"That's the point. I don't need to fit in. They're taking women, *Aermian women*, women who look like me."

'Woman' was a stretch. Maisy was beautiful—but she was still a girl, with an air of innocence surrounding her. It was one of the reasons she was such a damn good spy. No one suspected her cherubic face to be listening in.

"That may be true, but I need you here."

"My sister needs me!" Her voice echoed in the room.

He'd been waiting for this moment. All his girls hit a wall when they'd lost someone. Maisy had kept it together for longer than he'd expected, but she was starting to crack.

She dashed angry tears from her cheeks. "How can I stay here when they're doing God-knows-what to her?"

His heart clenched, and he pulled her into a hug, patting her back. Since he'd released the information about what was happening to the women in Scythia to his network, his girls had been on edge, and he didn't blame them. It was a person's worst nightmare.

"As I laid in bed last night, I wished she was dead," Maisy hiccupped, "if that was the only way to spare her the horror of those monsters. What kind of person does that make me?"

Sam pulled back and cupped her face between his hands. "It means that you're a caring, merciful person, and you don't want those you love to suffer."

She blinked her big, watery eyes up at him. "I miss her."

"Me too," he whispered and placed a kiss on the crown of her head, hugging her again.

He didn't offer platitudes or promises. There weren't any promises in their line of work, but he could hold her together while she crumbled until she was strong enough to put herself back together.

Her sobs quieted, and she pulled back, wiping her face on her sleeve.

"You okay?" he asked softly.

"Yeah." She stared at his shirt. "I'm sorry about all of that." She waved a hand at his splotchy shirt that looked like a dog had slobbered all over it.

"It's nothing."

She shuffled from foot to foot. "Is there anything you need from me tonight?"

"Are you working at the tavern later?"

"No."

"Then go and get some sleep."

Maisy nodded and spun on her heel, snatching her cloak off the ground. She clasped it around her neck, hiding her trousers beneath. She paused at the door and looked over her shoulder.

"You get some sleep, too, Sam."

"I'll try."

She lingered for a moment and then disappeared out the door, leaving him to the cold silence of the stones. The silence seemed accusing. It rang in his ears, reminding him of all the people he'd lost to Scythia.

He dragged a hand over his face, his scrub scratching at his palms. When was the last time he shaved? Hell. When was the last time he bathed?

From the smell of him, it had been a while.

He scanned the area one last time and blew out the remaining candles, casting the room into complete darkness. It engulfed him, seeming to caress his skin like an old lover. At one time, he'd been terrified by the darkness, but now he was more comfortable in the shadows than the light.

Slipping out the doors, Sam wove through a maze of hallways and staircases by touch. His fingertips ran along the stone walls as means of a guide, though he'd had the way memorized for years. It was an old habit that he'd started as a child. A way to ground himself in the dark, so it didn't feel like the darkness was swallowing him whole.

Sam ghosted from the bowels of the palace and snuck through the darkened kitchen. Cook snored in the corner on her cot, her mouth wide open. He pulled her blanket up over her shoulder before silently creeping away.

The older woman was a grim and gruff, but a gem nonetheless. She knew of his comings and goings and kept her mouth shut. His lips hitched up. Every now and again, she brought him little pieces of information.

He rounded a corner, the infirmary coming into view. Despite himself, his pace picked up. He hadn't been by to check on the village girl yet.

Immense heat greeted him as he entered the room on silent feet. Mira stared blankly into the blazing fire while Jacob snored softly in his rocking chair. Sam paused when he got a good look at the third person in the room. Colm sat hunched over, his eyes closed, head nodding. The poor man hadn't slept much in the last two weeks.

The man-eater, he had since learned was named Nali, cracked open a golden eye and chuffed at him, before closing it again. They'd made friends over the last few days. He'd filched a haunch of ham and a few steaks for the beast, which she'd sincerely appreciated, if he went by all the purring. If only women were that simple: bring them some food and they'd be your best friend. Unfortunately, they were a lot more complicated.

Sam halted next to the cot and placed a hand on Colm's shoulder. The older man immediately straightened and blinked his eyes as if to clear the sleep from them.

"Sam?" he said roughly.

"Yeah."

Colm patted him on the hand and slumped back into his chair. Mira glanced tiredly over her shoulder at them, before turning back to the fire.

"What are you doing here? You should go and get some sleep," Sam said.

The older man stared at Jasmine for a long moment. "She doesn't deserve to be alone. To be without family." He reached out a hand and ran it along the crown of the girl's head. "She helped my Sage and for that, I owe her, and anyone who Sage considers family is also mine." He pulled his hand back and rubbed it across his eyes. "I'll care for her as my own."

Sam stared down at Colm's head and hoped he ended up as good a man as Colm. His kindness and loyalty were something he admired.

"I'm going to sit here through the night. I'll make sure she's not alone. Go get some sleep in a bed with your wife," Sam said.

His friend gave him a wolfish smile, despite the fatigue clearly riding him. "Never been one to pass up a night in bed with my wife." His smile dimmed as he stared up at Sam. "You'll look over her?"

It was more than just a question. It was Colm asking if he would handle the responsibility the older man had deemed his own task.

"I will," Sam said.

"Okay. I will see you in the morning." Colm leaned close and placed a kiss on the village girl's forehead. "You need to wake up, little miss. There are many people waiting for you." He straightened and clapped Sam on the shoulder before strolling out of the room.

Sam pulled the chair closer and plopped down into it. He rested an elbow on the arm of the chair, and leaned his cheek against his fist, watching the pale girl before him. "How is she?" he whispered.

Mira sighed. "No worse, but no better."

If she became any worse, she'd die.

He shied away from that thought. For some reason, this girl mattered to him. Of course, he cared about all human life, but there was something intriguing about her. Not to mention, she'd be a wealth of information. Information that could win the war.

A drop of sweat trickled between his shoulder blades. How did the healers stand the heat? He loosened the ties at his throat. It was almost suffocating. Jasmine shivered. There was only one person in the room who wasn't practically melting.

He reached forward and plucked her clammy left hand from the cot and held it between his. "Today was an interesting day," he spoke softly. "You probably would've enjoyed it immensely. I got slapped by a fisherwoman today."

"You probably deserved it, too," Mira muttered.

Sam grinned and rubbed Jasmine's hand between his to work some heat back into her cool skin. "It depends which side of the story you heard, but I had a handprint on my face for several hours. Tehl, Gav, and—would you believe it—even Blaise, got in on the teasing."

His grin fell when Jasmine shivered so hard her teeth clacked together. He placed her hand underneath the blanket and fussed with the edge, despising the fact that he could do nothing but wait to see the outcome.

"Now that's a spectacle I would've liked to see," a rusty voice said.

Sam glanced to Jacob. The older man had stopped snoring when he'd come into the room. Cunning old coot. But they had more important things to speak about than his public slapping.

"I'm sure you would've enjoyed it." Sam eyed Mira and then glanced back to Jacob pointedly.

Jacob's unique bronze eyes traveled to Mira. "Darling, why don't you go get some sleep?"

"I'm not sleepy," she said, her words slightly slurring.

The Healer's expression hardened. "What is my rule about exhaustion?"

"Exhaustion—" A yawn. "—breeds mistakes."

"Exactly. You've pushed yourself beyond your limits. Please go and get a few hours of sleep."

Mira stared at her adopted father for a few moments before acquiescing. "I'll go and find my bed for a few hours, but then I'll be back," she said, pushing from her chair. She pressed a kiss to Jacob's weathered cheek before checking on the village girl and giving Nali a good scratch on the top of her head.

Sam watched with a smile, as she eventually wandered out of the room after making sure everyone was okay. Jacob was a lucky man to have such a daughter and healer at his side.

"She's remarkable."

Jacob stared at the closed door. "I am a lucky father, and, as a Healer, there's no one better to replace me when I die."

He scoffed. "You'll never die."

A bark of laughter slipped out of the old man. "And you'll settle down with a quiet-spoken girl someday."

"Who says I won't?" Sam crossed his arms and smirked at Jacob. "I might marry your own daughter."

Jacob sniggered. "If you think Mira is quiet-spoken, you haven't spent enough time around her."

"Isn't that the truth? She's got a bit of sauce to her, doesn't she?" he joked.

"That she does, but it's tempered by her sweetness."

"Indeed." Sam shifted in his chair to get comfortable and asked the question he'd been thinking about all day. "Have you discovered what was in that ring?"

"There wasn't much poison left in the ring to test. Gavriel and Lady Lilja have been helping. I think we might have come up with a similar poison, but I can't be sure. I have no one to test it on."

That posed a problem. If they could replicate the poison from Sage's ring, then it would give them an advantage in the war. From what he got from his sister-in-law's few words was that it worked as a paralytic. If needed, he could get his hands on a Scythian to test, but it would be dangerous.

Then there was the other option. Blaise. He could ask her to help with the experiment, but he didn't want to. She was their ally. What if something went wrong with the poison? They couldn't risk her death. But...she truly was the easiest route. All he had to do was walk down two corridors, up three flights of stairs to her, and ask.

He exhaled harshly. "I'll find you a subject."

"The sooner the better."

"You'll have your test subject by the end of the week."

"You're not going to do something terribly dangerous, are you?"

Sam smiled wickedly. "Why, no, I'm just going to do a little fishing."

"Fishing, you say?" Jacob asked, rocking in his chair.

"Yes, fishing."

Now all he needed was the proper bait, and Ruby would be just to their taste.

CHAPTER NINETEEN

Sage

"I'm ready to leave this blasted room," Sage said, glancing away from the velvety night sky.

Tehl glanced up from the book he was reading, his forehead all wrinkled. "What was that?"

A little bit of warmth seeped into her heart at how mussed and disoriented he appeared, like he'd been yanked from a completely different world. "What are you reading?"

He placed his book on his lap and shrugged. "A little bit of nonsense."

That she did not expect. Tehl was always so practical. Very few times had she ever seen him show a shred of whimsy. "You? Prone to a little bit of drivel, are we?" she teased.

"Everyone needs an escape once in a while," he reasoned.

His comment was offhand, but it was like cold water had been thrown over her. She was the reason he needed an escape. Each night, he barely slept, because she woke him with her thrashes and crying. Not once did he complain.

"I'll leave you to it," she murmured, turning back to the window.

"No," the crown prince said softly. He placed his book on the table next to the fire and gestured to the chair across from him. "I'm quite finished. Why don't you come and sit with me and tell me what's on your mind?"

She arched a brow and plopped into the other chair. "Why do you think there's anything on my mind?"

Tehl snorted and crossed his legs at the ankles. "You've been pacing for a good two hours, Sage."

She hadn't even noticed. Her mind had been a whirl with so many things, she'd hardly noticed how the night deepened.

Sage glanced at the fire and stared at the glowing embers, trying to figure out where to start. There were too many things to speak about and not enough time. It made her anxious. He wiggled in his chair to get more comfortable as the silence continued, and she peeked at Tehl from underneath her lashes. That's one thing she appreciated about him. He didn't have to fill the silence, and, yet, it didn't feel uncomfortable when they didn't speak.

"I'm ready to leave this room."

Tehl nodded but didn't look her way and continued to stare into the fire like it held the answers to every problem in the world.

Sage continued. "I'm strong enough to leave this room. I have been for a few days."

"I agree with you."

She blinked. Well, she hadn't expected that. She'd expected an argument. "I'm glad."

He turned to her and pinned her with his deep blue eyes.

"Physically, you are healthy enough to leave this room, but are you prepared for what is outside that door?"

No, she wasn't, but she didn't have time to wait for that. No one did. "I have to be."

"The choice is yours," he said, "but I want you to consider the cost. Little things trigger you. I won't always be with you, and that leaves you vulnerable to the prying eyes of others." He held up a hand when she opened her mouth to retort. "I don't care what others say, but I do care about how it will affect you. What affects you, affects me. Are you prepared for that?"

It was difficult letting Tehl help her when an episode overwhelmed her. But to have others witness her weakness? The thought alone made her shudder, but she knew she couldn't hide forever.

"I know what it will cost me, but the cost is worth it. I'm needed."

"You are needed, but we don't need to shove you in the middle of everything. I can make arrangements to ease you back into palace life."

"We don't have time for that." Her throat tightened with the fear that rose up from her belly. Every moment they dallied, was a moment they lost.

"What do you know of what's coming?" Tehl asked, his voice grave.

"If we do not band together, it will be the end of us all."

Her ominous words hung in the air, heavy, and as dark as black waves crashing against the bluff.

The crown prince rubbed a hand across his mouth. "What do you suggest we do?"

"That's precisely what I wished to speak to you about. In our acquaintance, we have two individuals who are the bridge to allies we desperately need if we are to win this war."

Tehl gazed at her thoughtfully. "You mean Lilja and Rafe?"

That surprised her. She suspected he knew about Lilja, but not about Rafe. "That's right. I'm astonished you know about Rafe."

"He didn't tell me willingly, but we've reached an understanding all the same."

"Good. It will help if he hates you a little less."

Tehl chuckled. "I think you'll be surprised how well we get along these days."

"Are you friends?"

"In loose terms." He leaned closer, clasping his hands together and hanging them between his knees. "So, you're proposing an alliance with a mythical race, which hasn't been seen in hundreds of years, and with the kingdom that just tried to overthrow our crown?"

She scowled at him. "Well, when you put it that way, it sounds idiotic."

He held his hands up. "It's not idiotic—insane maybe, but not idiotic." His lips twitched as if he was fighting a smile.

Sage gaped. "You're teasing me."

"Yes. What of it?"

Who was this man? Her Tehl rarely got the end of a punchline. *Her Tehl.* Some heat crept into her cheeks. When had she started thinking of him that way? "Nothing, just a delightful surprise."

"You think I'm delightful?"

Of course, he'd hone in on that. "As delightful as a burr in my boot," she retorted.

Tehl grinned at her with a twinkle in his eyes. "There she is. I was wondering where my fiery wife had gone."

Sage waved a hand at him as he leaned back into his chair, bumping his elbow into the table near the fire. Her eyes narrowed at the book sitting precariously on the edge. The foolish man would burn his book if he wasn't careful.

She popped up from her chair and rescued the book, tossing it onto the bed, before sitting back down.

"That's no way to treat books," Tehl commented.

"Neither is burning them."

"It wasn't going to burn."

"Says you."

The bickering made her smile. It was comfortable. It felt like home.

He mirrored her smile before sobering. "So, how do you propose we unite three kingdoms?"

"We need to approach Lilja and Rafe separately. I think Lilja will be the easier sell."

"Because she's been helping our people all this time?"

Sage ignored that comment. How much had she helped if she was hiding? "Because she's my family, and I know…" She forced the words out: "She's a good person." She knew it was the truth, but Sage was still hurt. "She's old enough to understand the stakes. Convincing Lilja will be the easiest."

"And Rafe?"

"He holds sway. How much—" She shrugged. "I don't know."

"He seems too highly educated to be someone lowly."

Those were her thoughts, too. Rafe was too arrogant to be common. "Those are my thoughts too, in a way, but he doesn't give much away. And he's an excellent liar."

"Indeed, he is. He's helped us so far, more or less, and after…" Tehl paused, pursing his lips. "After our broken delegation in

Scythia. I'm sure he's already reported to Methi."

She ignored his comment about the delegation. As it was, the memories were trying to creep up on her, but she wouldn't let them. "That will work to our benefit. They will already know how dangerous the threat is if they do nothing. Plus, if Aermia falls, so does Methi," she said. It was the sad, grim truth of it.

"When would you like to meet with them?"

"I've already sent for Lilja."

Tehl nodded. "I can approach Rafe tomorrow."

"I would like us to meet with them in private, if it's acceptable to you."

He blinked. "Together?"

"Well, we are to rule together, are we not?" she asked, a little stung.

"It's not that I don't desire that, it's just... You've always kept to those you view as yours, and I to mine."

"I think it's time to change that. We can't afford miscommunications; the stakes are too high."

"I agree. What time would you like me to be here to meet with Lilja?"

"After dinner perhaps."

"Would you like me to take dinner with you?"

The request was shy, so sweet that it made her feel both happy and unworthy. Happy that he'd want to eat with her. Unworthy that he'd spend his time with a soiled creature.

"I'd like that. Maybe we should send for dinner for Lilja and Hayjen as well. Negotiations are always better on a full stomach."

"You are quite right."

They lapsed into silence, each lost to their own thoughts. Sage watched him from the corner of her eye, marveling at how lucky she was to have such a friend.

"You're my friend."

Tehl startled, his eyes widening. "Where did that come from?"

"The proper response is 'Sage, you're my friend as well.'"

"Sage, you're much more than my friend. You're my consort."

His words echoed in her ears, and her fingernails sunk into the arms of the seat. "Don't call me that." Her words were full of venom and darkness. She was no one's consort. Never again.

Tehl reached between their chairs and brushed his fingertips along her left hand. "I won't call you that again."

"Ever," she whispered.

"Ever," he promised. "Release the chair, love, or you'll hurt your hands."

She didn't move.

"I'd hate for you to damage your hands. Think of all the daggers you won't be able to throw."

Sage gritted her teeth and focused on her husband's face. "That's not as funny as you thought it was."

He graced her with a lopsided grin. "True, but it got you back to the present, didn't it?"

It did. "Thank you," she said, forcing her hands to release their death grip on the chair.

The warlord seemed to haunt her every waking hour, but there was one thing in particular she'd been dreaming about that terrified her, even in the bright light of day. One nightmare she could put to rest if she did one simple thing.

"I'm having Mira examine me tomorrow."

Tehl jerked, his mouth bobbing. "Sage…"

She held up her hand. "My mind has been made up. It needs to be done."

His gaze took a tender edge, and he clasped her right hand between his own. "I don't expect that of you. It's not needed. I trust your word."

Tears clogged her throat. "I was drugged many times. I don't know what happened to my body." Her voice cracked. "I'd like to think I would know, but the truth is I don't. And despite everything *he* said... He's a mad man, not to be trusted." She swallowed heavily. "Our children could be called into question; that is reason enough."

His nostrils flared. "They'll accept any child from you if I accept it."

"That's what makes you a good man, but I can't live with that. Also—" She squeezed her eyes closed, keeping her tears at bay. "I need to know for myself. I can't keep imagining the worst."

His jaw worked as he thought about it. From the surly expression on his face, he clearly didn't like it. "Do you want me to go with you?" he asked, hesitantly, looking in every direction but at her.

Her heart squeezed, and the world shifted around her. Of all the things he could have done or said to make Sage love him. It was that. Clearly, it made him uncomfortable, and, to be honest, she was, too. Not to mention that it wasn't done. Men didn't accompany women to examinations, let alone princes. But he knew it would be hard for her, and he didn't want her to be alone. That was true companionship.

"No, thank you."

He nodded, still not looking her way.

Sage scooted to the edge of her seat and placed a hand on his cheek, causing his gaze to clash with hers. "I am lucky, indeed, to be married to such a fine man." She dropped a small kiss on to his left cheek and leaned back.

Tehl reached up and held her hand to his cheek. "We'll make it through this."

"Together."

"Together," he whispered back.

CHAPTER TWENTY

Sage

"You're pacing."

Sage cast a glance Tehl's way, and then she continued her route across his study. When he'd suggested they meet Lilja in his study, she'd jumped at the chance. But the longer she was away from something familiar, the more jittery she became.

She shook out her hands and bounced on the tips of her toes as she stopped in front of a huge wall lined with books. Her hands itched to pull out the old tomes from the shelves and crack them open, just to see what secrets they held. Her nose wrinkled as she peered closer at the ones at her eyeline. *Royal House of Aermia* and the *Laws of Aermia*. Maybe those held *too* many secrets.

Her gaze flitted up the bookshelf, her attention snagging on a deep blue book with faded gold filigree adorning the spine. It looked out of place among the sea of brown, tan, and black spines surrounding it.

Without meaning to, she stretched for it, but it was well beyond her reach. Sage stepped up onto the bookshelf and extended again, barely missing her mark. A gurgle sounded behind her, and heat swamped her back as a solid arm slid around her waist.

"I look away for one moment and you climb things," Tehl growled. "What part of 'take it easy' did you not comprehend?"

Sage scowled at the books and wiggled in his grasp. "I was trying to reach a book."

"Clearly." A sigh. "Which one?"

She tipped her head back and pointed to the elusive blue book. "That one."

He chuckled, ruffling the hair at her neck. "I should have known."

Tehl reached over her head and deftly pulled the book from the shelf with ease. She glared at his hand as he pulled her from the bookshelf and held the book out to her. Tall people sure had it easy.

She plucked it from his hand and stepped away from him. "Thank you," she said mulishly.

A snort. "Don't sound too grateful," he retorted, his voice drifting away.

A sigh escaped her. She wasn't unthankful; she was tired of others doing things for her when she could do them for herself. But she needed to be reasonable. They were just helping. Turning on her heel, she strode to Tehl's desk and crowded next to him until he looked up at her with a raised brow.

"Thank you."

He studied her for a moment and dipped his chin. "You're welcome." He pointed his quill at her treasure. "Are you going to open it?"

Sage brushed her hand gently across the cover and opened it with care. A smile graced her face as she read the title.

Gifts from the Sea.

Of all the books to pick up, she'd picked one about the sea. She turned another page, the musty scents of aged paper and old ink greeting her like old friends. How long had it been since she'd read a book? It seemed like such a luxury.

Her gaze bounced back to the practical tomes adorning the shelves. "This doesn't seem like it fits."

"It doesn't." Tehl shuffled a few papers to the side and leaned back in his chair, his gaze distant as he stared out of the adjacent windows toward his balcony. "My father spent a great deal of time in this room. My mother snuck in here to work on her correspondence." A smile. "Misery loves company. But when she didn't have work, she came and read. My parents didn't need to talk, they just enjoyed being in the company of each other."

Her gaze darted down to the book in her hands. "This is your mother's?" she asked.

"It is."

She held it out to him, feeling uncomfortable. She didn't mean to touch something that was clearly precious to his family. He looked up at her and gently pushed it back toward her. "You take it. It's collecting dust on that shelf anyway. My mum gained joy from trading books with others. I'm sure she would have given it to you herself if she were here. Plus—" He glanced at the bookshelves and to the chairs clustered next to the open balcony doors. "It would do Father's heart good to find you here reading sometime."

That sounded like an invitation. "And you wouldn't mind?"

"You're quiet enough." His lips curved into a smile. "I've found

I like company when I'm being forced to do something I hate."

Her lips tipped up. "Misery loves company?"

"Something like that."

A knock.

Sage straightened and placed her book carefully on the desk.

"Enter," Tehl called.

Garreth opened the door. "Lilja and Hayjen are here for you."

"Send them in."

She braced herself as Hayjen strolled into the room. His face was placid, but his ice blue eyes held a wealth of emotion that she promptly ignored. Emotion had no place in this conversation. Lilja commanded Sage's attention as she swept into the room, her citrus scent teasing the air.

Tehl stood and gestured to the chairs and refreshments near the balcony. "Please sit."

Sage jumped when a hand settled on the small of her back. She glanced up into Tehl's heartbreakingly handsome face. "Yes?"

"You ready to sit down?"

"Yes."

She allowed him to guide her to the chairs and sat much less gracefully than the Sirenidae, now staring at her with fathomless magenta eyes, had.

An awkward silence settled over the group as Sage stared at her friends-turned-family. The ones who'd lied to her. She blew out a breath. Today wasn't about personal feelings. Today was about bridging divides.

"You know why you're here," she said.

Lilja nodded. "You want a meeting."

"We do," Tehl rumbled.

"They won't help," her aunt said. Her tone was matter-of-fact.

"They will," Sage said. There wasn't any other choice.

"In hundreds of years, they've done nothing, despite my entreaties. What makes you think they will now when they wouldn't listen to one of their own?"

"Ezra." Saying his name hurt her.

Lilja's brow furrowed in confusion. "Who's Ezra?"

"A Sirenidae I met in Scythia." Sage bowed her head. "He was my doctor."

"Your doctor?" Hayjen asked. "As in he worked with the warlord?"

"Something like that," she murmured. "I thought he was my friend...until he tried to drown me."

Tehl sucked in a sharp breath.

"I was bathing one day when he appeared by my side."

The memory rose to the forefront of her mind, unbidden.

Ezra knelt beside the pool, his face looking infinitely sad as he leaned toward her.

"Wh-what are you doing here?" she screeched, blinking water out of her eyes. "Get out!"

He dipped his finger into the water and drew a pattern. "You're too good for our world, Sage. You shouldn't be here."

She took a tiny step away from him. Something in his voice was off. It sounded as if someone had died. "Thank you. If you give me a moment, I'll get dressed and come out to you."

His lips tipped up, but he didn't look up from his water drawings. "Do you remember when we spoke of peace?"

Chills erupted along her arms. Something wasn't right. Why was he bringing that up now? She glided back another step, eyeing the stairs that led out of the pool. She darted a look to the open door. No guards. Could she make it out of the pool, to the outer door?

184

Unlikely.

"Yes," she said, slowly twisting toward the Sirenidae. She jerked when her gaze clashed with his.

"I want to give you peace," he whispered, and something akin to determination altered his expression. "I'm going to help you end your suffering."

She balked and opened her mouth to scream, but he lunged. Water closed around her face as he shoved her under. What the bloody hell? Her feet touched the bottom, and she propelled herself to the surface.

Gasping for air, she pushed toward the stairs, panic building in her breast. All she needed to do was make it to the stairs. Her foot landed on one stair, then two, and then three. Hope blossomed. Maybe she would make it.

A shriek flew out of her as a hand grabbed her ankle. Her palms slammed against the stone, and her chin cracked against the step's edge, clicking her teeth together. Dark spots dotted her vision, and the room swirled. She dug her fingers into the stone as she was pulled back and kicked at his hand.

"Let GO!"

He jerked harder, and her nails broke, her hands slipping. She sucked in another breath and screamed, the sound piercing the air, and echoing around the empty room.

She scrambled forward when the hand released her ankle, but she didn't make it far. Ezra's arm wrapped around her torso, and his hand slapped across her mouth, cutting off her screams. He towed her back into the pool, kicking and screaming.

"Don't do this," she pleaded from behind his hand.

"I'm sorry..." His voice broke. "I have to save you from him. I won't let you be used. You deserve peace after everything you've suffered.

I'm going to grant you at least that."

Her eyes widened. He was really going to do it. Ezra was going to drown her.

She pulled in a deep breath through her nose when he kissed the top of her head and pulled her under. All sound disappeared except for Ezra's soft humming. She struggled against him, bit at his hand, raked her broken nails down his arms. But he didn't budge. Panic filled her as her lungs burned, begging for air. She flung her head back and crashed it into his face in a blind panic. She needed air. Now. But even that didn't help. It earned her a hand around her throat.

Unable to hold her breath any longer, she sucked in a breath and choked. Her body spasmed at the invasion in her lungs. It burned. Stories said drowning was peaceful, but those were lies. Her body seized, trying to get rid of the fluid. She tried to claw her way to the air, the surface of the pool just above her, taunting her. She gazed at her hair floating around the pool and closed her eyes. This was how she would die.

Suddenly, something slammed into her, breaking the vise around her torso and throat.

She touched her throat, flinching at the rough texture, her story dying off. She could still feel the echo of his hands around her throat.

Sage met Lilja's pained gaze. "He didn't want to hurt me. He wanted to spare me the pain of what he knew was coming." She swallowed. "There were many times I wished I had died then."

Tehl cursed under his breath as Lilja's eyes became watery. But Sage continued.

"That's everyone's future if we do not band together and fight. The Sirenidae are naïve if they don't think Scythia will come for them. If Ezra was working with him, what makes you think others won't to save their families, their friends?" She let the question hang in the air before she continued. "I know what I would do for my family. Anything. No one is safe until he is gone."

"We don't disagree with you," Lilja said softly.

"Good, then you'll arrange a meeting," Tehl said.

Hayjen and Lilja exchanged a glance before looking between the two of them.

"We will do our best, and you'll have your meeting, but I can't make any promises that they'll listen. However, know this, we'll be on your side."

"Will that make a difference?" Tehl asked.

Her uncle cast a sharp look his way.

The crown prince held up a hand. "Your support means something to us, but, when it comes to negotiation, only those who possess power matter."

Blunt as ever. Tehl wasn't wrong. Sage arched a brow at her silent aunt as if to say, 'do you want me to tell him or will you?'

"That won't be an issue," her aunt supplied. "I may be banished, but I'm still a daughter of the king."

Tehl blinked but otherwise didn't react. "Well, that's... fortuitous."

"Indeed," Sage said.

Lilja pinned her with an unreadable look. "We will arrange the meeting within the next two weeks in exchange for something."

Of course, she wanted something. The woman was a bloody pirate for heaven's sakes.

"Next week," Tehl cut in. "Time is against us."

She nodded gracefully. "Within the week." Her attention turned back to Sage. "I'd like to have a conversation with you in private."

That worked perfectly. Sage also wished to speak to her aunt in private. "Then it's agreed."

Tehl held out his hand, and Lilja clasped his forearm.

"We're in accord."

"We are."

The Sireniade turned her attention back to Sage. "Can we speak now?"

"Yes." She turned to Tehl who watched her. "Would you like us to go someplace else?"

He shook his head. "I'm in need of a bout or two." He jerked his chin at Hayjen. "Would you like to join me in the ring?"

Her uncle smiled, and it was a bit feral. "I always enjoy a good bout." He pushed from his chair and smacked a kiss against his wife's cheek as Tehl stood. The crown prince moved around his chair and placed a hand on Sage's shoulder, squeezing.

"If you need me, send for me."

"I'll be fine," she said softly.

"I know." He said it simply. Like he believed it to be the honest truth.

Sage smiled at him and reached up to give his hand a squeeze. "Once we're done, maybe you could bring your book back?" The question hung in the air.

He blinked. "I'd like that."

"Okay." She fought a blush as he stared at her like he was trying to see inside her mind. The fact was that she didn't want to be alone, and she enjoyed his company. When she was alone, her monsters liked to come out and play.

He released her and strode across the room, each step purposeful, and flung open the door. Hayjen followed him, and a rush of nervousness and anger slammed into Sage as the door quietly clicked shut.

Sage turned to her aunt and cocked her head. "You've gotten me alone. What do you want?"

CHAPTER TWENTY-ONE

Lilja

Hostility and anger radiated off Sage. It was evident in every line of her niece's body. Even the way she tilted her head spoke of her readiness to fight. It pained Lilja to see her like that, but she knew it well. She'd been there herself. It had been years, but some days, it felt like yesterday.

"I want nothing from you," she said softly.

Sage tossed her head with an unladylike snort. "You and I both know you don't want nothing. Stop lying to me, or is it such a habit by now that it comes naturally?"

"That was earned," Lilja said. "It's natural to be angry when someone keeps the truth from you. I can't change the past, but I can apologize. I am sorry."

Her niece gazed out the windows. "I know you're sorry, but it doesn't make it okay."

"You're right. Apologizing is only half of it. Taking the steps to correct the misdeed is what matters."

Sage nodded and bit her lips as if to keep from saying what was on her mind.

"Ma fleur, tell me what's troubling you," Lilja asked gently.

"I can't understand why you did nothing. The women," Sage choked, her green eyes flashing. "They are suffering so much and yet you kept silent. I don't understand why you didn't say anything to me months ago. I would have believed you. I would have pressed the crown."

"You weren't ready."

"Not ready? No, you weren't ready to let go of your freedom."

A spark of anger flared in her chest, but Lilja tamped it down. Sage was hurt, lost, and looking for someone to blame for the atrocities she'd gone through. She needed to be calm. She could handle her niece's rage and pain. She needed someone like Lilja to help her, because they were more alike than she knew.

"There was a time when I felt the same as you. When I came out of Scythia, I was more broken than a person should be." Lilja looked at her hands, still able to feel the weight of her tiny daughter in her arms. "I lost more than just myself in that hellhole. I lost my daughter."

Sage's eyes widened, and Lilja's breath hitched. Even now, after all these years, a pain unlike anything she'd ever known welled up inside her. "They took my first and greatest love from me, and left me a broken, wretched carcass. When I finally escaped, I sought solace in my family." She smiled bitterly. "They helped for a time, but when I came out of my sorrow and demanded vengeance, no one lifted a finger. They claimed it was too dangerous to leave the sea. They also thought to use it as an example of what would happen if anyone disobeyed their laws."

"Those bastards," Sage spat, her green eyes sparking with anger.

"Indeed," Lilja said. "They were supportive as long as they didn't have to leave their bubble of safety. It was there and then, that I left. I refused to reside with a people who were so apathetic that they wouldn't fight for those they loved."

"What did you do?"

"I fought. I caused mayhem. I mourned. Then, I found my purpose."

Sage leaned closer. "And what was that?"

"I only had so much power at my disposal. So, I did my best to protect those who could not protect themselves, and I made sacrifices."

"So, you pirated."

"I did."

"Not for selfish gain, but to keep others from Scythia."

"Yes." Lilja scooted forward in her chair. "I didn't tell you this to excuse the choices I've made in life. I'm imperfect and I make mistakes, but I also stand by the choices I make. The reason I have explained my story, ma fleur, is so that you know you're not alone. You will *never* experience what I experienced. I will fight for you with my dying breath. I will not turn a blind eye to your rage, pain, and sorrow. I will stand beside you and support you when you need it. You will never be made to feel like this was somehow your fault, and your horrors will not be turned into a life lesson." She held out her hand to Sage. "I will always hold my hand out when you're drowning, because that's what you do when you love someone. That's the meaning of true family and friendship."

Sage stared at her hand, her eyes becoming glossy. "What was her name?" she whispered.

Soul-wrenching pain stabbed her. "Gem."

"Gem," Sage said softly. Slowly, she stretched out a hand and placed it in Lilja's. "I won't ever let another girl face what you and I went through. I'll fight for them. I'll fight for Gem."

Lilja squeezed her niece's hand, relief washing over her. Sometimes a person could lose themselves to bitterness and rage. But Sage hadn't surrendered herself to the darkness; she was just lost.

"As will I."

Lilja tugged on Sage and stood, pulling her into a hug.

Sage stiffened for a moment then embraced Lilja in return, until her lungs felt like they would burst.

"How do I survive this?" Sage whispered against her shoulder. "How do I come back from this?"

"One day at a time, ma fleur." Lilja pulled back and clasped Sage's face between her palms. "Each day will be a fight, but it will get easier. I promise."

Her niece nodded. "I can fight."

Lilja smiled. "I know you can." She pulled her into another hug and then stepped back.

Sage met her gaze squarely. "I'm visiting Mira." Her gaze dropped to her toes. "I need to be examined."

Lilja cursed, her rage almost choking her. So help her, if that fool prince asked that of her, she'd tie him to a rock and drown him, or maybe drop him in leviathan-infested water. "Did Tehl ask that of you?" she asked calmly.

"No." Sage shook her head. "He told me it wasn't necessary, but I need to know."

"Sometimes knowing isn't always better."

"True, but this might help the nightmares, and if there is a child..."

Lilja clasped and squeezed her hands. "We'll love it no differently."

Sage nodded, a tear dripping down her face. "I need to know. Will you come with me?"

Stunned, she stared at her niece and again pulled her into a hug. "Of course, I'll come with you. But wouldn't you rather your mother was there?"

"My mum has been through enough. This is one thing she doesn't need to know, unless Mira finds something. I don't want to worry her more than I already have." She pulled back and wiped at her face. "You, my dear aunt, can handle it. You will stand by my side?"

Lilja nodded. "I will."

She wouldn't let Sage suffer alone. She would give her what no one else did.

Vengeance.

CHAPTER TWENTY-TWO

Sage

She was going to puke.

"Ma fleur, it's going to be okay."

Lilja ran her hand over Sage's arm in a soothing motion, but it did nothing to calm her nerves. She wanted to object to everything about the situation. The longer she lay on Mira's table, the more she wanted to bolt from the room.

"You don't have to do this," her aunt said in a hushed tone.

Sage stared up at the ceiling. If only that was true. Much rode on the outcome of the examination.

Mira walked through the door, and Sage's stomach lurched. The blond healer closed the door, shutting off Jacob's quiet humming from the main section of the infirmary.

Mira moved to her right side and grinned at her. Sage gave her a wobbly smile and groped for Lilja's hand. Long fingers clasped hers, and her heart slowed just a touch. She wasn't alone.

Everything would be okay.

"Sage. I'll be gentle, and it'll be over before you know it." Mira hesitated, her face a mask of concern. "Are you sure you want me to...?"

"Yes."

She really wanted to shout 'no,' but she didn't have a choice. The examination had to be done. She hadn't thought about it when she was in Scythia, but her flow had never come. It became glaringly apparent when she'd been lying in bed several days prior in the infirmary.

Sage focused on the white-washed ceiling as Mira moved around to the end of the cot.

"Please scoot down to the end," Mira's calm voice said.

She complied and blew out a breath as the healer gently touched her knees.

"Please let your legs fall to the side."

Sage gritted her teeth and closed her eyes, obeying Mira's command. Lilja squeezed her hand in support which she squeezed in return. Breathe. That's all she had to do. Breathe through the violation that was necessary because of *him.*

She bit her lip as Mira began the examination. Her eyes teared up at the slight pinch, but it wasn't the worst thing she'd ever experienced. Red flashed through her mind. Pain. Blood. Helplessness.

"Almost over," her friend said softly.

Sage swallowed hard and focused on the swirls inside her lids. This was for the best. Not knowing was the worst. If she was with child, then she'd deal with it, but she couldn't stand the nightmares that came each night when she imagined the worst. Dreaming of the warlord taking what wasn't his while she slept and couldn't move. She inhaled deeply to keep the contents of her stomach *in* her stomach.

Her right hand moved from the table to her belly. She'd made the decision the day before that she'd love and adore the child with every single breath she took, despite how it was begotten. Children were innocent, and she'd not condemn an innocent for the sins of the damned.

"All done." Mira straightened and pulled the sheet over Sage's legs.

Sage forced her eyes open and lifted her head, meeting the deep blue gaze of one of her dearest friends. Mira broke into a huge smile, and Sage's breath caught.

"You're intact, Sage. There's no child. There's been no ravishment."

A choked sob escaped her, and she lay back, tears streaking down her cheeks. No child. No violation. Zane had kept his word.

She cried louder, hating that she'd used his name unbidden. That she was thankful he'd kept his word.

"It's okay, ma fleur," Lilja murmured, stroking the hair at her temple.

Sage untangled her left hand from her aunt and pressed the heels of her hands to her eyes, hoping to stop the flow of tears. Relief. She felt sheer bloody relief.

Mira placed a hand on her right shoulder. "It's over, Sage. It's over."

It was far from over. But it was one less nightmare that would plague her each night.

Glass shattered, startling her. She met Mira's widened eyes as Jacob cursed loudly from the other room.

"Missy, everything is all right," Jacob said loudly.

"Who the bloody hell are you?"

Sage bolted upright, almost cracking her head against Mira's. "Jasmine."

CHAPTER TWENTY-THREE

Jasmine

She swiped at her eyes and tried to make sense of where she was. Her throat ached something fierce, and she longed for a drink of water. But what she wanted more were answers.

Her fingers slipped along the petite dagger she'd snatched off the table near her side. An old man held both hands up placatingly as she shifted to the side, eyeing the basin she'd thrown at him.

"It's okay, missy. My name is Jacob."

She blinked the sweat from her eyes and held the dagger out in front of her. Her arm shook, and each breath was wheezed and horridly painful. Her eyes felt like they were full of sand, and her lids weighed a million pounds. All she wanted to do was lie down and go to sleep, but fear had her holding the blade higher.

Had the Scythians gotten her again? The little old man didn't look Scythian, but that didn't mean anything. All it meant was that they'd captured an old man who looked to be Aermian, although there was something about his eyes. They shone like copper behind his spectacles. She'd not seen eyes like those before.

"I will only ask one time. What do you want with me?" she rasped. He opened his mouth, but she shook her head. "Think carefully of your answer, or I might be tempted to slit you from your navel to your gullet."

"I'm Jacob, Royal Healer of Aermia."

She scoffed. Why would the royal Healer be tending to her? Likely story. "Listen here, you old coot—"

"Jas," a familiar voice whispered.

Jasmine froze then peeked over her shoulder at the one person she had been to hell with. "Sage?"

The green-eyed beauty slowly approached her like she approached a dangerous animal. "I'm here, Jas. We're both safe."

"Safe?" she asked.

Sage gave her a wobbly smile. "Yeah, relatively."

Jas's time in Scythia had taught her that nowhere was safe. People only experienced the appearance of safety. She shakily gestured to the old man edging around her cot. "And him?"

"He's harmless. Jacob is the palace Healer. He and Mira." Sage gestured to the blond woman with huge blue eyes behind her. "They've been taking care of you. You're very ill."

Stars above, her fatigued body agreed with that statement. It was worse than when she'd been thrown from her horse when she was thirteen. Everything pained her, but it was her labored breathing that bothered her the most. It was like breathing with a wet rag stuffed inside her mouth.

A growl startled her, and she stared down at the beast in which her fingers had found purchase. She gaped at the large golden eyes staring at her. A leren. A bloody leren. Flashes of the man-eater surfaced in her mind.

"Nali?" Jasmine asked.

The beast chuffed and settled down while Jasmine tried to process everything around her. The room began to spin, and she placed her hand with the dagger on the cot to steady herself. She lifted her head to stare at Sage. "The twins?"

Sage smiled. "They're here. In the palace."

The blade slid from her fingers and clattered noisily to the floor. All that mattered were the children. The room spun, and Jasmine smiled as everything dimmed.

Her family was safe.

***

The second time she woke, it was much more peaceful.

Jasmine opened her eyes and stretched, a huge yawn cracking her jaw.

"Jasmine?" a soft-spoken voice called.

Glancing to the right, she locked eyes with the lovely blond she vaguely remembered. "Who are you?"

The blond smiled at her, flashing white straight teeth. "I'm Mira. I'm your healer." She abandoned her herbs on a sturdy wooden table, wove through the cots, and paused by her side. "How are you feeling?"

Like someone had punched her in the chest repeatedly. "I've been better."

Mira knelt by her side and held out her hand. "Will you permit me to check your temperature?"

She snorted, the motion causing her throat to scream in pain. "I think we passed pleasantries and manners by now if you've been tending to me," she rasped. Her brows furrowed. How long exactly had the healers been taking care of her. "How long have I been here?" she asked, as Mira lay cool fingers against her brow.

"Almost three weeks."

Jasmine flinched. Three weeks? "As long as that?"

The healer pulled away and placed two fingertips on the underside of her wrist. "You've been very ill, Jasmine. It's a miracle that your fever broke."

The severe expression of the healer's face chilled Jasmine. She must have been at death's door.

"How surprised are you that I'm awake and speaking to you right now?" She studied the blond's features carefully. Reading people was a particular skill of hers. Most of the time, she could tell when someone lied to her.

But the healer didn't shy away from her question. "I didn't think you'd survive. You sustained grievous injuries on your way to Aermia. Then, being exposed to the elements and taking a swim in the chilly water so late in the year did nothing for your health. The sickness settled in your lungs, and we've battled it ever since."

Jasmine rubbed a hand over her chest. Her breaths now weren't exactly painful, but they weren't comfortable. Her thoughts turned to her niece and nephew. She *needed* to see them. "Am I contagious?"

"No. Otherwise, the princess would not have been allowed to visit you."

"Sage has been visiting?"

"Every single day. You actually just missed her. The crown prince summoned her, or she'd still be here by your side."

She was beyond lucky to have such a friend to care and watch over her. Jasmine eyed Mira as she tucked the blanket around her feet and bustled to the fireplace, pulling a kettle with care from the heat. She didn't doubt that this woman had much to do with her survival. The infirmary was clearly her domain. It was evident by the way she moved with confidence.

"Thank you," Jasmine said.

The healer glanced over her shoulder and smiled. "There's no need to thank me. I did what anyone else would."

"That I highly doubt. And I would be grateful to anyone who brought me back to my littles." She paused. "Can I see them?"

Mira slipped around the cot with a cup of tea in her hand and sat in the chair next to Jas. She placed the cup on a little side table and wiggled an arm underneath her shoulders. "Can you sit up?"

Jasmine nodded, but she gasped out a breath when pain slammed into her.

"Yep, those are the broken ribs. Luckily for you, you've slept through the worst of it."

If this wasn't the worst of it, broken ribs must be something truly heinous. She gritted her teeth and sat up slowly with the help of Mira. The healer plucked the cup of tea from the table with her other hand and held it to her lips.

"Drink up. It will soothe your throat and help with the pain."

Jas obeyed and blew on the liquid before taking a swallow. It burned a little, but it soothed her dry, scratchy throat, which was a godsend.

After a few more gulps, Mira pulled the cup away, and she licked her lips. She hadn't forgotten that the healer hadn't answered her question. If she wouldn't get the children sick, there was no one who could keep them from her. She'd drag herself from the damn room if that's what it took.

"My children," she stated. "I want to see them."

The healer nodded and placed the cup back on the table before lowering her back to the cot. "I promise you will see them soon."

"Do they know I'm here?" *Alive.*

"No, they do not."

Anger was her first emotion. "Why?" she bit out.

Serious blue eyes peered into her own stormy gaze. "We didn't know if you'd make it. I did everything in my power to bring you back to your little ones. There was talk of letting them know you were here, but, in the end, it was decided no. Could you imagine if we let them see you and then you died?" she murmured.

Jasmine's anger melted away. That made sense. These people were only looking out for Jade and Ethan. She reached out and clasped the blond's hand. "Thank you. I understand the decision you made. But what about now?"

"I think it will be best if you gained more strength before we brought them in."

Her heart screamed 'no,' but her head told her it was a good plan. The children wouldn't suffer in her absence. She'd be the only one to suffer, but she knew she wasn't strong enough to care for them now, nor let them leave her again. They'd never leave her sight again.

***

The next week passed with long, boring bouts of silence and naps. Each day, her body gained strength. She'd come to enjoy her visits with the Royal Healer, Jacob. He had an interesting mind and an even more interesting sense of humor.

She looked forward to her daily visits with Sage. Her friend tried her best to be positive, but darkness clung to her like a cloak. Jas couldn't imagine the horrors that had been rent on her during their time in Scythia. Her own short visit to the warlord's chamber would haunt her for the rest of her life, and that was only a handful of minutes. Sage had been there for months.

Jasmine glanced down to her shoulder and ran her finger over the long thin scar that she'd carry until she died. What kind of scars did her friend carry?

She closed her eyes and paused in her rocking. Over the last week, nausea would strike at the oddest times and leave just as quickly. The worst part was that she didn't have an appetite, so all she did was dry-heave. Then there was the fatigue. It was like she couldn't keep her eyes open. All she wanted to do was sleep.

Her stomach churned, and she leaned forward, her head between her knees, and panted. Sometimes if she breathed just right, she wouldn't dry-heave.

A weathered hand appeared underneath her nose, and, with it, the bitter scent of peppermint. "Thank you, Jacob," she croaked. She inhaled deeply through her nose while the Healer ran a palm across the top of her back.

"My pleasure, missy."

He continued his ministrations until the bout passed, and she straightened in the rocking chair she had absconded from the elderly man. Jacob moved around her chair and eased himself into the one across from her.

"How are you feeling today?" he asked.

Jasmine waved a hand at him. "Better and stronger each day."

He pierced her with his unique gaze and then tapped his right temple. "How about up here?"

She shrugged a shoulder. "I'm tired. Honestly? Awful." She paused and glanced toward the door for eavesdroppers.

"You can speak freely here."

"I know, but I just don't want anyone overhearing one word."

She turned back to Jacob and heaved a sigh. "I feel guilty."

"Why?"

"Because I didn't suffer what Sage did." She shook her head and stared into the fire. "I can see the torment clinging to the princess, the pain. But I didn't experience that. The worst I suffered was fear. Fear of not being able to come back. Fear of not seeing Jade and Ethan again." She swallowed. "The men weren't bad. They had strict rules—but those were to protect me. They never hurt me."

In the past week, she'd found herself even missing them. They weren't bad men. They were just stuck in a bad situation.

The side of her face prickled the longer Jacob stared. "What?" she asked tiredly, turning to the Healer. "You clearly have something on your mind."

The old man steepled his fingers and closed his eyes. He sighed and then scooted his chair closer to her. Jasmine frowned as he pulled her hand between his. "Jasmine. Those men weren't good people."

Her frown deepened. "Just because they're Scythian doesn't make them bad people. That's prejudice of a nasty kind, and I'm surprised to hear such generalities from you."

"That's not what I meant, missy."

He stared at her with a sorrow that made her breath catch. "Then, what do you mean?"

His face creased, and his lips flattened. "Jasmine, love, I have some news that might distress you."

Her mind flashed to the twins. "Are the twins okay?" she asked, squeezing his hand.

"The twins are just fine. It's you whom I'm worried about."

"Pah, I'm just fine."

His face creased even more. "Love, I believe you are with child."

"What?"

"You have all the signs," he said gently. "Fatigue, nausea, lack of the flow."

She flinched, and her gaze dropped to her belly. "It's not possible," she muttered while staring at the little bulge she'd not given a second glance at until now.

"I'm so sorry, Jasmine."

She yanked her eyes from her belly. "It-it can't be possible. I've never…" Bile flooded her mouth, and she swallowed, feeling sick. "I can't be!" Her voice was shrill even in her own ears. "They never touched me." He squeezed her hand, but she barely felt it.

"Are there any timeframes, any days, you cannot remember? Sometimes, certain drugs…"

His voice became fuzzy as she stared blankly at the fire, its heat not warming her in the slightest. She did have missing periods of time. Every night was a blank after dinner. She slept well through the night, and nothing ever disturbed her. That she knew of.

"But they protected me," she said, her voice wobbly. "They cared for me."

"Jasmine. Those who love and care for us, don't take without asking. They don't steal from and harm those they love."

Her lip trembled. "I can't believe it."

"We can do an examination whenever you wish." His lips pressed harder together. "But it's my opinion that you are, indeed, with child."

She pulled her hand from the Healer's and laced her fingers together. "As soon as Mira returns, she'll do the examination and prove you wrong."

She folded her arms. They'd see.

***

"So?" Jasmine asked, sitting up.

Mira stepped away from her and washed her hands in the bowl behind her. Slowly, the woman turned to her, her face desolate, no expression at all.

Her stomach dropped. "No." Mira blinked and moved to touch her arm, but Jasmine yanked her arm away. "No!"

"You are, indeed, with child, Jasmine."

"But they took care of me." How could they do this? Heat filled her eyes as a big ugly sob erupted from her chest. Chills broke out along her arms as her body flashed hot and then cold.

Mira wrapped her arms around Jasmine, pulled her into a hug, and began to rock her. "It's okay. We'll get through this. You're not alone."

Alone. She was alone. She had no husband. No memory of the creation of the being that was now growing inside her without her permission.

Darkness began to creep into her vision, and the room spun as ice crept through her body. Someone was screaming, a horrible, ugly, gut-wrenching sound of pain and sorrow, but she couldn't lift her head to see who it was.

Huge arms wrapped around her, and she turned into the warmth, trying to burrow into it. Hoping, praying that it would keep the stabbing chill of betrayal from completely freezing what was left of her broken heart.

CHAPTER TWENTY-FOUR

Sam

He tightened his arms around the woman breaking apart in his arms. Her gut-wrenching sobs tore at his heart. "It's okay," he soothed, staring over Jasmine's head at Mira, who looked like she was about to break into tears herself.

Jasmine jerked away from him, almost clipping him in the chin, her tear-stained face turned upward. Something in his chest clenched when her glazed, blue eyes met his.

"They destroyed me," she cried, her eyes rolling into her head, and she slumped into his arms.

"What in the bloody hell?" he whispered, staring wide-eyed at the woman in his arms. "What happened?"

"It's not my place to say," Mira hiccupped, her eyes liquid. "Keep her head elevated."

"Like hell, it isn't," Sam barked, rearranging Jasmine so her neck wasn't crooked. He narrowed his eyes at the healer. "So help me, Mira. I'll shake it out of you if I have to. No one cries like that unless an atrocity has happened." His stomach dropped. The only thing Jasmine had really spoken about were the twins. "Are her children all right?"

"The twins are fine, but..." Mira swallowed and shook her head. "Bring her to the other room where we can warm her by a proper fire. I'll explain more then, once I've had a chance to care for her."

Sam rose and followed Mira out of the room. Jacob rocked in the rocking chair, his white hair sticking up in every direction like he'd been running his hands through it. He watched them enter the room, his mouth turned downward. Sam placed Jasmine down gently and stepped aside, so Mira could make her comfortable. He crossed his arms and shifted on his feet, feeling restless. He hated being in the dark.

"For the second time, I ask, what is wrong?"

Mira cast a glance to her father, and they stared at each other, a silent conversation passing between the two of them. Jacob broke first and met his gaze.

"I'd hoped to be wrong," the old man rasped. "She's been sick for so long, but the nausea, fatigue, and lack of appetite..."

A ringing filled Sam's ears. Most other men wouldn't understand what the healer was alluding to, but not him. He'd met many girls with the same symptoms over the years. "She's with child?" he croaked. It hurt even saying it.

"Yes," Mira said softly while tucking a blanket around the unconscious Jasmine.

He dropped his head to stare at his boots, sorrow for the woman washing over him. The injustice in the world never ceased to amaze him. No one deserved ravishment, to have their choices stolen from them in such a brutal manner.

"She told you what happened?" he asked.

"No, she doesn't have any recollection of the conception at all." Jacob muttered a dark oath. "She defended the men who held her captive. She didn't believe me, so she asked for an examination." He shook his head. "I should have waited. It was too soon."

"She would have noticed, father," Mira said, placing a hand on Jasmine's forehead before sinking down into the chair next to the cot. "We had no choice."

A rage unlike anything Sam had ever experience ignited in his chest. How dare someone touch a woman without her consent. It was one of the most disgusting things he could think of.

His hands twitched by his sides, wanting to strangle someone. This was why men killed for women. This reason right here. They provoked a deep-seated feeling of possessiveness that called for men to protect them.

Mira eyed him, her face hardening. "You reek of unchecked anger. You need to calm down."

"I've got it under control."

"Not from where I'm sitting," she retorted. "If you want to truly help Jasmine, you need to calm down right now, or I'll bar you from the infirmary."

Sam scoffed and smiled arrogantly, even though all he really wanted to do was beat someone into a bloody pulp. "I'm a prince and the spymaster. You couldn't keep me out of here if you wanted to."

Mira pushed from her chair and threw her shoulders back, a steely glint in her eyes. "Listen to me and listen well. You've been in here every night since Sage and Jasmine arrived. Don't think I didn't see you lurking in the dark." She stabbed a finger at Jasmine. "She has been through hell, and she doesn't even know it. From this moment on, she'll need stability and a calm environment. Pregnancies with too much stress will cause damage to the babe and could kill her. She's delicate enough without you bringing a barrage of messy emotions into her life. So, you either calm down and help, or you get the hell out. You better believe me when I say, I'll cut you open before I let you hurt this girl."

He swallowed and forced his anger down. Mira was right. "I'm sorry. I am angry."

"As we all are." Mira tossed her hands in the air, a tear leaking from the corner of her eye. She scrubbed at it angrily. "Which is why I'm going to leave the room until I can regain my composure, and I suggest *you* do the same as well." It was more of a command, not a suggestion.

Mira strode to her father's side and dropped a kiss on his whiskered cheek. "I'll be back soon."

Jacob cupped her cheek. "Take your time. I'll stay here with her."

"I know, but I don't think she should be alone with men right now, so I'll hurry."

The healer nodded, his gaze returning to the fire.

"Sam?"

He glanced at Mira. She snatched a leather pouch off the long table covered with jars of herbs.

"You speak of this to no one."

"I'm as silent as the grave." He'd not breathe a word of it. Once it was out that she was with child and not married, well... He ground his teeth and hissed out a breath. The way of the world was not kind to unmarried pregnant women, no matter how they'd become that way. Again, his rage flared up.

Mira waved her leather bag at him. "You fancy throwing

daggers?"

Stabbing something would most definitely help. "May I accompany you?"

"You needn't ask. Come along," she called, moving through the infirmary door. "Let's stab something. Maybe I can exercise the anger and disgust out of my system."

He followed her but didn't reply. Sam already knew the truth. There was no way to rid oneself of those emotions. He'd tried for years. The best he could come up with was to forge it into something else.

The time would come for him to unleash his rage on the world, but it wasn't this day.

Today, he would hone his self-control, so he didn't hurt the little, broken brunette in the infirmary.

Chapter Twenty-Five

Tehl

"There's been an attack along the northern border, near Nagali," Garreth reported. He leaned over Tehl's desk and handed him the missive.

"Our northern border?" Tehl asked, his brows furrowing.

He'd been waiting for the warlord to strike, but this was rather anticlimactic. Why had he attacked there? What used to be a lush farm area was nearly a desolate wasteland. In fact, it had been that way for over two hundred years. There were only a few stubborn Aermians who stayed in the area. But it was a rough way to live between the sand storms and the attacks from predators.

Tehl cut open the missive, scowling further at the letter. There wasn't much information. Basically, only what Garreth had reported. "Is there no further news? Nothing at all?"

"I'm sorry, but no. The only other piece of information I was able to glean from the messenger was that there were few casualties."

"That's good news," he muttered.

"But there were disappearances."

Sage, who had stayed silent until that moment, sat up from the chair she'd been slumped in. "How many?" she asked sharply.

"Ten."

"All women?"

"No. They took three men."

Sage pushed from the chair and strode to the window overlooking the balcony, but not before Tehl saw a flash of pain cross her face. He stared at his wife's back for a moment before glancing at Garreth. "Has Sam dispatched anyone?"

"Yes. We'll have word within a few days."

"All right. Thank you, Garreth."

The Elite bowed to him and exited the room, a slight hitch to his gait. Tehl stared at the missive as the door closed silently behind his friend. "What are you up to?" he muttered.

"He's playing a game," Sage said.

Tehl scowled and glared up at his wife, who'd moved across the room like a wraith. "You're as bad as Sam."

A ghost of a smile flitted across her mouth then disappeared as she leveled a serious look on him. "This wasn't a random attack."

Tehl leaned back in his chair, the leather creaking. "There's nothing out there."

Sage shrugged and sat on the edge of his desk while fingering the feather of his quill. "Make no mistake." She tapped the missive with her knuckles. "He struck here for a reason. He does nothing without a purpose."

He met Sage's haunted green gaze. "What are we really up against, Sage?" She'd said very little about the warlord. Only that he was dangerous.

Her face crumpled, and she turned away from him to pace from one side of the room to the other. "He's calculating. Each move he makes serves a purpose to further his agenda. To say he's intelligent would be like saying the sun is bright." She scrubbed a hand over her face. "The warlord is charismatic, charming. His enthusiasm makes you want to believe what he believes. And if that wasn't enough, he's..." She swallowed, her gaze darting to him. "Well, you know, handsome." Her hands curled into fists.

Tehl pressed his lips together, hating that just speaking about that monster brought her such pain. "You know I wouldn't ask unless it was important."

She chuckled, the sound bitter. "It's more than important. It's dire. I don't have a choice."

"You always have a choice." Even as he said the words he knew they were a lie.

"I've never heard you tell such a bald lie before, Tehl." Sage flopped into her chair and slung her legs over the arm of it. "This was just the beginning." She rolled her head to the side, staring at him. "It will get worse from here. We don't know his angle right now, but we know where this leads." A pause. "War."

War. It was only three letters long, but it held a sinister edge to it and left a bad taste in his mouth. "We need to meet with Rafe tonight."

Sage nodded and closed her eyes. "It needs to be private. I have questions that need to be answered, and he owes me." She cracked one eyelid to peer at him. "I also need to speak to him privately."

He bristled a little but tamped it down. He trusted Sage...and now he trusted the rebellion leader, too. "All right."

"All right?" she arched a brow at him.

"Yes."

"That's different," she whispered. "What's changed?"

"Rafe has proven himself honorable when it comes to you." That and he seemed to have turned his attention to a certain Scythian beauty.

Her eyes narrowed. "What do you know that I don't?"

"Nothing that needs to be said."

"You're keeping secrets from me?"

He frowned at her. "It's not my secret to tell."

Her lips twitched. She was teasing him. He blinked. It was odd, but he liked it. He'd seen her tease and play with others, but she'd never engaged him before. "Maybe if you're nice, I'll tell you."

Her jaw dropped open, and her eyes narrowed further into slits, causing him to stifle his grin.

"You don't want to play this game with me."

Oh, he most definitely did. Each day was filled with its own anxieties, worries, and dangers. But he'd seize each opportunity to invite laughter and light in. It was a rare gift. One he'd not take for granted again.

***

Tehl arched a brow at the rebellion leader as he strolled into the room like he owned the place. His arrogance never ceased to surprise him. Rafe pulled the lid from the decanter and gave it a heavy sniff before pouring it into an ornate goblet and throwing it back.

"Help yourself," Tehl said dryly.

"Long day?" Sage called from the balcony. She turned from the sunset and abandoned her vigil, strolling into the room.

He sighed, his body relaxing as she moved away from the drop.

217

Sage had been standing at the balcony for so long, Tehl hadn't been able to focus on the letters scattered across his desk. His mind kept imagining her swinging a leg over the railing and disappearing from view. She'd never mentioned her conversation with his father, nor her attempt, but she spent enough time on their balconies that he could never forget what had happened.

Sage gave him a funny look, and he shook himself, realizing he'd been staring for quite some time. He pulled his gaze from his wife and met golden eyes watching him with amusement. If he had been prone to blushing, he would have done so. He knew what the rebellion leader thought. That he was gawking at Sage.

Tehl scowled and crossed his arms over his chest. Even if he was staring, it was his right. She, by law, belonged to him. If he wanted to gawk at his wife, he bloody well would.

Rafe cocked an eyebrow at him as if saying, 'Really? We're back to this?'

Tehl rolled his shoulders and placed his hands on the desk. The rebellion leader was right. There was no need to be so defensive. Rafe eyed him for a moment more then turned to Sage with a warm smile.

"Nothing I can't handle, little one."

Sage winced but quickly wiped the expression from her face. "We're about to add to your burden."

"Is that so?" He leaned against the bookshelf, his gaze bouncing between Tehl and Sage. "Out with it," he said, reaching for the decanter again.

"We need you to deliver a message to your people."

He froze for only a moment before slowly pouring more spirits into his goblet. "Oh?"

"We need your people to align with us."

Rafe took a measured sip. "That is a huge undertaking. I'm not sure I can guarantee much of anything. I don't hold as much power as you think."

Sage scoffed, her eyes narrowing. "Cut the lies. You and I both know you hold a great deal of power. I'm not sure what your station is, but I know you can arrange for us to meet with the crown of Methi. Not only that, we need you to do it quickly and quietly."

"How quickly?" Rafe questioned.

"Within the week," Tehl said.

The rebellion leader barked out a laugh. "You expect me to arrange a meeting with the Methi crown within the week? It's impossible. Travel and negotiations would take months."

"We don't have months," he said. "Scythia has attacked again."

Rafe growled. "When?"

"Within the last several days."

"The causalities?"

"Minor, but still disturbing," Tehl answered. "We don't know when Scythia will strike again, but we know this is just the beginning. It will only get worse from here."

"And you expect Methi to aid you without an incentive?"

"If Methi does not support us, they will be next."

"That sounds like a threat, little one."

Sage shook her head. "Not from Aermia. There won't be any Aermia left. All there will be is Scythia. The warlord is coming, and it's not just for us. If Aermia falls, so do all the kingdoms."

"Methi is not without its own defenses."

"True," she mused, perching on the arm of the leather chair. "But if you think your prowess in battle and your mountains will protect you, you are a fool. When he sets his mind to something, he will gain it."

"And you believe he's set his mind on Methi?"

Her face hardened, even as it paled. "He wants it *all*." The way she said the words sent a chill down Tehl's spine as her gaze emptied of all emotion. She turned her blank gaze from him to the rebellion leader. "We will all perish if we do not unite."

Rafe studied Sage, his expression grim. "It will not be an easy thing to unite the world."

"It's not easy to escape the depths of hell, and, yet, here I am," she said, holding her arms out to her sides. "And it was only done with the help of all the races. Aermian, Sirenidae, Methi, and Scythian. If we do not work together, we will all perish."

"I will do my best."

Sage stared at him before glancing out of the window at the darkening sky. "I know you will."

Rafe swallowed another sip of spirits and placed his goblet on the bookcase, nodding to Tehl. "There is no time to waste, it seems. I'll send a missive immediately."

Sage chuckled and glanced over her shoulder. "Don't pretend you don't have your people nearby."

The rebellion leader's lips curled into a satisfied smile. "You were always my best pupil."

"No, just your favorite."

His expression softened. "That's true as well."

Tehl watched Rafe and Sage stare at each other, and he smiled inwardly. Their friendship had healed. He'd been threatened by the rebellion leader when he'd acted so dishonorably with Sage, but, now, it was clear there was nothing but the kind of love friends shared.

His wife pushed off her chair and strolled to his side. Tehl tipped his head back to stare into her face. She leaned close and pressed a kiss to his cheek. A jolt went through him at the simple touch that made him want to yank her into his lap, but she pulled back and slipped her hand into his.

"You remember what I asked earlier?" she murmured.

Tehl stared at her lips for longer than was polite as her words sunk in. He blinked. She wanted to speak with Rafe in private. He nodded and pushed from his chair.

"I have many other engagements this evening before I seek my bed. So, if you'll excuse me," he said.

Rafe tugged on his vest. "I'll follow you out."

"I wish to speak with you," Sage said.

"If you insist," the rebellion leader said, settling back against the bookshelf.

Sage squeezed Tehl's hand once and let go. Tehl surprised himself by snatching her retreating hand and bringing it to his lips to kiss the inside of her wrist. Her eyes widened as he lingered.

The devil inside him, that he kept a tight leash on, grinned in delight. "I'll see you tonight." He breathed across her skin, and a little shiver visibly worked through her that made him want to cheer.

"I'll see you tonight," she said, a little breathy.

He smiled, dropped a kiss on top of her head, and tried not to strut toward the door.

One step forward. Many more to go.

And he looked forward to each one of them.

Life with Sage wasn't simple. It was exhilarating.

CHAPTER TWENTY-SIX

Sage

The door clicked shut behind Tehl, leaving her alone with Rafe for the first time in months. She glanced at him and then away. His golden eyes always saw too much, and today wasn't about her. It was about him.

She rubbed her forehead and then gestured to the chairs. "Would you like to sit down?"

"If it will make you more comfortable, little one."

Sage nodded and stalked to her favorite chair. The buttery leather seemed to give her a hug every time she slid into it. Rafe prowled to the other chair and sat, dwarfing it much like Tehl did. She studied him for long moments, and he let her. His deep wine-colored hair was longer than it had been when she'd met him. It was the lone braid at the front that surprised her.

Dark, beaded hair curtained around her face...

She gritted her teeth and dug her fingers into the chair arms to ground herself. *You are not there. You are here, in Tehl's study.*

"Are you all right?" Rafe's deep voice asked.

Sage opened her eyes, not realizing she'd closed them in the first place. He stared at her, concern clear in his reflective eyes. "I'm fine."

"No, you are not."

She glared at him. It was easier to be angry than accept his pity. "Why haven't you visited me?" she demanded. It had been bothering her for the last week. She'd even sought him out, but couldn't find him before she grew so tired she had to retreat back to her room.

"I figured you needed time," he said softly. "After the last time we spoke... I wasn't sure if I was welcome."

She glanced away from him. He'd hurt her before, but it paled in comparison to everything she'd experienced in Scythia. It actually made her feel ashamed. She'd been petty and vindictive at times. "I'm sorry," she said, turning back to him.

Rafe blinked slowly and blinked again; she'd surprised him. Rarely did the man ever show surprise.

"You don't owe me any apologies," he said softly.

"I do." She straightened and lifted her chin. "I let my personal feelings get involved in decisions that would change the kingdom. You were doing the best you could. I see that now."

A pained expression crossed his face. "Little one, don't justify what I did. It was wrong, no matter the circumstances, and I hurt you. That still pains me."

She waved a hand at him. "There are worse things in life." The statement was flippant even though her heart sped up. She understood true evil beings now. Rafe was not an evil being. He was human. He made mistakes just like herself.

"I don't deserve forgiveness just because there is a bigger monster out there."

It was uncanny. He'd always been able to read her.

"Tehl and I spoke about this the other night. No one deserves forgiveness, and that's what makes it precious. It's a gift. Please let me make it right between us." The telltale heat began behind her eyes.

Rafe pushed from his chair and knelt in front of her, placing his palms on either side of her face. "I'm sorry to my very bones, Sage, for what has taken place between us. If you need my forgiveness to move on, I forgive you. Even though there's nothing to forgive."

Some of her guilt eased at his word.

He continued. "It's I who should be begging for your forgiveness." He pressed his lips together and glanced away. "I'm ashamed of the way I acted. I'm not that type of man."

He turned back to her, and she placed her right hand over his, on her cheek. "Please let there be peace between us."

"Until my dying breath," he said. His thumb swiped something from her cheek. "I also must atone for my broken promises. I promised you that I'd protect you, that I'd make Rhys pay."

She stiffened as an assortment of images assaulted her.

"I'm to blame." He said it with so much pain, it snapped her out of her spiral.

Sage pulled his hands from her cheeks and held them in her hands. "No one is to blame for that animal's actions, except himself."

"Is he..." A hesitation. "Did he hurt you?"

Her skin cooled as another memory crept up on her.

Rhys leaned down until the tip of his nose brushed hers, as if they were lovers. Fear paralyzed her as she stared into the mud-brown of his eyes.

"If you weren't property, I would've torn you apart already." His eyes ran over her face, an unholy glee in his gaze. "Maybe I already did."

One of the warriors pushed a flask against his mouth and another pinched his nose. He fought harder, spewing the brew everywhere. Sage watched in horror as liquid and drool dripped down his chin, and he mouthed, 'You're mine.'

Not like he could have. "No."

Rafe scanned her face. "You never could lie to me. Don't start now."

"He's dead. Does it really matter?" she asked dully.

"He's dead?" Her friend squeezed her hand. "Did you kill him?"

"No, that honor was taken from me."

"Murder is not honorable."

"But vengeance is." She shivered and stared over Rafe's shoulder blankly. "He should have been made to suffer, experience the pain and suffering he'd brought on others. But he was gone in the blink of an eye."

"What happened?" Rafe asked, his voice soft and smooth.

"The warlord," she said flatly, as one of her nightmares rushed to the forefront of her mind. "Rhys brought me before the warlord." She could remember how beautiful and untouchable he'd looked sitting on his throne with his imposing leren sitting on either side. "Rhys had warned me to keep my mouth shut." She smiled bitterly, focusing for a moment on Rafe. "But you know, I was never one to keep silent. I spoke out and was rewarded for such the perceived embarrassment." Sage touched her mouth where Rhys had backhanded her. "I found myself on the floor, then a hand reached out to help me up…"

"Take it, please," his smooth voice said.

With no other option, Sage slipped her hand into his. He lifted her from the floor, and she swore she heard her bones creak. She met his gaze and dipped her chin as she pulled her hand away. "Thank you."

A nod. He scanned her face slowly, taking all the time in the world. Then, he moved down the rest of her body, stopping here and there to examine a scar, a cut, a bruise. Was he admiring his man's handy work? Looking for ways he could hurt her? She held herself stock-still as he walked around her as if he were inspecting chattel.

"What happened to her clothing?" he murmured, only loud enough for Rhys to hear.

"The other woman needed medical attention. Sage had to use her shirt as punishment for insubordination."

The warlord hummed and paused by her side.

"Is she still pure?" The question lingered in the air.

"Of course, my lord. We wouldn't dare touch what is yours."

She forced herself to hold still when he caressed a scar along her hip and then her wrist.

"How did she come by the scars?"

"She and I had…a disagreement, if you will," Rhys replied smugly.

Her stomach churned at his lies.

"And the rest? She's been beaten badly."

"All deserved, I can assure you. She brought them on herself. She never stopped fighting."

Another hum. "What do I cherish most in the world?" the warlord asked conversationally.

"Perfection." Rhys's response was automatic.

"What comes second?"

"Our line."

"True," the warlord answered, circling her again. "And who bears our lines?"

"Our women," Rhys drawled.

Sage turned her head to follow the prowling warlord. All his pacing had her on edge. He stopped between Rhys and herself.

"Do we ever hurt our women?"

"No," the monster replied, his mud-brown gaze darting from her to the warlord.

He glanced at her arm, and the warlord's lips thinned just a touch. Slowly, he began circling her again. This time, she turned to keep her back from him. She was finished with his inspection.

A small smile tipped up his sensual lips. "I wondered when you would give up your submissive pose. You don't have it in you to bend to someone else's will."

She bared her teeth at him, countering his movements. "You know nothing about me."

"On the contrary, I know everything." The warlord slid behind Rhys and whispered, "You shouldn't have marred her. You know how I feel about that, and yet you disobey me."

One moment, Rhys was staring smugly at her, and, the next, he was gurgling on the floor, scarlet liquid slipping from his neck.

Her body flashed hot and cold, and a high ringing filled her ears. A tremor rippled through her body as Rhys gasped and writhed on the floor. Even as death claimed him, he managed to choke out something that would surely haunt her dreams.

"I'll always be on your skin," he coughed, and the light in his eyes dimmed.

She blinked. No.

Sage scrambled toward Rhys and dropped to her knees next to him. Carefully, she held a hand over his parted lips, shaking. Not one breath. "No," she uttered as she frantically grabbed his wrist to feel for a pulse. Nothing. "No, no, no, no, no, no!"

Her eyes darted back to his face, and she gagged at his empty, unseeing eyes. He was gone. Dead in a matter of heartbeats.

No pain. A clean death. No suffering.

An ember of rage caught flame in her gut. How dare he die! "You bastard!" she screamed and slammed her fists on Rhys's unmoving chest. "You don't get to die! Breathe, damn it."

Still, his chest didn't move. He was dead.

He didn't deserve a quick death. He didn't deserve death at all! He deserved to rot and suffer in eternal hell like she did every day. A wail came out of her that didn't seem physically possible. "Death was too good for him!"

Sage pulled her hands back and held up her shaking palms. They were red. Covered in blood. She retched, bile burning her throat and flooding her mouth. In a frenzy, she scrubbed her hands over her pants and half-corset, sobbing. She didn't want him on her. Pushing up from her knees, she tried to stand, only for her feet to slip in the gore. Again, she gagged and scrubbed harder, but only succeeded in making it worse. Her body now looked like a garish painting of red, brown, and black.

Even in death, Rhys seemed to win.

Sage blinked back to the present, the room a blur of colors around her. "The warlord took him from me. The warlord was observing, completely calm, utterly unaffected by the murder he'd just committed. I cursed him. You know what he did?"

Rafe shook his head.

"He shrugged, shrugged like it was nothing, and said Rhys deserved to die for his actions." Sage shook her head. "He didn't deserve to die. He deserved to suffer. When I told him that, he said the reason he'd executed Rhys was because he'd touched me. For that, he had a price to pay, and that I was too valuable to ruin." She laughed hollowly. "No, that was the warlord's right. He wanted to ruin me himself."

"I am so sorry, little one," Rafe whispered brokenly.

Sage focused on his golden eyes, her body numb. "Sorry doesn't fix what happened."

"No, it doesn't," he said sadly. She gasped as he yanked her off the chair and pulled her into a rib-crushing hug. "I promise to do my best, as will my people."

"I know you will."

Rafe pulled back, rubbing his hands up and down her arms. "Stars above, your skin is like ice." He glanced around the room, spotting what he was looking for. He tugged a blanket off the back of his chair and wrapped it around her shoulders. "I hate that you went through that. Hate it."

The only thing she could do was nod. She hated it as well, but there was nothing for it. What was done, was done.

"The only consolation I can find is that he's gone. Rhys can't hurt you anymore."

She chuckled, the sound dark and haunting. "Maybe from the mortal world, but he haunts me most nights." She glanced out at the balcony to the night sky, stars just barely appearing. "Rhys was a rabid dog compared to the monster that's ruling Scythia." She turned back to a grave Rafe. "He cannot succeed, Rafe. We cannot allow it. The warlord kills everything in his path."

"He won't."

"Will you fight with me?" she asked.

"I will fight with you. I vow it."

He held his forearm out to her. Sage reached a shaking hand

out and clasped forearms.

"I missed you, friend," she said.

He squeezed her other hand. "As I missed you."

CHAPTER TWENTY-SEVEN

Rafe

His smile dropped as he exited the study. He nodded curtly to the Elite stationed outside the door, both relief and worry at war inside him. Sage's words whirled in his mind as he strode down the wide hallway, turning to his left, and jogged down the steps, ignoring the stares he always seemed to draw. It was the eyes he knew. In Aermia, they were unique, but in his kingdom, he was one of many.

Many who would fight in the upcoming battle.

Rafe had always known his actions would lead to war. That much wasn't a surprise. His people had been preparing for Scythia's attack for over fifty years. But now that it was upon them, he found himself anxious. Before, the people in Aermia were just another part of the plan, but now? Now they had names and faces. They were friends. Friends he'd watch die because of the blackguard on the Scythian throne.

Sage's empty green eyes flashed through his mind. The warlord had damaged Sage. A deep-seated fury brewed in his gut. No one hurt those he loved. The abomination that called himself lord would die.

He barely noticed when a maid scampered out of his way, her eyes wide as he stalked by. Even after everything Sage had gone through with Rafe, she'd never given up. She'd fought. Rafe could always see her fire brewing right underneath the surface. But today? He rubbed at his chest as he pushed through the exterior doors leading to the training ground. Today, he'd truly seen how broken she was. Her fire was still there, but it flickered and sputtered, hardly alive.

It was his fault. He should have tried harder to find Rhys. But even as the thought passed through his mind, he knew the truth. If it hadn't been that traitor, it would have been someone else. No one can control everything, no matter how much he tried. It just wasn't possible.

Rafe passed through the gate and jogged down the slope into Sanee, weaving through alleys and then running across roofs. He squatted on the edge of a tavern roof and listened to the medley of music, shouting, and crass jokes below. He whistled a five-note song. An answering tune floated softly through the air.

He dropped from the roof, landed on his feet, and rolled to absorb the impact.

"I hate it when you do that," a male voice commented from the dark. "You're going to break your neck one of these times, and I will be blamed for it."

Rafe straightened and swept his cloak back. He could have dropped from three times that height and been just fine. "You've seen me attempt much more dangerous feats."

Badiah stepped from the darkened corner and pulled his pipe from his mouth, shaking his head. "And I'm not completely over those experiences. You scared ten years off my life."

He leaned a shoulder against the tavern and smiled at the shorter man. Even after all these years, Rafe had no clue how old Badiah really was. There were a few lines around his eyes and mouth to indicate he was older. "I'm sure you have many more left yet," he said.

Badiah puffed on his pipe, eyeing Rafe. "I've not seen much of you lately. How is our girl?" he asked softly.

He pressed his lips together and shook his head. "She's not the same as she once was."

Sadness crossed his companion's face. "But at least she's out of his grasp. He can't hurt her anymore."

"The damage is already done."

"Then we kill him," Badiah said without inflection. "That girl deserves peace, and we will give it to her."

"We will." Rafe reached into his pocket and handed the wiry man the note. "Deliver this as fast as you can. It's time."

Badiah straightened. "It'll be done. I'll have news for you soon."

"Thank you."

His companion nodded and turned on his heel, disappearing down the alley. It still amazed him how easily the man blended into his surroundings. Rafe tugged his hood up to cover his face and went the other direction.

There was much to do and little time.

War was brewing.

Chapter Twenty-Eight

Sage

She sat on the bed, staring at the fire.

Today had been more emotionally exhausting than she expected. Speaking to Rafe about what had occurred with Rhys in Scythia had been liberating and draining. The flames danced, casting shadows on the wall that writhed and twisted together in mesmerizing patterns.

"How did your conversation go with Rafe?" Tehl asked quietly.

She glanced over her shoulder as the bed sank behind her. The crown prince sat with his back to her, rubbing the back of his head. "It went about as well as I expected."

He grunted but didn't say anything further.

Sage stared at his back for a beat before turning to the fire. Her eyelids drooped, but she didn't want to sleep. Sleep opened her to the horrors she'd rather forget.

"I forgave him," she blurted.

"What?"

She scooted onto the bed as Tehl twisted to look at her. "It was time," she said, picking at her linen shirt. "I've come to realize that friendship is one of the most important things in the world. And Rafe's been my friend for a long time. He's fought for me, and that means something."

"That's well-done, Sage."

His reaction was curious to her. Rafe and Tehl never saw eye to eye, but, after today, she'd say they were...friends? She peeked at him through her lashes. "I'm surprised how amicable today was."

Tehl stretched his leg out on the bed and leaned back on his hands, brows furrowed. "Why wouldn't it be?"

"You weren't the best of friends before."

"We came to an understanding and then fought together for something important." He shrugged. "That bonds people."

"That I—"

A knock interrupted her.

Tehl pushed from the bed and opened the door. Sam nodded to Tehl and strode into the room without an invitation.

"That is the second time someone has walked into *my* room like he owns it," the crown prince muttered.

Sage hid her smile at his grumpy tone.

Sam plopped into a chair by the fire and held out a note. "I know it's late," he said wearily. "But Lilja sent news."

She froze. This was it.

"A meeting has been set for tonight. I'll escort you to the place."

Sage sprung from the bed and begun to tug on her boots. Lilja had done the impossible. They had a meeting with the Sirenidae. Her movements were quick as she strapped her daggers to her body. There was no time to lose.

"Have you notified anyone else?" Tehl asked, clasping his cloak around his shoulders.

"Lilja said it was only to be both of you and myself. The Sirenidae are skittish enough. It could damage our chances if we arrived with a large party."

Tehl pulled her cloak from a chair and held it out. Sage paused for a moment then turned so he could help her with the cloak. A small burst of warmth suffused her at the simple gesture of kindness. She'd seen her papa do that for her mum her entire life.

"Thank you," she said, her fingers brushing his as she clasped it closed.

Sam yawned and slowly rose from the chair, his movements stiff.

"What have you been up to today?" she asked. "You're moving like an old man."

Her brother-in-law winced. "I've been training with Blaise."

"Truly?"

"She walloped me today. I'll be feeling it for quite some time."

Sage sniggered. She'd have loved to see that.

Tehl pinned his brother with a serious look. "Did Lilja say anything else?"

"Just to prepare a convincing argument."

Sage nodded and moved toward the door. "Tehl and I have been working on it since we spoke with Lilja."

"Good."

She yanked open the door and stepped outside, followed by the two princes. They jogged through the quiet corridors of the sleeping palace. Sage sighed when they exited the palace, inhaling the crisp night air. There was nothing like being outdoors. The knot in her chest loosened when she was outside.

It meant freedom.

Sage opened her eyes and trailed behind the princes. Hay and horses surrounded her when they entered the stables.

"Horses?" she asked. The docks weren't too far away. The walk would be easy. "They're not really inconspicuous."

Sam led a dapple-gray horse from the stall. "Lilja isn't in the port. We'll travel about an hour and meet her."

"Am I to ride with you?" Sage asked turned to Tehl.

He smiled and brushed his hand along the silky face of a mare. The bold face with the uneven stripe made for a striking contrast. With twinkling eyes, he led the mare to Sage.

"This is your mare."

Sage blinked at him and then the horse. He'd purchased her a horse? She reached a hand out and let the tall mare sniff her palm. A smile curled her lips as the curious mount lipped her shirt and then headbutted her in the chest, almost toppling her.

"She's spirited, isn't she?" she said, planting her feet, while stroking the mount's velvety nose.

Tehl ran a hand down the mare's neck. "Just like her owner."

She smiled, loving the animal already. Her family had always owned a horse, but Sage had never owned one herself. "What's her name?"

"She doesn't have a name."

Sage scowled at Tehl. "Why doesn't she have a name?"

"I thought you'd like to do the honors." He avoided her gaze as he said it, focusing on the horse.

Her heart warmed as she stared at her husband. Tehl was clueless sometimes when it came to emotions, but he made up for it by being observant and thoughtful.

Sage placed a hand on his arm and smiled at him when he

looked at her. "Thank you so much. I love her."

He nodded and coughed into his hand. "I'm glad." His attention turned back to the mare. "What will you name her? She's gone quite some time without a name."

She patted the horse's neck. "I'm not sure. I'll figure it out soon."

Tehl handed the reins to her and then opened the stall for the huge black war horse that had been staring at them since they'd arrived. He strode right up to Sage and blew air into her face before sniffing around her pockets. Her husband scowled.

"Listen here, Wraith, you don't need apples all the time. Leave the ladies alone."

Wraith sidled up to her mare, who eyed him suspiciously.

Tehl chuckled and led Wraith from the stable. "Easy there, boy, or she'll bite you again."

"Again?" Sage asked.

"Wraith thinks himself the boss." He nodded to her mare. "Your mount taught him otherwise." He glanced at her. "Do you need help up?"

Sage eyed the tall horse. She could manage. Barely. "I can do it."

Tehl said nothing for moment, staring from her to the mare, before turning his back and mounting Wraith.

She turned to her own horse and brushed her hand along the mare's muscular shoulder. "Hello there, pretty girl," she whispered, stroking the horse. "My name is Sage, and you and I are going to be best friends."

Sage placed her foot in the stirrup and swung up onto the horse. "Easy, girl," she murmured as the mare pranced before settling down.

She glanced to the left. Tehl and Sam spoke quietly between the two of them.

Sam straightened and nudged his mount with his heels. The beast responded immediately. Tehl glanced at her. "Are you ready?"

Excitement vibrated through her. It had been ages since she'd ridden. "Let's go."

***

She couldn't wipe the grin from her face if she tried. Sage pulled on the reins and slowed next to Sam. He grinned at her and swung from his horse.

"You enjoyed your ride?" he asked taking her reins from her.

"It was invigorating."

Her mare was made to run. Her movements were so fluid, it was like flying. Sage had felt utterly free. Tehl stepped close as she swung her right leg over the horse, his large hands settling on her waist, lowering her to the ground. Sage grabbed his forearms to steady herself and smiled up at him.

"So, you like her?" he asked.

There was a hint of uncertainty to his voice. Sage popped up onto her toes and pecked his cheek. "I love Peg."

"Peg?"

"Yeah," she said, turning back to her mare. "Riding her was like flying so I thought Pegasus was an appropriate name, or Peg for short."

Tehl stepped around her and scratched Peg between the ears. Her mare leaned into Tehl. Sage hid her smile. It seemed that Sage wasn't the only one who loved him.

She stiffened as she stared at the crown prince.

Stars above, she loved the man.

He glanced at her and frowned. "Is something wrong?"

"No," she said shakily. Could he see it on her face? "Just worried about tonight."

He shifted, shadows covering his face, hiding his expression from her. Tehl reached out and brushed her cheek with one finger. "You'll do just fine. You always do."

Sage exhaled and stuffed her new-found feelings deep. She'd deal with them later.

Tehl

His brother groaned. "The ship didn't look this far away. My arms are killing me."

Sage smirked at Sam. "That's all you got?"

"Why don't you take a turn, if it's so easy?"

"I'll leave that in your capable hands," she murmured, reaching out to touch the water.

Tehl snapped a hand out and caught her. She glanced at him questioningly. He lifted his chin to the sleek dark fin slicing through the water.

Sam followed his gaze and scowled. "Of course, we have to take a row boat through leviathan-infested waters," he muttered with a curse.

Sage pulled her hand from his and smiled. "They won't hurt us. They're here for Lilja."

"Lilja?" he asked.

"They are her...companions of sorts."

Sam blinked. "Like a pet?"

"No. A leviathan is no one's pet."

"Can she control the beasts?" Tehl asked.

"No, but she can give them her request, and they choose whether or not to follow."

"So, she communicates with them?" he pried. The idea intrigued him.

"In a way," she answered, staring out at the waves.

The moonlight disappeared as they neared the boat. He stood and held a hand out to Sage. She placed her hand in his and carefully stepped up the rope ladder hanging over the side of the ship.

"Be careful," he said softly.

"Always."

He watched as she nimbly climbed the ladder.

"Now seems like the perfect time to make a comment about what a nice looking—"

Tehl glared at his brother. "Finish that thought, and I'll throw you into the water."

Sam held his hands up with a grin. "I was going to comment on nice *form*." He wiggled his brows. "Where was your mind, dear brother?"

On the woman above them.

Tehl rolled his eyes at his brother and tied the dingy to the ship before climbing up. Hand over hand, he ascended the ship and hauled himself over the railing. Sage stood next to Hayjen and Lilja.

The older man turned to him and held a hand out. Tehl clasped his hand then turned to the Sirenidae. She wore one of her complex knotted dresses with her silvery hair straight down her back. He'd never seen her hair not in a braid. "You look well."

Lilja inclined her head. "Thank you," she said as Sam joined them. "They will arrive shortly, but I need to warn you about the Lure. When they arrive, you'll be tempted to go to them, touch them."

"What?" Tehl demanded.

"How?" Sam asked.

"Pheromones. The seawater reacts with their skin, making them almost irresistible," Hayjen muttered. "It's disconcerting the first time. We wanted to make you aware of this before it happened."

"As if they needed something else to make them more desirable," Sage grumbled.

Lilja flashed a smile at her niece, but it melted into determination. "They're here."

Tehl scanned the darkened water lit with moonlight. Nothing. "How do you know?"

She tapped her ear. "The leviathans' song changed."

"Intriguing," Sam whispered as the group lapsed into silence.

Tehl strained to hear something, but all he heard were the waves lapping gently against the hull. The ship creaked ominously, and a long-fingered hand curled over the deck railing edge. Startling magenta eyes peered up, over the edge. A moment passed, and then the Sirenidae catapulted herself over the railing and landed with grace. She flipped her wet, white hair over her shoulder and stood in nothing but a sealskin suit.

Lilja glided forward and handed the girl a robe. "Mer."

Mer slipped the robe on and hugged Lilja. "Aunt." She released Lilja and rushed to Hayjen, who threw his arms wide and pulled her into a hug.

"Hello, Mer," Hayjen said gruffly.

The girl pulled back and turned toward him. Tehl's knees weakened. She was beautiful, but not his taste. Despite that, he felt the need to be closer to her, to touch her skin. He managed to tear his gaze from the girl and forced his feet toward Sage.

She glanced over her shoulder at him as he pressed himself against her back and wrapped his arms around her.

"What are you doing?" she whispered.

"If I do not hold on to you, I might throw myself at her," he panted harshly.

Sam cursed. "Bloody unfair."

The Sirenidae offered an apologetic smile. "I'm sorry." She backed away. "I'd introduce myself, but I'll wait until I'm dry." She whistled softly and planted herself in front of the railing.

Even from here, Tehl wanted to grab her and hunt for the intoxicating scent. He yanked his eyes from the Sirenidae and pressed his face into Sage's neck, pulling in deep breaths. She shivered in his arms, and his hands began to wander. Tehl curled his hands into fists. Stars above, this was brutal.

Sage gasped. Tehl peeked over her shoulder as two males swung over the railing, both tall and muscular in a wiry sort of way. His gaze narrowed on the sealskin loin cloths. Lilja held out robes for each of the men.

His wife shifted in his arms and arched into his body. He blinked and stared down in shock as her fingers wove through his own and pressed them harder against her body. The older Sirenidae surveyed the boat, pausing briefly on Hayjen, and then turned back to Lilja.

"Daughter," he said, his voice like thundering waves.

Lilja dipped her chin. "Father." She glanced to the other man. "Cousin."

"It's been a long time," the younger man said.

"It has, Lareme."

Tehl's shoulders drooped with relief as the burning need to get closer to the Sirenidae lessened. He lifted his head and made to step back when Sage's fingers tightened.

"Not yet," she whispered, her tone panicked.

Tehl paused and cuddled her close.

The Sirenidae king turned in their direction, his white brows raising. "It's been a long time since I've met someone able to fight the Lure."

Sam stumbled next to his side. "It packs a punch."

Lareme chuckled. "That it does."

Sage sighed, released her death grip on his hands, and stepped out of his embrace, her legs a little wobbly. She sank into a curtsey. "Thank you for agreeing to meet with us, my lord."

"We weren't given much choice." The king cast a dark look toward Lilja. "My daughter is quite persuasive when she desires to be."

"Then we are thankful for that as well," Tehl said, moving to his wife's side. He held his forearm out. "Welcome to Aermia."

The king eyed him and then slowly clasped his forearm. "Well met." He cocked his head, studying Tehl's otherworldly eyes, his white braids framing his face. The king released him and Tehl felt like he'd gone through a test, but he had no clue if he'd passed or not.

Next, the king slowly turned his focus to Sage. A spark of pride filled Tehl at how his wife raised her chin and met the king's gaze without flinching.

The king eyed her. "You've caused quite a bit of commotion. More news has reached my ears about Sage Ramses than any other person in the last six months. You wreak havoc everywhere you go."

"I bring change," Sage corrected, not batting an eye.

The king's lips twitched. "I can see why Lilja loves you. You're just like her."

Tehl glanced at Lilja in surprise. The last part didn't sound like a compliment, and he wasn't the only one to notice, but Sage took it in her stride.

"Thank you. I always hoped to be a strong, capable woman who protected the ones she loves."

"Loyal, as well," the king murmured. "An admirable quality."

Sage dipped her chin but didn't answer.

The king turned on his heel and prowled back to the ship railing. "Let's cut to the chase. I know what you want, and we cannot give it to you."

Mer gasped and glared at the king, but she kept silent.

"You promised to listen," Lilja said softly.

"There's no need to draw it out if we all know what you want."

"Then why meet?" Sage asked. "If you already had decided, why meet at all?"

"I desired to meet the future rulers of Aermia."

"We won't be ruling if you don't unite with us," Tehl said. "War is brewing, and, if you don't stand with us, Aermia will fall. The kingdoms need to unite if we are to defeat the warlord. There's no other way."

The king shook his head. "It's too much risk. My people aren't warriors. I won't have them slaughtered for the sake of another kingdom."

Tehl schooled his face as Sage's jaw clenched next to him.

"You're being short-sighted. The fall of Aermia might not affect you now, but it will."

"The damage would be minor. The Sirenidae people are completely self-sufficient, and the warlord can't reach us," Lareme said. It was a bald statement, said without pride. It was spoken like a fact.

An eerie laugh erupted from Sage. A chill ran along Tehl's arms as he turned to his wife. It was devoid of humor.

"You're a fool."

Tehl blinked at his wife. Of all of the foolish things to say...

The king's magenta eyes narrowed on her. "Pardon me?"

Sage took a step forward. "You heard me." She flung her arm out, pointing at the sea. "You've hidden yourself from the world for so long that reality is now out of your reach."

"And what reality is that? Please, enlighten me, young one."

"The world is ending as we know it. Change is inevitable. It is our choice, though, whether it's for better or worse."

"Such ideals," the king said softly. "You only see what is right in front of you. I lived many generations and have come to this knowledge; crowns rise and fall. It's the way of life."

"And the annihilation of the Nagalian people? Was that a way of life?"

"It's the past."

"No." Sage shook her head. "It's our future. Do you really think the ocean will keep you safe?"

"No one can breach our depths."

"Maybe not now, but, mark my words, if Aermia falls, so will the Sirenidae." She glanced down at her boots. "I'm sure you're aware that I spent time in Scythia."

"I am," the king said gravely.

"In my time there, I met a Sirenidae."

The king stiffened.

"His name was Ezra," Sage continued. "He cared for me but followed the warlord's bidding."

Tehl crossed his arms and glanced at Sam, who was busy cataloguing the Sirenidae.

"Not possible," Lareme scoffed.

"The warlord has many ways to control people. It is the epitome of arrogance to think yourself infallible to his machinations. Ezra was not a bad person. He was doing his best to protect his family, and he was not the only Sirenidae in his service. Your people are not safe. Some have been enslaved for years."

Sage bridged the space between herself and the king. Tehl admired his wife as she braced her feet and stared up at the imposing king defiantly. She pushed her hair over her shoulders exposing her neck. "Do you know how this happened?"

The king kept silent as he stared at the healing wounds of Sage's neck.

"This is the product of the warlord. He collared me with a broken crown made of metal thorns. I wore that cursed collar for months." She gingerly touched the wounds. "This will be the fate of your people. Slavery and cruelty."

The king stared down at Sage, his expression unreadable. "I'm sorry for what you've experienced. But one does not justify the many. I have a duty to my people."

Sage swallowed then nodded. "True. It's one kingdom, but it'll mean thousands of lives. I hope you can live another hundred years carrying the deaths of thousands on your shoulder, because it will be you condemning them to slavery when it was within your power to help."

"You have a barbed tongue, young one," the king said.

"The truth is painful."

The king chuckled, but it wasn't happy. "Well spoken." He held his arm out. "I'm sorry we cannot do more."

Sage inclined her head and clasped his forearm. "You say *cannot*. I say *will not*, but I thank you for listening. It was interesting meeting some of my kin."

"Kin?" Mer piped in.

"Lilja is my aunt," Sage said, stepping back from the king.

The Sirenidae king's attention snapped to Lilja. "Daughter?"

"What she speaks is true. Sage is our kin."

The king frowned. "I am sorry. Truly, I am."

"So are we," Tehl said, striding to Sage's side. "Thank you for meeting with us. I hope you'll reconsider your decision. This is a battle no one race can win. We have to stand together."

"I wish you both the best."

The king nodded to each of them and strolled to Lilja. He kissed her forehead. "You're welcome to come home."

"My home is with my husband, family, and people. *I* will not abandon them and disappear into the sea. It's without honor."

Tehl's eyes widened at the jab.

The king stared at his daughter silently then pulled off the robe and handed it back to Lilja. "Then we are at odds."

"It's nothing new. Farewell, Father."

He sighed and turned away. He spared them one last glance before stepping onto the railing and diving off, disappearing into the black water below.

Lareme stared at the dark water and then back to them. "My

uncle is a wise man, but, sometimes, it takes time for him to think things over."

"Time is short," Tehl said.

The Sirenidae nodded and hugged Lilja. "I'll do what I can," he said, handing his robe over. He smiled at them and took off running, launching over the railing.

"Show off," Mer muttered. She slowly turned to Sage. "I'll change his mind."

Sage smiled ruefully. "I don't think there's much that can change his mind."

Mer smiled, every bit of it devious. "If I can't change his mind, I'll lead the people myself."

"Mer," Hayjen growled.

She waved a hand at the burly man. "Someone has to do something if he will not." Mer clasped Sage's hands and then his. "It was wonderful to meet my extended family. Know that you're not alone. Even if he won't fight, my sword is with you."

She skipped over to Lilja and Hayjen, hugging each of them fiercely. "Love you both. Send for me if you need me." She waved and disappeared off the side of the ship with a complex dive.

"The little imp will be the death of me," Hayjen grumped. "Why can't she do anything the safe way?

Lilja patted his cheek. "That was safe."

Tehl tuned them out to stare at the dark sea. Sam appeared on the other side of Sage and leaned heavily against the railing.

"That could've gone better," his brother said.

"He's blind to the danger," Sage whispered.

"Ruling is difficult," Tehl began, "Every decision made could mean someone's life. He's ruled longer than we have lived, longer than our grandparents lived. I don't agree with his decision, but I can understand it."

Sage peered up at him. "It doesn't make it right."

"No, it doesn't."

Tehl rubbed her back and tried to see if he could perceive anything in the deep water. It was a heavy blow for Aermia, but now he could only put his hope in Methi.

War was on the horizon.

Now they had to stand up and fight.

CHAPTER THIRTY

Tehl

"That makes three more strikes in the last ten days!" Jeren exclaimed. "We have to do something."

"Steps have already been taken. Soldiers have been sent out to defend the affected areas," William said sharply. "But they're too late each time. The Scythians attack and then disappear like smoke."

"Can you show me the areas that have been attacked?" Sage asked.

Lelbiel and the gruff Noah rolled open the huge map of Aermia and pointed to the four towns that had been hit. Tehl took a closer look even though he knew it wouldn't make much of a difference. He'd studied the map with his father and brother for most of the night prior. It didn't make sense. There wasn't a pattern.

Sage rounded the table and pushed between Noah and Lelbiel, her eyes narrowing. "The attacks are scattered."

"Indeed, my lady," Zachael answered.

She placed her palms on the table and scanned the map again. "What has been taken in each place?"

"Not much," Sam said, leaning back in his chair. "They didn't touch the weapons or gold. There have been abductions, but even that's not consistent. They left most of the women during the last two attacks."

Most was the key word. Women were what the Scythians consistently stole. Unmarried woman. Sage flicked a look his way like she heard his thoughts.

She glanced back to the map and pointed to the most recent attack. "What happened there?"

"They burned the town to the ground. It's the most populated area that they've attacked so far," Garreth said.

"They're escalating," the king commented while stroking his neat beard. "The question is, to what? We already know we'll have war, but why the attacks? For misdirection?"

"No," Lilja said. "That's too simple to him. This is one move of many. We need to look at these like they are chess pieces."

"So, he's playing with us," Rafe said.

Tehl turned to Blaise, who stared intensely at the map. She'd stayed silent almost the entire time. "Blaise, what do you think?" he asked.

Deep brown eyes snapped at him. "I think this is just the beginning. He's testing you."

"To see how we'll react?" Tehl concluded.

The Scythian woman nodded. "He's a master when it comes to planning. The warlord has lived long enough that he can usually predict an outcome. Your choice in how you approach these attacks will decide which move he makes next."

"So, he doesn't know what he's doing next?" Jeren asked, his face a mask of confusion. "You just said he plans everything."

Blaise chuckled. "Oh no, he knows what he's doing. He never has just one plan, but many. So many, they're like the strands of a spiderweb."

"So, we're back to our original question. What do we do?" William said tiredly.

"We could send an Elite team to track the Scythians," Noah suggested.

"No. It would be a death sentence. Those men wouldn't come back alive. I've lost enough men to know that," Sam said bitterly.

"I agree with the spymaster," Sage added. "I've run free through our forests all my life, but their jungle? It's nothing like our forests. I would've died the first day if not for the warriors. The Elite wouldn't survive."

"We can't leave our people unprotected," Garreth said, staring hard at the red dots on the map.

"We're not doing nothing." Tehl pushed from his seat and circled the points of each attack. "The attack areas have no rhyme or reason." He traced a path between the attack sites. "All of these villages have been near the Mort Wall. So, we evacuate our people nearest to the wall and bring our soldiers back."

"You'd leave our border vulnerable?" William demanded.

"Our border is already vulnerable. We have our soldiers spread too thin and that's why the Scythians are getting through undetected. We need to shrink our protection zone."

Zachael and William both leaned closer. The weapons master brushed a finger along the Aermian-Nagalian border.

"The Scythians will not come through the deserts of Nagali. It would take too many resources and too much time. We can pull our men from that part of the border and station them along the Aermian-Scythian border and across the north end of Aermia. That way there will be extra support in the fiefdoms of the north."

"That's wise, but it still feels like we're giving the Scythians ground," Garreth said.

"No, we're protecting what's most important. The north end is scarcely populated as it is," the king commented. "I approve of this plan. Tehl?"

"It's a sound plan. Sage?"

Sage nodded. "Tighten the noose. We can't afford to let them sneak right through our boundaries."

Garreth stood and bowed, exiting the room with William, Zachael, and Sam in his wake. By the end of the day, they'd have everything in place.

Tehl glared at the map. What was the warlord up to?

CHAPTER THIRTY-ONE

Sage

"This seems frivolous," Sage called from the bathroom.

"We have no choice."

She gathered up the slight train of the dress and bustled out of the bathing room. Tehl sat on the bed, his head in his hands.

"Are you all right?" she asked while trying to adjust the pins stabbing her in the head.

Some days, she longed to cut her hair off. It would be so freeing to not carry all the weight around. Her lips pulled down as she stared into the mirror above her vanity. She still hadn't gotten used to the creature that looked back at her in the mirror. Lifting a hand up, she placed it on the mirror just to remind herself that she was indeed real. She wasn't a specter, even though she felt like one.

A soft hiss pulled her attention to the man also reflected in the mirror. He stared from the bed with unabashed male appreciation. Her body warmed as his gaze wandered down her body, so strong it was like a physical touch.

"Sage," he began, and then cleared his throat. "You look lovely."

That was one of the things she loved about Tehl. He was honest. She eyed the corseted, peachy silk dress and tugged at one of the straps that kept falling down her shoulders. "If only these straps would stay up," she muttered.

"I believe, love, they're supposed to fall off the shoulders."

"And how would you know?"

"I'm not blind. Many ladies wear dresses like that. Now, stop fussing with them."

She growled and let them slide off her shoulders. It wasn't that revealing, but it felt exposing. Her hand clasped at the front of her throat as she realized the problem with a sickening lurch. Her neck looked too empty. A choker would've looked beautiful.

"Sage?"

"Will I ever be free of him?" she whispered, staring into the mirror in horror. She'd hated the collar the warlord had forced on her and yet... part of her felt comfortable with it on. It grounded her, because she knew what her place in the world was. Who she was.

The foreign creature in the mirror didn't know who she was.

Tehl stepped behind her, and his hands slipped around her waist, pulling her into a hug. He rested his chin on her shoulder and stared at her in the mirror, his blue eyes fathomless.

"He's not here. He has no place here."

His breath brushed her ear as he spoke, his scent curling around, settling some of the fear in her gut. Sage pulled her hand from her throat and laced her fingers with his, drawing comfort from his touch.

"I need a necklace."

It was such a simple statement. To anyone else, it wouldn't have meant anything, but to Tehl, well...she knew he understood. Her ladies in waiting had tried to get her to wear necklaces since she'd arrived, but she'd turned them down, not able to think about having anything around her throat.

His gaze dropped to her healed throat. There weren't any scars, but she still felt the collar's weight, the bite of pain, the warm metal heated by her skin.

There's nothing more satisfying than to see my collar on your skin. Beautiful," the warlord whispered.

She sucked in a deep breath, focusing on their laced hands and the man behind her. She wasn't there. She was here, in Tehl's arms. Safe.

"You don't need jewelry to look beautiful."

"The dress needs it." She needed it. To prove that she could. She wouldn't let the warlord control her life.

Tehl detangled himself from her without a word and strode into the wardrobe. She sagged against the vanity and closed her eyes, counting her breaths. It was just a necklace. That's it.

"What about this?" Tehl rounded the vanity and held a simple silver chain with a deep, blue gem for the pendant. "I thought you'd like this one. It's simple."

It was simple. Any other woman might have been offended at the simple offering, but not her. It was exactly the type of thing she'd pick out for herself. Understated, but of high quality.

He held it out further. "Go on, take it."

She didn't want to take it, but with trembling fingers, she plucked the necklace from Tehl's hand. The cool dainty chain slid through her fingers as she held it up.

"Put it on," he urged.

Another simple action. But simple actions these days turned out to be some of the most difficult.

Clumsily, she unclasped the necklace and lifted it to her throat. Her hands shook, but Tehl didn't help her. He just smiled at her encouragingly.

Her stomach lurched as she clasped the chain. She stared at the necklace, the sapphire nestled in the hollow of her throat.

He grinned at her like she'd single-handedly slain an enemy. "The chain is lightweight, so if you can't get the clasp, you can pull on it and it'll break."

She swallowed hard. This man. Sometimes, he destroyed her. "Thank you."

"My pleasure." He offered her his arm. "Are you ready?"

"Ready to eat." She placed her hand on her stomach. She'd hardly eaten anything all day.

"Me too," he grumbled. "I'm starving to death."

Sage eyed him and took his arm. "That I highly doubt."

Tehl made a face. "They fed me greens and fruit today."

Her mouth watered. "That sounds delicious."

He scowled. "A man needs meat." A pause. "And gravy."

Spoken much like her brothers. Sage smiled and patted him on the arm. "Let's find you some meat before you waste away." *Big baby.*

"I don't appreciate your tone, wife."

Sage hid her smile. "I don't know what you're referring to."

He snorted. "Mmhmmm...you may be spending too much time with Jasmine."

Her fiery friend had a quick wit that made Sage laugh more often than not. Her smile dimmed. Jas had not been her normal self for the last few weeks.

"I'm worried about her," she found herself saying as they exited their bedroom.

Tehl sobered and squeezed her arm. "She'll heal. It takes time."

That was something she understood keenly. "The twins make her better."

Jade and Ethan were the light of Jasmine's day. As soon as she was healthy, the twins had been taken to her. Sage choked up just thinking about the reunion. They'd not left Jasmine's side since.

"Children tend to do that. Speaking of which... Isa told me you were taking her riding."

Sage rolled her eyes. "I told her I'd take her to meet Peg."

"Well, you better say that to Gav. He's kept her from the stables."

"Because of her mother."

"Yes."

Sage frowned. She could understand being afraid, but riding was a part of life he couldn't keep Isa from or it would hobble her.

"I'll make sure to speak with him."

"The sooner the better or he'll come looking for you. His temper is something fearsome."

Her lips pursed. She'd need to have a talk with Gav. He'd been standoffish since she'd gotten home, and it bothered her. A lot.

She and Tehl descended the stairs, and she plastered her court smile onto her face. Thoughts for another time.

***

What in the hell was happening?

Sage tried to keep the horror and embarrassment off her face. Not for herself but for Jas. Her friend was currently in a group of men, smiling coyly and flirting. It was worse than flirting. She didn't even have a name for it.

"She's drawing attention," Tehl muttered underneath his breath.

Sage scanned the room and grimaced as Rose and her posse were giggling behind fans while watching the catastrophe. "I don't know what's gotten into her. Jasmine would never act like this."

"You're sure you don't know?" Tehl asked quietly while eyeing the spectacle.

A retort was on the tip of her tongue, but she swallowed it. She didn't really know. They survived something extraordinary together that had bonded them, but, other than that, Sage didn't know much about her. But Jasmine didn't strike her as a flighty, frivolous type of woman.

She studied her friend and frowned when Jasmine ran her fan up the lapel of a young man with sandy-blond hair. The hair rose on Sage's arms at the hungry look the man cast her and the secret smiles passed to his friends.

"I need to stop this," she whispered scooting back from the table.

Tehl stood and held his arm out. "I'll accompany you."

They descended the dais and strolled toward the group. Jasmine smiled widely at Sage and curtsied. The vultures surrounding her friend bowed and engaged Tehl in conversation almost immediately.

Sage sidled up to Jasmine and wound her arm in her own. "Walk with me?"

"Gladly," Jas said, smiling at the sandy-haired fellow, and allowed Sage to moved her away.

"You make friends quickly," she said, smiling at those they

passed.

"They're not really my friends. I amuse them. The wild girl from the village."

Startled, Sage stared at her. "Are they laughing at you?"

"Stars above, no." Jasmine waved a hand at her, her smile sharp and bitter. "They just want to bed me."

"You look stunning." And she did. Earlier in the day, she'd taken a stormy blue, green dress to Jas for tonight. She had so many, and the color had reminded her of her friend. She was right. The color did make her eyes shine like jewels. Jasmine was slightly more endowed than she was, so the sweetheart cut showed more of her assets than Sage would've been comfortable with, but to each their own.

Jasmine snorted. "I look like a china doll dressed up like this."

Sage smirked, knowing the feeling well. She still wasn't comfortable wearing such expensive clothing, but she'd stopped fighting her ladies-in-waiting as long as there were not jewels on the dresses. She drew the line there. "You fit right in."

"I fit in with all the strutting peacocks, eating and drinking like we're not on the verge of war," Jasmine said in a disgusted tone.

If Sage hadn't experienced the court before, she would've thought the same thing. The people may have seemed carefree, but there was an underlying tension that thrummed through the air. Everyone was scared, but they had to go on with their day-to-day lives.

"Not everything is as it seems."

Jasmine flashed her a brilliant smile that would make any courtier proud in its veneer. "That is the first truthful statement I heard tonight." Her gaze wandered to the wolfish blond.

Sage followed her gaze and kept her face blank. "He's not as nice as he looks."

"Maybe I'm not looking for nice."

She turned to Jas, brows raised. "I don't want to see you hurt, or the twins," she tacked on.

"He won't get near the twins," Jas murmured. "This means nothing."

"Okay. Don't get yourself in too deep. I'm always here for you."

"And that's why I love you." Jasmine steered them toward the group of men.

Tehl glanced at Sage, giving her a half smile.

"Speaking of deep, your prince can't keep his eyes off of you. I'm glad he's worthy of your love."

Startled, Sage gaped at her friend. "Who said anything of love?"

Jasmine chuckled. "It was written across your face and his when he found you."

She blushed. Could Tehl see it, too?

"My advice?" Jas said softly. "Life is too short to waste on misunderstandings. One thing I learned in that godforsaken place was to cherish every day you have with those you love. Don't be a coward." She lowered her voice to a whisper. "I've seen you stand up to horrid monsters. You can take the first step and seize your happiness. You deserve it."

Wise advice, indeed, albeit scary. Even thinking about saying those three little words out loud caused her heart to speed up.

"What about yourself? If you're giving advice, you might as well be able to take it yourself."

"Love is not in the cards for me. I have two little ones I have to raise. I don't have time for that."

"And the blond?"

Jasmine smiled. "A diversion."

"Be careful," Sage whispered as they neared the group.

Her friend squeezed her arm. "Always."

Jasmine released Sage's arm and smiled at the group. "What sort of things have you all been speaking about?"

"Things that will shock your womanly sensibilities," the blond commented.

"That I can't believe. There's not much that can shock me."

"Joshua and I were speaking of hunting," Tehl interrupted as awkward as ever.

Sage grinned at Jasmine and slipped her arm into the crook of Tehl's elbow. At least she knew the wolf's name. "And what do you hunt?"

"A number of things, my lady," he said, a small smile tugging at his mouth as he stared at Jasmine.

Sage smiled at him, but it was more of a baring of teeth. The bastard couldn't have been more suggestive if he tried. "You should try your hand in the training ring."

He laughed, the sound haughty. "I'm much too busy for such things."

Sage tensed. "Such things as protecting your kingdom?" She smiled at Tehl, despite the blank expression on his face. "My lord, my husband, spends a *great* deal of time there."

She hid her smug smile as Joshua's smile slipped.

"Forgive me, I meant no offense." He sketched a bow.

"No offense taken." Sage waved him away and cuddled closer to Tehl's arm. "I find myself quite exhausted after the day's events, my lord."

Tehl eyed her. "It has been quite harrowing." He smiled blandly at the group. "Good evening."

Murmured goodnights followed them as Tehl towed her away

from the group, his steps brisk. Swamp apples. The crown prince was not happy. "Will you tell me what I did that angered you, or will you brood all the way back to our room?"

"You can't help yourself?" Tehl sighed. "You just made an enemy of a duke's son."

"He was a pompous windbag who looked at Jasmine in a way I didn't like."

"I'm sure Jasmine could have handled it on her own, love."

She frowned. "I'm not so sure." She peeked up at Tehl. "I'm worried about her, and he's a snake in the grass. I can feel it."

He paused at the bottom of the stairs and tipped his chin down to look at her. "Don't worry. Sam is watching over her."

"Sam?"

"Yes. Sam knows of Joshua's tricks. He won't allow anything to happen to Jasmine."

Somewhat soothed, Sage followed Tehl up the stairs.

At least she wouldn't have to deal with the fool.

Chapter Thirty-Two

Jasmine

She gazed past the blond duke's shoulder, blankly staring at the deep blue velvet curtain. Had the twins been put to bed already? Of course, they had. It was past their bedtime.

His lips traveled down her jaw to her neck. Her gaze traced the silver scrolls on the draperies, feeling nothing.

"You're so beautiful, love," he muttered against her skin.

Love. How cliché. She doubted he even knew her name.

Jasmine squinted, her brow furrowing. Damn. She didn't know his name, either. What was it? Jesse? James? Josh... Joshua! That's what it was. Not that it mattered. She wouldn't remember his face an hour from now. She never remembered any of them. They didn't matter. None of this mattered.

Joshua pulled back, his grey eyes smug as he pressed her back into the stone wall. "As soon as I laid eyes on you tonight, I was enchanted."

She sighed. The last thing she wanted was to hear him speak. She wanted oblivion, the numbness and condemning silence that came with hands upon her skin.

Jas ran her hands up his silk vest and seized his lapels in her hands, crushing the dainty, expensive fabric. A snort almost escaped her. The pink silk was the most ridiculous thing she'd ever seen on a man.

He grinned wolfishly and pressed his palms on the wall above her head. "You're not much for talking, are you?"

"Talking is overrated," she whispered.

"On that, my fair lady, I must agree," he said, bridging the gap between them.

Her eyes closed of their own volition as Joshua attacked her mouth in what she thought was supposed to be a kiss. It was more of a mauling.

She shifted her face to the side, and Joshua happily continued to kiss whatever skin he could get to. A shiver worked through her when he breathed near her ear.

"You like that, do you?" he rasped.

It tickled.

His hands left the wall and made their presence known low on her hips. Jasmine stared into the darkness wishing she could just disappear. Maybe if she concentrated hard enough, she'd disappear into the wind like the seeds of a wishing flower. Forever scattered.

A sigh escaped her, and his lips curled into a smile. "Like that?"

No. She couldn't feel anything. Her soul was numb. There wasn't a flicker of disgust or heat. Just a gaping maw of nothingness. It was a pressing of skin together. Nothing more.

His hand drew circles on her hips and then skated forward.

Every muscle locked up in her body as his fingers grazed her belly. Her breathing became shallow as she fought the heat behind her eyes. Her fingers curled into fists, and she blinked repeatedly. He didn't notice the slight swell, but she felt it keenly. No matter how much she tried, there was no forgetting. Nothing could undo the crimes. The knowledge of what had been taken.

Jasmine squinted as light flooded into the cove, and she glanced away, trying to clear her vision.

"If you do not wish to be betrothed by morning, I suggest you leave now," a cultured voice said with humor.

She got control of herself and avoided Samuel's gaze. No matter where she went, he seemed to pop up. He wasn't her caretaker. If only he'd leave her alone.

Joshua jerked away from her as if burnt and turned to grin at the man she could scarcely escape.

Sam leaned against the wall, the picture of relaxation as he took in the scene. Jasmine tugged her gown into place and dropped her eyes to the floor as she felt for any hair that might have escaped its confines. It was time to go. She wouldn't wait around for the lecture that would surely come. Just because he knew her secret didn't mean he knew her, or what was best for her.

"I appreciate the warning," Joshua said, his tone light, if not a little thwarted. "I'll take my leave." A finger brushed her cheek, causing her to look up.

Grey eyes crinkled when he smiled at her. "Goodnight, love."

"I'm not your love," she said, brushing out her skirts. She'd never be anyone's love.

"I always did like my women feisty," he murmured. "Until next time." He bowed and disappeared from view.

Good riddance. There would be no next time.

She rolled her neck and winced as she thought about the long walk to her room. The heeled shoes Sage had lent her were killing her feet. Why would anyone wear these torture devices when flat, soft boots were available?

She shook out her skirts one more time and brushed by the male still staring at her, ignoring him. If she never had to look at his smug face again, it would be too soon. Her cheeks heated as she remembered sobbing herself into oblivion in his arms. Never again. She'd never allow herself to be that vulnerable with a man again. The heat behind her eyes said otherwise.

"Not even a 'thank you' for getting rid of the toad?" he asked.

"I could have gotten rid of him without your help, thank you."

She gritted her teeth as footsteps approached behind her. She would not break down here. No breaking down. None. She was stronger than that.

"I really deserve thanks… unless you were trying to trap him into marriage."

The comment brought her up short. Her tears dried as anger took its place. Jasmine forced a chuckle out. She couldn't let him get to her. The prince enjoyed getting a rise out of others. She wouldn't give him the satisfaction.

"He wouldn't have married me over a few kisses, and I certainly wouldn't have married him." She'd never marry.

Men like Joshua didn't care for others. They took, and she had children she had to worry about. Children… Her gaze dropped to her belly. She swallowed thickly and stared straight ahead as she powered down the hallway as fast as she could, the heels rubbing against the blisters on her feet.

"Well, you and I both know you've been kissing your fair share of men recently."

Skidding to a stop, she whirled around to glare at the prince. "Excuse me?"

He smirked and sauntered closer. "You've collected quite the harem from what I've heard."

"That is none of your business," she hissed, glancing around. There were too many corners for her liking. Anyone could be listening. "Keep your mouth shut and leave me alone."

"I would leave you alone if you stopped leaving messes everywhere else," he retorted. "You have no idea how many of your little 'escapades' I've had to cover up in the last few weeks. You're being careless."

"I never asked you for that." She never asked him for anything. Being in debt to someone was not her cup of tea. "I can take care of my own affairs. Now, if you'll excuse me."

"No, I will not excuse you," he said, stepping closer, his blue eyes snapping with anger. "Things aren't roses and sunshine right now, but you need to abandon this path of self-destruction now before you get hurt."

She chuckled. The hurt was already done. No one could hurt her now. They'd have to get past the ice that encased her. "You know nothing about me."

"On the contrary," he whispered, his blue eyes darting between hers. "You'll be thrown from the palace and be forced to take care of the twins alone if your extracurricular activities are discovered."

"Sage wouldn't abandon me."

"There are some things that are too great. Do you think a woman considered having loose morals would be allowed to remain in the princess's inner circle?"

Jasmine flinched as if he'd slapped her. His words stung. A

woman with loose morals. His face fell as her eyes filled with tears.

"I didn't mean it that way," he said softly.

"Yes, you did." She was ruined, but it hurt for someone else to say it. She wiped her cheeks and smiled at him. "Thank you for the speech. I will keep that in mind the next time I tumble someone," she snarled before spinning on her heel. A large hand curled around her arm and spun her about.

"What are you—"

Sam backed her against the wall, his nose touching hers. Her heart pounded as he pressed more of his body along hers. What the hell?

"Is this what you want? What you've been looking for?" he murmured.

No, it wasn't. She didn't want to feel, and, anytime she was around the prince, all she did was feel. Her numbness melted away, leaving behind rage, pain, betrayal, and disgust.

His hands ghosted down her sides to her hips, and he nuzzled the side of her jaw. "I'll gladly give you what you seek." He pulled back and looked her in the eye. "All you have to say is 'no.'"

Jasmine stared at him with hate but hated herself more. He was like all the others. She'd heard about the prince's conquests. She placed her hand around his neck and smiled seductively at the prince, even as a voice in the back of her head told her not to do it. But she ignored the warning. She'd made her bed, and now she had to lie in it. Sam was known for his exploits and never staying with one woman. He was exactly what she was looking for.

"I'd like to see you try," she taunted.

His lips curled. "Challenge accepted, my lady."

She closed her eyes, expecting him to paw at her like every other man had, but he didn't. He breathed with her, chest to chest.

"Look at me," he said with a hint of iron in his voice.

Jasmine opened her eyes, and he brushed a finger along her top and bottom lips before leaning close and pressing a chaste kiss to her mouth. She didn't close her eyes, and neither did he. They stared at each other. What was this madness? This was the blessed numbness she wanted.

Samuel brushed a kiss along her cheekbone and then along her jaw. She tipped her head back to stare at the ceiling and sagged into the wall, the cool stone seeping through her gown, guilt pricking her. She pushed it away. What was one more sin to add to her already long list?

Cool air kissed her ankles, but she hardly cared. She closed her eyes and tried to forget everything around, imagining the cool forest on a morning hunt. How she missed the forests, the worn, smooth wood of her bow in her palm.

"Check mate," the prince whispered.

Her brows furrowed, and she opened her eyes, blinking.

"This is highly irregular," a prim voice snapped.

Jasmine's attention snapped toward the voice. Five well-dressed women glared at her with varying degrees of disgust.

A buzzing filled her ears. She'd been ruined publicly, and she didn't feel a thing.

CHAPTER THIRTY-THREE

Sam

Sam stared at Jasmine's blank face. Not a flicker of emotion while the women declared their degrees of shock. In that moment, he second-guessed himself. Had he done the right thing?

Sam knew what image they painted. Jasmine rumpled, his hand hoisting her skirts up as he pressed himself against her. It was the image he wanted. The image that would change his life forever.

He'd kept an eye on Jasmine since her breakdown. She put on a good show for everyone, but it was all a lie. He knew an actor when he saw one. The only time she lit up was when she was with the twins. She was a remarkable mother, and that's what had sealed his decision. He knew how her story would end if she didn't marry before the babe began to show more than it already was. Even now, he could feel the hard, proud little bump pressing against his stomach.

Jasmine had tried to help Sage when she didn't even know her, and that had cost her everything. He wanted to give her something in return, and this was the only way he could think of doing that. She was hell-bent on destroying herself. If she wouldn't protect herself, he had to.

Slowly, he lowered her skirts to the floor and smiled boyishly at the older women, wrapping an arm around the stiff Jasmine. He flicked another glance at Jasmine, praying she didn't ruin the ruse he'd orchestrated.

"Hello, ladies."

"My lord, we did not mean to intrude," the baroness said, her tone sharp and disapproving. Her lips thinned as she frowned at them, not hiding her thoughts whatsoever.

"That's quite all right," he said grinning. "We were celebrating our betrothal."

He kept his smile in place as her thin, graying brows practically climbed to her perfectly coiffed hair. "Betrothed?"

"Indeed," he said gaily, hugging Jasmine closer.

The old crones tittered between themselves, and the baroness pressed forward, reaching a hand out. "My congratulations," she said, her ember-like gaze sliding to Jasmine at his side. "You are one very lucky woman."

Jasmine said nothing. *Thank the stars.* Silence he could work with.

Sam tucked her underneath his arm and pressed a kiss to the baroness's hand. "I'm afraid it grows late, and I have to share the news. Ladies."

He winked at them, causing the older women to blush as he steered his new fiancée away from the gossip-mongers. The news of their engagement would be spread all over the palace by morning. It would be an affair to remember, but that was okay. A quick marriage would fade from mind, but a bastard child? Not so much.

They rounded the corner, and Jasmine yanked her arm from his and spun to face him. "What the hell was that?" she hissed, her stormy eyes wild.

Anger. He could handle anger.

Sam wove around her and picked up his speed. She was about to explode. Words would be had, but he needed to get her away from hearing ears for that conversation. She'd ruin everything if she lost control now.

"Don't you dare walk away from me."

"I'm not walking away from you." *He was leading her away from the harpies who would love to tear her apart.*

She stomped behind him. Sam eyed the empty hallway. Good enough. He spun, snagging her wrist and pulled her into one of the secret coves.

Jasmine yanked her arm from his grasp and glared at him. "Don't touch me."

He held his hands up and took a step back.

"What was that?" she demanded. "What have you done?"

"That was me saving your life." He leaned a hip against the wall. She was justifiably angry, but, in the end, she'd understand he was doing what was best for her and the twins. He wouldn't allow another girl to be destroyed by the Scythians when it was within his power to do something.

"My life? You just *lied* to those women."

"I didn't lie to them."

"You told them we're *betrothed*." She said the word like it was something dirty.

"We are."

"No, we are not."

"Yes, we are," he said slowly. "What do you think those women would have done if we weren't, hmmm? I'll tell you. Word would have spread, like wild fire, of our little tête-à-tête." Her face paled. "You would've been well and truly ruined in the court's eyes. It's a dangerous game you've been playing. You've been lucky so far."

"So, you made up a lie?" she said flatly.

"No, I saved your reputation and just provided for the twins and yourself for the rest of your life."

"I won't go along with this," she whispered.

He chuckled, hating each moment he played the bad guy. That's what he got for trying to be the knight in shining armor. "You will. You will not make a fool out of a prince of Aermia, and you certainly won't turn away the best life you could offer to the twins. We have but one choice. To marry. If you won't do it for yourself, you need to do it for the children. They don't deserve to suffer for the outrageous mistakes of other men."

Sam held firm as one tear dripped from the corner of her eye.

"And what do you expect to get from this arrangement?" she asked.

That was not the question he expected. "Nothing."

A bitter laugh followed as she wiped away the lone tear. "Nothing? No one does anything for nothing."

That was the bold truth, he knew. He sighed. "I need a wife and a family. I'm not as respectable as I should be, I am told." She'd believe that. It wasn't quite true, but it was close enough to the truth for now.

"A wife in truth or in name only?"

"In name only." For now.

She scoffed. "What of heirs?"

His gaze dropped to her belly. "The one you carry will be sufficient." He'd give the child his name. She deserved that much after everything she'd given for Aermia. His stomach twisted as he remembered her tear-streaked face. He'd make those bastards suffer; they couldn't expect to get away with causing her pain.

Her hand fluttered near her belly, and she glanced away, her bottom lip trembling. "I hate you."

So be it. "Good. It'll make the next part easier," he whispered.

CHAPTER THIRTY-FOUR

Sage

She stared at the mirror and slowly pulled the pins from her hair. A necessary evil she was told. They helped form a beautiful visage, but she wasn't sure it was worth the pain. Her gaze flicked to Tehl's reflection. The crown prince had his back to her as he began to tug his shirt over his head.

Nervousness ran down her spine, like ants marching across her skin, as she watched him. She admired the burnished skin he revealed and a blush touched her cheeks. She was staring at him like a wanton woman. She jerked her gaze back to her own reflection as he looked over his shoulder as if he felt her gaze.

Internally, she cursed herself. What in the blazes? He'd always been handsome, but since her revelation at the coastline, she'd found her attention lingering on him far longer than it should have. *Wanton, indeed.*

She pulled the last pesky pin from her head and shook her hair free, so it fell in waves down her back. Thank goodness only warm candlelight illuminated the room or he'd have seen the blush scorching her cheeks.

"You're quiet tonight," Tehl said softly as he tugged his belt from his waist then placed his daggers on his side table.

"There's a lot on my mind."

He turned and slung a hip against the bed. "Like what?"

Like how she loved him. Her breath hitched at the thought. It still baffled her how she hadn't seen it before, and how it had slapped her in the face, leaving her elated and terrified. "I'm worried about Jasmine," she said instead.

Coward, her inner voice whispered.

He frowned and stared at the fire. "She's going through an adjustment period. Healing takes time. She'll be okay."

"I don't know." Sage turned, kicking the train of her dress out of the way. "Something happened, and now she's changed."

Tehl turned to her, a line of tension entering his shoulders. "That's to be expected after a trauma."

His words were soft, but they still felt like a blow. He wasn't just speaking of Jasmine. Sage spun and placed her hands on the vanity, her eyes squeezing shut. He spoke the truth. She wasn't the same girl. Hell, she didn't even know the girl she used to be. The old Sage had died in Scythia, and a creature of nightmares and vengeance had been born.

Large hands settled on her shoulders, and only years of practice kept her from jumping. She hadn't even heard him move.

"I didn't mean to upset—"

"You didn't," she cut him off, peeking at him from under her lashes. Hunched over like she was, he towered over her. A little thrill of fear went through her, but she pushed it away. This was

Tehl, and he'd never hurt her.

Sage straightened and reached back to place her right hand on top of his. "You're right. Trauma does change people." And she was sorry for it. "But Jasmine changed right before she was released from the infirmary. She went from her bright, sarcastic self to…" An image of Jasmine's empty blue eyes floated to the forefront of her mind. "It's like part of her died."

Tehl squeezed her shoulders, and she blinked, focusing on his deep blue eyes.

"It hurts to watch someone you care about suffer and battle demons that you can neither see nor protect them from," he rasped. Her fingers clenched around his at the emotion leaking through his voice. "You can't take away the pain, but you can be the best friend possible."

Like he had. "Sound advice," she murmured. "Thank you for being my friend."

His fingers tightened for a moment. "It's been a pleasure being your friend."

She snorted. "Let's not get carried away. The sleepless nights are no walk in the park."

"That's true. But, in being your friend, I've gained much more. Losing a little sleep is well worth it."

Her heart picked up speed. This man. "And why is that?"

He smiled, causing her breath to hitch. "I gained a friend of my own." A shrug. "I've never had many. Sam and Gav are family. There are the men… but it's different with you."

A heartfelt confession so honest that it made her want to weep. Sage ignored the heat gathering behind her eyes. "I don't think I could put it any more eloquently."

Tehl rolled his eyes. "Now that, I don't believe. You and I both know I'm terrible with words."

"That you are." She smiled at him, and he returned the expression, both grinning like idiots. Her smile faded first. "But, in all honesty, I mean it. Your friendship is a gift I could never afford."

His smile faded into something more serious as he dropped his gaze. His thumbs ran along the tops of her shoulders and underneath her hair, causing her to shiver. He paused, a little line forming between his brows. He ran his thumbs up the sides of her neck. Goosebumps rose along her arms at the soft touch.

She watched his eyes flicker as his left thumb brushed the heated chain of her necklace. He caught her eye in the mirror. Her breath caught, but not in fear. Her pulse picked up as she saw the look in his eyes. *Desire.*

She'd seen that look on men. On *him.* But all those men only saw one part of her, or what they believed her to be. Tehl *knew* her. He'd seen all the ugly and yet...he still looked at her like she was the most beautiful thing in the world.

"Do you want me to take it off?" he whispered.

She blinked. Then blinked again. He meant the necklace. She wanted to slap herself when a nervous giggle slipped out. "Please."

He slowly swept her long hair over her left shoulder and fumbled with the latch. Sage hid her smile when he cursed underneath his breath and glared at the necklace. After two more tries, he unlatched it with a growl.

"Stupid design."

She hissed when the chain caught some of the hair at her nape.

"I'm sorry," he muttered before dropping a kiss to the back of her neck.

She froze, his heated breath leaving her skin. She stared at his reflection and he stared back, both of them silent. She couldn't even hear his breath.

"It's okay. Half the time, I want to cut my hair off." There. She'd said something to dispel the awkward silence.

"No."

"No?" She arched a brow.

Tehl gently placed the necklace on the vanity, his heated chest brushing her arm, and then straightened. "I love your hair. It's shiny and smells nice. I even find myself sniffing it sometimes. Cinnamon. I smell it all the time..." He sucked in his cheeks, embarrassment clear on his face as he rambled.

"So, I shouldn't cut it?" she asked, throwing him a line.

He puffed out a breath. "No." Even though he was obviously embarrassed, he didn't look away. He didn't hide from her. Honesty. She'd always treasured it, and Tehl encompassed it.

Sage turned her cheek and kissed his fingers still cupping her shoulder. "Then I shan't."

Tehl shifted behind her, his body grazing hers, causing everything to heat. Her lips parted as he leaned close and placed an open mouth kiss on the top of her shoulder, never losing eye contact in the mirror.

Part of her wanted to run and hide, but that part was small. Her fear and nervousness had no place here. This was Tehl. Her awkward, honest, kind husband who carried the weight of the kingdom upon his shoulders and managed to look out for everyone around him.

His lips found her throat, and then his teeth grazed the tender skin there, and he never looked away from her. Each move was slow, like he was waiting for her to pull away from him. But that was the furthest thing from her mind.

His touch didn't cause bile to burn her throat, or disgust and shame to drown her. It soothed and yet burned her all at once.

"So beautiful," he murmured against her skin, his callused hands drifting down her arm and across her torso, catching on the fine fabric of her dress.

Sage trembled and slowly spun in his arms. She tilted her head back, and Tehl stared down at her. She knew he would step away if that's what she wanted. He wouldn't push anything. But she didn't want him to step away; she wanted him to hold her. To love her.

Slowly, she moved, sliding her hands up his arms, and pressed her palms against his chest, feeling the rapid thud of his heartbeat. She looked up. His mouth was closer, his breath whispering over her forehead. The throb of his heartbeat increased its tempo beneath her hand. She licked her lips, and a thrill went through her as he watched her movement, obviously transfixed.

She looped her arms around his neck and pressed up onto her toes as his arms banded around her waist. Her belly trembled as the words she'd been rehearsing in her head tumbled from her lips. "Let me love you."

Four little words. That was it. But it changed everything.

Emotions flitted across his face, too fast for her to catalogue them as he held perfectly still. Sage's heart pounded, and a whooshing sound filled her ears. What if he rejected her again? Could she handle it? Surely, it would break what was left of her.

She dropped her eyes to the small spattering of hair on his chest, afraid of his answer. The silence felt condemning, suffocating.

A finger slid underneath her chin and lifted, forcing her to meet his deep blue eyes. He searched her face, his fingers caressing the soft underside of her jaw. Whatever he was looking for, he found.

His lips curled, and his mouth drifted closer.

"No." Her heart stuttered. "It will be my pleasure to love you," he whispered before kissing her.

Lips brushed against lips, and, as she took a breath, she stole his. Tehl cupped her cheeks with both his hands and pressed closer, his mouth opening over hers as he tasted her, a faint hint of his tongue flickering over her lips. *Stars above.*

Her hands flexed against his neck and as he pulled back to brush his nose against hers, an odd sound rose in her throat, one that sounded suspiciously like a sigh. His gaze flicked to hers as if to make sure she was all right.

Sage swallowed and smiled. "I trust you."

He didn't ask for the words, but she needed to say them all the same. She trusted him more than she trusted herself most of the time.

A groan erupted from his throat, and then his hands were on her, lifting her onto the vanity, her back pressed against the mirror. She leaned forward, her hands sliding over the smooth skin of his shoulders. How had she gotten so lucky?

He shuddered and caught her face in his hands, and then his mouth swooped across hers in a kiss that caused her to go up in flames. Her fingers wandered into his silky black hair and a rumbling sound vibrated from his chest.

His hands skimmed down her waist and slowly began to lift her skirts.

"This is enough," he rasped, between kisses. "This is all I need, love. You can say no."

"It's not nearly enough," she said, tugging on his hair, so he met her gaze. "This is my choice. *Our choice.* This is our future."

Tehl curled his hands against the back of her knees and pulled her forward until the insides of her thighs caressed his hips, and he settled her there. "For so long, I've wanted you more than I've wanted anything."

His tender words caused a fat tear to sneak out.

He cupped her face and gently stroked her cheeks as he stared into her eyes. "I don't want to hurt you. I want to make you happy."

She pulled his left hand from her face and kissed his palm. "That's what I know: you will never hurt me," she whispered. Her other hand went to his nape, and she pulled his head down, so his mouth went back to hers. "You are mine, and I am yours."

He brushed his lips across hers. "I'm happy to call you mine and to be yours."

"Then make it so," she breathed, her cheeks heating.

"I intend to, love," he whispered.

A knock.

They froze, staring at each other.

"Maybe they'll go away," Tehl whispered, kissing her neck.

Another knock.

Disappointment filled her as he growled.

"Who in the hell would be calling at this hour?" he all but snarled.

"It's likely important," she said softly.

Tehl pressed his forehead against hers. "So is this."

"I'm not going anywhere."

His disgruntled expression caused a small giggle to escape her. He blinked, and the corners of his mouth curled.

She couldn't remember the last time she giggled.

A third knock.

Tehl glared at the door. "Stars above, I'm coming." He turned back to her and arched an eyebrow before kissing her hungrily, and then, leaving her breathless, he pulled back.

"Are you ready for this?" he asked, tugging her skirts down and holding a hand out for her.

Sage tried not to blush as she accepted his hand and glanced at the vanity. He followed her gaze and squeezed her hand, pulling her attention back to him.

"This is the beginning, you know," he said softly.

"The beginning?"

"The beginning of us."

CHAPTER THIRTY-FIVE

Sage

"Hello, pretty girl," Sage crooned at Peg. The mare nickered a hello and butted her in the chest affectionately. She grinned and stroked Pegasus's velvety nose. "I don't have any treats for you." Peg ignored her and nosed around her pockets.

"Are you ready?" Gav asked, his face shadowed by the hooded cloak he wore.

She craned her neck to look at her friend. "Yes."

He stared at her for a beat then nodded. "Make sure to tell her about your shadow."

"Nali," she breathed. That sneaky beast. She turned back to Peg and gave her another pat on her chest. "Don't worry about the kitty-cat out there. She'll not harm you." Peg snorted in answer.

Sage led her out of her stall, the earthy smell of hay and horse fading as they moved out of the stable. Zachael, William, Rafe, and

Marq sat on their horses, only lit by the soft moonlight. She glanced at Tehl. He had already mounted Wraith, his mammoth of a horse, and leaned down to speak quietly with Gav. She watched them, feeling a little left out, and fiddled with the clasp of her cloak.

Since she'd come home, Gav had been different. He'd been quieter, more withdrawn. She couldn't help but think she'd done something to upset him, but, for the life of her, she couldn't imagine what it was. He hadn't spent enough time around her for Sage to offend him. But those were thoughts for another time. Tonight, they had to seal an alliance with Methi. Rafe had arranged a meeting. Aermia's future rested on the decisions made tonight.

Pegasus jerked and shied to the side, yanking her from her thoughts. Sage pulled on the reins and planted her feet, reeling the mare in as she reacted to the huge feline. "It's okay, Peg. Nali won't hurt you." The whites of Peg's eyes showed as she backed up another step. "It's okay."

Warmth suffused her back as two hands reached around her to hold Peg.

"Get back, Sage. It's okay. I got it."

She blinked at the anger in Gav's voice. Why was he so angry? Peg was still getting used to her.

"This is dangerous," he growled, elbowing her out of the way.

Her eyes narrowed on him, and she pushed the hood from her head to scowl at her friend. What was wrong with him? She hadn't done anything wrong. It was natural for a horse to be afraid of a predator. Plus, it was her responsibility to care for her mount, and Peg needed to learn to trust her.

Sage ducked underneath Gav's arms and curled her fingers around the mare's cheek piece once again. "She's mine. Now, move."

"Why are you so bloody stubborn?" his voice raised.

Peg jerked again. Gav was making it worse. His agitation was affecting her horse. Sage let go of the cheek piece and pulled on the reins. "You're frightening her. Calm down and back away," she growled.

He gritted his teeth and glared at her. "No. It's not safe."

His words penetrated her confusion. She'd never seen him lose his temper, and he certainly had never spoken to her in such a manner. It was the horses. The horses set him on edge, because of his wife. Sage moved her hand to his arm and squeezed, her heart going out to him.

"It's okay," she said softly. "I'm okay. I'm not going to get hurt."

Gav squeezed his eyes, a tremble moving through his body.

"I've got her," she said.

He nodded and slowly released her horse. Gav stormed to his dapple-gray mount and swung up into the saddle. Sage watched his hands clench and unclench on the reins. She glanced at Tehl, who was staring at his cousin with sympathy. The poor man.

Sage turned to Peg and ran her hands along the mare's neck. "You're okay, sweet girl. Are you ready to go on a ride?" she whispered. The horse's ears flicked forward at the word 'ride.' "That's right. We're going on a long ride." She gathered the reins in her left hand, placed her left foot in the stirrup, and climbed into the saddle without a fuss. She leaned forward and patted the mare's neck. "Good girl. Now let's ride."

***

The wind whipped Sage's hair around her face, and she grinned, wanting to whoop with joy. Riding Pegasus was unlike anything she'd ever experienced. It was true freedom. The moon painted the road and surrounding trees in soft whites, like the world had been gilded in silver.

The thundering of Peg's hooves kept pace with her heartbeat, almost as if they were one creature. Rafe reined in his mount and slowed ahead of her. The ride had gone too quickly. Peg's sides heaved as they slowed and took another offshoot from the road. The trees grew in arches over the path, like they were bowing to the heavens above them.

The men closed around Marq, and Sage shivered as the path darkened, only to be broken up by small puddles of moonlight. She scanned the area around them and froze as something dark darted through the trees. Her hand crept to the dagger at her waist. A flash of golden eyes. Her shoulders slumped, and she glared at the darkened forest. "Bloody cat," she whispered.

"What was that, my dear?" the king asked, his voice barely above a whisper.

"Nali."

A huff. "She's quite the protector."

"That she is," she murmured, focusing on their surroundings again, the hair on the back of her neck standing on edge. She had the feeling she was being watched. Sage tipped her head back and scanned above them thinking of the snake that had almost killed them in Scythia. They were too confined.

Her left hand clenched around the pommel of her saddle, and she focused on her breathing while squeezing the reins in her right. Panicking would do no one any good. She counted down her breaths from one hundred and sighed when the pathway opened to a small meadow with what looked like a rundown cottage.

Rafe paused and slid off his horse. "We leave the horses here."

"Here?" Zachael asked, his salt-and-pepper brows furrowing.

"You will thank me for it."

Rafe met Sage's gaze, his amber eyes practically glowing in the moonlight. What was he trying to tell her? She stared at the stone cottage. It wasn't small by any stretch of the imagination, but there was something off about it. It looked to be abandoned, and yet... the roof was in fine condition, as was the masonry. This place was used often.

She nodded to Rafe and swung off of Peg. Why did he want her to know it was in use? And what about the horses? Was there something that would spook them? She froze, the reins hanging limply from her fingers. What sort of predators did the Methians bring with them? At that moment she was beyond thankful that Nali had accompanied them. There wasn't a thing that feline couldn't detect.

Brushing the hair from her face, she pulled her hood up, shielding her face. It would be best to disguise the fact she was a woman. Not all men appreciated an outspoken woman.

Tehl stood to her right, his arm brushing her shoulder, and Gav to her left. Rafe scanned their group and nodded before striding out into the meadow confidently. Her lips twitched. The man wore arrogance well. Many would see it as stupidity, but she knew his capabilities. He'd catalogued every potential danger before his feet had even touched the ground.

Nali stalked from the trees and pushed in between Sage and Gav, her lips pulled back and the hair along her spine slightly on end. Gav missed a step and moved to make more room. Sage studied her feline companion, and then scanned the trees. There was clearly something Nali didn't like out there.

Rafe stopped in the middle of the meadow, allowing them to

catch up. Sage paused, her cloak swishing around her boots as a group of tall, cloaked figures emerged from the other side of the clearing.

She placed a hand on Nali's head as a chilling growl rumbled in the feline's throat, never taking her eyes from the hooded warriors. And that's what they were. Warriors. Sage still remembered the first time she met Rafe. Each move he had made was fluid, calculated, predatorial. These men moved the same way.

They halted several strides away, and the whole forest seemed to hold its breath.

Marq stepped forward and pushed his hood back, his head held high. "Well met, my brothers."

"Well met, my brothers," the tallest warrior said. "I have to say, I'm surprised that you risk yourself." It wasn't a taunt, but a simple statement.

"Times are dangerous, and my people need me. I'll do whatever is necessary to help them. As is my duty."

The shortest warrior stepped around the warrior who spoke first and pushed back her hood. Sage's breath caught in her throat as one of the most beautiful women she'd ever seen stepped forward. Her long hair was deep-wine in color, streaked with silver, and braided into an intricate rope that draped over her shoulder. Lines bracketed her mouth, and her eyes said she laughed often, but it was the color of her eyes that struck Sage the most.

They were amber. The exact shade of Rafe's.

The tall warrior pushed back his hood, revealing himself to also bear a striking resemblance to Rafe. He indicated the woman with a quick movement of his hands. "My mother, Queen Osir."

Sage's fingers curled into fists. That lying weasel. Rafe had kept more secrets. She stared at his hood, and Rafe slowly glanced in her direction as if he felt her gaze. He pushed back his hood, not glancing away from her. There was an apology lurking in his gaze. She puffed out a breath and looked away from him. They would be having words later. The bastard was royal. A damn royal spy.

Marq stepped forward and held his hand out. Queen Osir scanned him from head to toe, her shrewd eyes missing nothing. It was an examination, and, by her smile, she hadn't found him wanting.

She stepped forward and placed her hand in his. "My lord," she murmured.

"My lady." He placed a chaste kiss on the back of her hand and straightened. The two royals stared as if sizing each other up.

The Methian queen swept her arm out toward the cottage. "Shall we?"

King Marq dipped his chin. "After you."

The queen's lips twitched, a ghost of a smile. "So polite," she murmured. Sweeping aside her cloak, she strode purposefully toward the cottage.

"Brave," Gav said under his breath. "To turn her back."

"I am among friends, no?" she called, pausing several strides ahead.

Gav's eyes widened.

Marq strolled by her side. "Indeed, my lady."

She huffed a small laugh as both Aermian and Methian men circled them. "Uneasy friends."

"New friends."

Sage stayed put and ran a hand over Nali's fur. Apparently, Rafe had inherited his acute hearing from his mother. Curious.

Tehl paused, waiting for Sage to catch up. She rolled her shoulders and followed the group.

Here went nothing.

CHAPTER THIRTY-SIX

Sage

Sage stepped to the door, and Nali darted in front of her, blocking the way. Tehl paused just inside the threshold, watching. Gav moved closer to her side, and scanned the darkened forest.

"What is it?" she whispered. Something had set off the feline.

Nali sniffed the air, and her ears laid flat against her head. She back-pedaled and nudged Sage from behind. Sage cast one last look around the meadow and allowed Nali to herd her inside. Her hand crept to the dagger at her waist as she entered the cottage. Whatever the danger was, it was outside.

Sage shuffled to the side to make room for Gav as Nali pressed against her leg, her hackles still raised. She brushed her hand along the leren's neck, and surveyed the room from beneath her lashes.

Her suspicions had been right. Someone had been using this house for quite some time, though it looked rundown from the outside. Furs covered the stone floor, and a fire roared in the hearth. Large comfy chairs were set in a rough circle around the room.

Sage's people spread out as one of the Methian men yanked the heavy, tan draperies closed and took the cloak from the queen.

Queen Osir placed her hands on the back of a large, brown leather, winged-back chair. Long scars ran down her arms in crisscross patterns that made Sage shudder. They looked painful. What had done that to her?

The queen scanned the group and then paused on Sage, before sliding to Nali. "A bonded couple," she murmured. "It's a pleasure to see a leren. It's been so many years."

Sage sank her fingers into Nali's fur, as the queen rounded the chair and approached them slowly. The leren growled softly and bared her fangs. "Easy," she whispered. It wouldn't do to have her feline attack a potential ally.

The queen paused. "I mean neither of you harm. I'm partial to felines. They hold a special place in my heart." Her piercing amber gaze wandered back to Sage. "There's no need to hide what you are. You won't find enemies here because of your sex."

Sage pushed her hood from her head and met the queen's probing gaze. "Not everyone has those ideals."

A sharp smile touched the queen's mouth. "Then they are stupid, indeed."

An answering smile tugged on Sage's lips. She liked the queen already. "As you say."

"I've heard much about you, Sage Ramses. Since you've entered the fray, you've changed much in Aermia." The queen drew in a deep breath, her expression turning grave. "I've also heard of your trials in Scythia. I am most sorry for what you've suffered."

Sage's throat tightened, and she swallowed down the grief and anger that always seemed to hover just at the edge of her control. "It's in the past."

"No, experiences like that are never in the past. They may fade, but we carry them for the rest of our lives. They shape who we are. Who are you?"

"Whatever the Crown needs me to be."

A ghost of a smile followed from the queen. "You have many names. The Rebel's Blade, Crown's Shield, Enemy's Queen." That one made Sage wince. "King's Warrior. But I don't think just one of those names could encompass who you truly are."

"And who do you think I am?" she asked warily.

"You, my sweet, are the end of our worlds."

She jerked back as if slapped, and Nali snarled. She'd done everything in her power to avoid that exact thing.

"It's not a bad thing. It's exactly what we need."

"The world needs shaking up," Marq commented, casting Sage an unreadable look. He gestured toward the chairs. "Shall we begin?"

"Yes. Time is against us." The queen nodded to Sage and took her seat, followed by Marq.

Tehl brushed his fingers along her knuckles, raising an eyebrow as if to say, 'Are you okay?' She nodded and trailed behind him to take a seat to his right. Nali placed herself on Sage's other side and leaned into her leg.

"We'd like to thank you for meeting with us on such short notice," Marq said.

The Methian queen waved a hand at him. "There's no need to mince words. War is upon us, and we'll fight beside you."

Sage blinked and peeked at Tehl who stared, his brow

furrowed. That was blunt, and she wasn't the only one to notice, but her king just smiled, completely composed.

"I'm glad to hear that. I, myself, hate to skirt around an issue. Aermia is grateful for your assistance."

"We're always willing to help a neighbor, but in this case, it also helps Methi."

The king cocked his head, studying Queen Osir. "If Aermia falls to the warlord, so does the world."

"True, and that's why we will defend it like it is our own home."

"I wish everyone had your views," Tehl commented.

The queen's eyes narrowed. "They are fools. If there's one thing I've learned as I've grown older, it's that older doesn't always mean wiser. Many years of life breeds apathy."

"True." The king crossed his arms. "I can see what you stand to gain with this alliance, but what I truly want to know is what you'll want in exchange."

The queen grinned at him, her eyes twinkling. "That's always the question, isn't it?"

"It's the way of the world. No one does anything for free, especially those who rule. We can't."

"Spoken like a true king." She tipped her chin up and tapped her fingers on the arm of the chair. "We want access to the seas around Aermia. The schools have migrated from the Maekin Sea to your part of the world."

"We will allow you access to our waters at certain times of the year when the fish population is high. If we over-fish, then we both will be in the same boat." The king cracked a smile. "Pun intended."

The queen chuckled and shook her head. "Agreed, and you are not what I expected."

"My wife said the same thing when she met me."

"I was sorry to hear of her death." She placed a hand over Marq's. "I, too, have lost a mate. So I understand your suffering."

"Thank you. I'm sorry for your loss as well. No one should have to experience that type of pain."

She nodded and pulled her hand back. "We have one more condition, and I'm afraid it's non-negotiable." Queen Osir's face turned to stone. "You seem like a good man, but even good men are prone to envy. I am about to show you something the Methian people have guarded with their lives. I warn you now, if you hurt those we love, we'll kill you."

Marq's brows rose. "I think there was a compliment somewhere among the threats. Clearly, our alliance puts someone you love in danger, so I'll ignore the threats. What is it that you want?"

She blew out a breath and glanced to her son, who'd stood like a stone statue at her side. "It'll be easier to show you. Raziel?" She held her hand out, and her son helped her from the chair, as the men around the room stood. She eyed the group. "If you attack, we will. You have been warned."

Marq glanced at Tehl and Sage. "I assure you, my men will keep control of themselves."

"As you say."

Queen Osir swept from the room, disappearing into the darkness outside. Gav, Zachael, and William surrounded the king.

Rafe stopped halfway to the door and turned toward the Aermian group. "Don't be afraid. This is not a trap."

"Says the son of the Methian queen," Sage growled, glaring at Rafe.

"I'll explain later."

299

"Yes, you will," Tehl said softly. Sage glanced at her husband. She wasn't the only one stung by Rafe's secrets if she went by his expression.

Marq stared at Rafe and then exited the home, his men encircling him. Sage followed, Nali on her left, Tehl on her right.

"You run if it's dangerous," Tehl whispered.

She shot him a sharp look. "I'm not going anywhere."

The crown prince stared at her. "Bloody stubborn woman."

Sage grinned, and stepped out into the moonlit glen, her eyes immediately searching for danger. Nali's ears flattened, and the hair along her spine stood on edge again. "What is it, girl?"

Nali pressed closer to her thigh as the queen whistled, the sound piercing the air. For a moment, there was complete silence, and then, it was as if the forest had exploded. Sage's breath froze in her lungs, as huge winged creatures burst through the trees, and landed in the glen between the Methians and Aermians.

"Wicked hell," Tehl whispered.

Sage placed her hand on Nali's head as the feline snarled at the menacing interlopers.

"They will not hurt you," Queen Osir called.

Sage would've retorted if she could have spoken at all. It wasn't possible to turn away from the spectacle even had she wanted to.

The creature in front of them crouched and growled at Nali, its tail, white with black speckles, whipping back and forth as its brethren pressed closer to its side. A name came unbidden to Sage's mind. Fiilee. Felines as huge as horses with leathery wings. A creature from story books. Was every myth rooted in truth?

The fiilee's dark gray wings flared as it snarled again at Nali, causing the other three at its side to snarl. The hair rose on Sage's arms. They were huge and terrifying. She barely noticed when the leren moved in front of her, each step slow. They made Nail look like a kitten.

Queen Osir moved through the fiilee like she wasn't strolling through a herd of the most dangerous creatures to ever be recorded. She placed a hand on the creature's white speckled shoulder, and whispered a few soft words. The light blue eyes of the fiilee flicked to the queen and back to Nali. Sage tensed, and clenched her fingers in the leren's fur. There was no way she would let Nali fight with that thing.

"There's no need to be afraid. They will not harm you."

"They don't look very friendly," Sage called.

"They, like your leren, only wish to protect us." The queen stroked the beast's white and gray fur. "Now that they know you're not a danger, they'll leave you in peace."

"You speak to them?" Tehl asked.

"More or less. Our ancestors were able to devise a way of communication. They're highly intelligent."

"And deadly," Zachael commented.

"I see now why you were so worried," Marq said. "They provide you a source of protection that none have had since the dragons were wiped out."

The queen lifted her chin. "You know of the origin stories?"

"I do, and I promise we mean these creatures no harm. It's truly a privilege to see one alive and well, let alone three. They will give us an advantage."

"Scythia is an enemy like none we've known. To survive, we will need every resource at our disposal."

The fiilee slowly closed its giant wings and leaned into the queen.

Crown Prince Raziel stepped forward and placed a hand on the darker fiilee to the right. It was broader across the chest, and its spots were so many that it looked more black than white. He ran his hand along the arch of the wing where fur faded into leather. "An áerial advantage will mean everything."

A deep purr rumbled out of the beast, vibrating into Sage's chest. How magnificent! Even though the raised hair on the back of her neck told her to stay far away, she still wanted to sink her fingers into the fiilee's fur.

The Methian crown prince smiled at Sage, his eyes dancing. "If you'd like to meet the living legends, step closer."

She cocked her head and took a step forward, but Tehl slid in front of her, his body blocking her view. "What are you doing?" she hissed, a little put out.

"Keeping you from being eaten," he retorted.

Sage rolled her eyes and glanced at Rafe, who watched the exchange with a calculating glint in his eyes. The man saw way too much. "Do you think Rafe would let me get hurt?"

Tehl's shoulders lowered, and he glanced over his shoulder. "No."

"Then, step aside."

He surprised her by doing just that and then looping her arm through his.

"Where you go, I go."

She hid her smile. It wasn't the time to moon over her husband. Tehl led them forward, no hesitation in his steps. He stopped an arm's reach away. "Is this close enough?"

Sage shook her head and met Raziel's familiar amber eyes. "Can I touch him?"

The Methian prince stroked the beast behind the ear, earning another purr of contentment. "Skye would like that."

"Hello, Skye," she said softly, staring at the fiilee with awe. The beast perked up, his light blue eyes practically glowing in the moonlight.

Tehl squeezed her hand once as she took a step closer and then followed her.

Sage held her palm out for Skye and locked her legs as he snuffled her hand. Her heart nearly stopped when a huge rough tongue darted out and wrapped around her wrist before retreating.

"That's his way of saying hello."

"It's a pleasure to meet you," she murmured as Tehl held his hand out as well. Skye sniffed him and then bathed his hand in saliva in the same welcome.

A booming laugh pulled her attention as Marq grinned at the queen's fiilee who'd licked him from chin to hair line, saliva clear on his face. She smiled, and then glanced at Tehl when he cursed. He rocked back a step as Skye butted him in the chest, releasing a rumbling purr that Sage felt to her toes.

"He's quite friendly, isn't he?"

"Only to those he deems worthy of his friendship."

"What does he do to those he doesn't care for?"

Raziel's smile turned sharp. "They disappear."

"Lovely," Tehl said, scratching the huge feline behind the ear.

Sage placed a hand on Skye's shoulder and ran her fingers through the thick fur along his spine. It was much thicker than Nali's. Speaking of Nali...

She glanced over her shoulder and spotted the leren. Nali sat just out of reach, eyeing Skye and then Sage like she was a traitor.

"All's well. He won't hurt you," Sage assured.

Nali huffed and flicked her tail.

"Stubborn beast," Sage muttered as she turned back to Skye. There was something about the fiilee that made her want to wrap her arms around it. So, she did. Warmth suffused her as Skye sniffed her head and nuzzled close. "You're just a big sweetheart, aren't you?"

"He's a pain in the ass," Rafe grumbled, sidling up to his brother. "Since he was a cub, he's always caused mischief."

"Zeefa was always worse, brother."

"Zeefa?" she asked.

"My companion."

Her brows furrowed. Companion?

"My fiilee."

Her gaze narrowed. When she got him alone, she would rip him apart, the dirty, secret-keeping liar.

"We will need to introduce your men to the fiilee before battle. They need to get acquainted with our companions." The queen's voice floated toward them.

"It will be arranged."

Sage released Skye and turned toward the two rulers.

"It's been a pleasure to meet with you, King Marq."

"And I you, Queen Osir. May the wind favor your return home."

The queen grinned and swung up onto her fiilee's back, sitting just behind its shoulder blades. "Thank you and safe travels. If you have need, you know how to reach us." She straightened, looking everything like the heroine of a story book on the back of her mythical steed.

Marq stepped back as the fiilee's wings spread, readying for flight.

Sage turned to Raziel and held her hand out. "Well met."

He glanced to Rafe and back to her before clasping her forearm.

"I would have enjoyed calling you family," he said with a glint in his eyes.

Sage squeezed his forearm a little harder than necessary. The man had a little bit of the devil inside him. He obviously knew of her past with Rafe. "Don't be so sure. I'm a tough woman to live with. Too much independence." Heat suffused her back.

"She's a challenge, but well worth it. Life is never dull."

Raziel gazed over her head at Tehl. "Of that I'm sure."

Tehl slipped his hand into hers and led her away from Skye. Nali huffed as they approached her, her tail flicking in annoyance.

"Oh, stop pouting," Sage said. "You know I love you best."

Marq, Zachael, Gav, and William joined them and watched as the warriors mounted the fiilee.

Queen Osir smiled. "Until we meet again."

Marq lifted a hand and the fiilee launched upward, their huge wings stirring the air around them. Sage brushed her hair from her eyes and watched until she couldn't see them any longer.

"You have much explaining to do," the king said, turning to Rafe.

"You understand why I couldn't tell you."

"I do, and that's why I'm not angry. But I am curious as to how a Methian prince ends up in my kingdom, on my council."

Rafe winced and swept a hand toward where they'd left the horses. "A story I'd be happy to tell when we're at the palace."

"All right." The king patted Rafe on the shoulder. "Don't think you can avoid me. I have two sons and a nephew."

Sage smiled and glanced at Tehl and Gav who exchanged smiles that were a bit evil. "I can't wait to hear this story as well."

Rafe sighed. "How angry are you?" he asked as they strode after the king.

"She hasn't started yelling," Gav said. "That's a good sign."

"Yet," she said.

He had so much explaining to do.

CHAPTER THIRTY-SEVEN

Tehl

Sage stumbled into their room, and Tehl shut the door behind them. He hid his smile as she yanked her boots off and tossed them across the room before crawling into their bed.

"You're not going to change?" he asked, pulling his belt and sword from his waist.

A grumble.

"What was that?"

"Too tired," came the muffled reply.

He chuckled and splashed water on his face from the wash basin. He was exhausted and yet... something buzzed in his veins. Something all Sage's doing. Tehl ran his wet fingers through his hair and smiled to himself. During what he'd remember as Rafe's confession, she'd cuddled into his side, her head on his shoulder. It was the best feeling. For the first time since his mother died, he'd felt like he was home.

He tugged his shirt off. Everything had changed tonight. The Methians and their fiilee were a godsend. "I half expected you to climb onto Skye tonight and fly away," he joked. "You couldn't stop touching the beast. I'm sure you made a friend for life." A light snore caught his attention. "Sage?"

He spun and leaned against the dresser, crossing his arms. Sage had sprawled out in the middle of the bed, her dark hair fanned out around her, lips parted in sleep. Tenderness flooded him at the sight of his woman.

His woman.

A streak of possessiveness went through him. She was unequivocally his, and he found that he liked it. A lot.

He shook his head and pushed off the dresser, rounding the bed. He grinned as a stubborn strand of tangled hair lay across her face, dangerously close to being sucked into her mouth.

"What am I going to do with you?" he muttered, and exhaled a soft laugh. Another snore answered him. He brushed the hair from her cheek, shaking his head. Sage was a beautiful disaster.

Tehl blew out the candle and gingerly crawled into the bed. He stared at her face, bathed in soft firelight. For once, she didn't look like she was in pain, her expression clear and at peace. He wished she'd stay that way. But inevitably, the nightmares would strike. He couldn't remember the last time either of them had slept the night through.

He reached out and traced one of her eyebrows and then the bridge of her nose, her skin like silk. Tehl froze as her lashes fluttered, but she didn't wake. She snuggled into his chest, her sigh heating his cheek.

This woman. She changed everything.

He brushed her shoulder and then curled his arm around her

waist, her body molding to his. She had suffered horrors and, yet, she'd given him her trust. Something he'd not take lightly. This was the feeling his father had talked about, and now that Tehl had it in his arms?

He pulled her a little closer, his fingers splayed across her back. He would never let her go.

This was everything.

CHAPTER THIRTY-EIGHT

Sage

Awareness slowly crept in, and with it, the feeling of being suffocated. She cracked her eyes open and discovered the source of her affliction.

Tehl had thrown his leg over hers and was currently wrapped around her like an octopus. She lifted her head a smidge and squinted at the windows. It was too early to tell what time it was. Sage lowered her head and stared at the ceiling. What had woken her up? Usually, it was nightmares, but those left her with a pounding heart and bile in her mouth. She suffered neither of those things.

She turned her head and stared at Tehl. Stars above, there was so much love in her heart for that man. Her husband was a diamond in the rough. Her gaze dropped to her belly as his hand moved, his fingers caressing the skin between her trousers and shirt. Sage glanced back at his face, her breath catching.

He stared at her, sleepiness clinging to him in way that was beyond appealing.

"Nightmare?" he rumbled.

No. More like the best dream she'd had in a long time.

He shifted closer, his fingers brushing the skin of her belly, causing it to swoop. All she had to do was say the words. It would be easy to give in to his curious touches without saying what needed to be said.

His brows furrowed. "What's wrong?"

"Nothing," she whispered, twisting her hands together as anxiety fluttered through her. She'd been planning what she wanted to say. But now that the moment was here? She wasn't ready.

"That's a lie if I ever heard one."

Sage winced. "Life keeps surprising me. I made a vow when I woke up in the infirmary, but it's proving more difficult than I anticipated."

"How so, love?"

Her heart fluttered at the endearment. "It's hard to explain."

"You've never been one to beat around the bush. Out with it."

All the things she wanted to say tripped over in her head, but nothing escaped her lips. Tehl smiled at her and squeezed her hip as if encouraging her. But, somehow, she'd lost her voice. Why was this so hard to say?

"Could you close your eyes?"

"What?"

"Close your eyes, please."

He arched a brow at her, but did as she asked.

Sage stared at him, her pulse picking up speed as she collected her thoughts.

"When I met you," she began haltingly.

"You mean when I caught you," he said, cracking an eye.

She smacked him on the arm and gave him a hard look. Tehl grinned and closed his eyes once again. She pulled in a deep breath and tried again. "When you caught me in that alley, I thought you were the vilest knave on the surface of the earth."

His brows slashed together, but he kept his eyes closed.

"Then, I was forced into the company of your friends and family. I still didn't like you, but I figured someone who was surrounded by such wonderful people had to have redeeming qualities."

"Charming," he muttered.

"Hush, you," she chastised. "Let me finish. Then I was sold to you." His eyes flew open, and she held her hand up. "You gave me the choice. *You*, not them. I appreciated that, even if I didn't show it at the time. We've fought each other, invisible enemies, and the ghosts of our pasts." Specifically, hers.

"In Scythia, you kept me sane," she whispered. "You were with me every step of the way. You protected me, urged me to never give up, and, even when I ignored you, you never abandoned me. You kept me from dying there, from giving in."

"Sage," he murmured, his sapphire gaze drawing her in, robbing her of her breath. His fingers caressed her cheek. "I wish you never were there in the first place."

Her eyes slid closed as she gripped his wrist, and held his palm to her cheek. "As do I, but we can't change the past, no matter how much we wish to. I'm just so sorry that it took me this long to realize what it all meant."

"Realize what?" His question was quiet, and had an edge to it.

She brushed a finger over his stubbled jawline and leaned

forward, gently brushing her lips across his. Easing back, she boldly met his gaze. She'd never been a coward, and she wouldn't be one now by having him close his eyes.

"You were the one my mind chose to protect me. Not my mum, Lilja, or Gav. *You*. All along, I'd cast you as the monster, but you never were. You are the hero to my story. You are my epic love."

His eyes widened, emotion tightening his features. "You love me?"

She nodded, as tears gathered at the corners of her eyes. "I have for a long time, but Peg sealed it."

He grinned, his gaze suspiciously shiny. "I knew you'd love that damn horse. She is the equine version of you." He pressed his forehead to hers and closed his eyes. "Since the moment I met you, I wanted you." He puffed out a breath. "I couldn't understand why. You were the enemy, mouthy, and as prickly as a porcupine. But I liked you."

He opened his eyes and pulled back, apparently searching her face for something. "Are you sure it's me you want? I know things can be confusing for you at times," he asked.

"I'm more sure about loving you than I've been about anything else in my life."

He stilled, and his eyes seemed to burn her. His hand curled around the back of her neck and he pulled her close, his lips brushing hers. "You slay me. Lead, sweet wife, and I will follow. Everything I am is bound to you until we depart this world."

She blinked hard as he repeated part of their vows. "Until we depart this world," she whispered across his lips.

That was the breaking point.

His lips crushed hers, fierce and demanding. It wasn't gentle. It wasn't skilled. *It was everything.* He kissed her like his life depended on it. She looped her arms around his neck and kissed him with every fiber of her being.

Her hands sank into his hair, as he deepened the kiss. Warmth swept through her middle when his fingers slid down her neck and over her shoulder. He pulled her hard against him and turned. Sage gasped as he came down on top of her, his weight pressing her into the bed.

As the room started to spin, she tore her mouth from his and panted for air. He instantly claimed her jaw, lips trailing up to her ear, then along the side of her neck.

"Lucky," he murmured. His teeth grazed her skin and she shivered.

"What?" she breathed, staring blurrily at the low fire.

He pulled away and pushed himself upright. Kneeling between her thighs, he stared down at her with glazed, burning eyes. "Lucky. I'm the luckiest man."

She swallowed hard, trying not to cry. *She* was the lucky one. She traced a pattern along his muscular thigh. "We both won."

He scanned her face and leaned down again, bracing himself on his elbows. "Sage." He clasped her cheeks between his palms and stared at her. Slowly, he kissed her, his lips tender, but edged with a desperation they both felt. "Let me love you?"

Heat flashed through her body, and a flush crept into her cheeks. This wasn't something she had to think about. She knew her answer already.

Sage curled her hand around his neck. "Yes."

He pulled in a deep breath, some of the tension in his body dispelling. Then he was kissing her again. Slow, deep, drugging kisses she never wanted to surface from. He found the buttons of her vest and undid them, brushing aside the leather. His mouth drifted to her chin, and Sage arched her neck as he kissed down her throat to the hollow between her collarbones.

A memory slammed into her.

She sucked a deep breath when his hand slid down, fingers brushing across the tender skin under her jaw then trailing over her abused neck.

She turned her head to the side to break the kiss. The warlord's mouth traveled across her jaw and along the side of her neck, following the path of his hand. His fingers caught the edge of her robe and pushed the fabric off her shoulder. The cold air made her shiver, and her eyes slammed open as he nipped at her collarbone.

Sage gasped, and squeezed her eyes closed. The warlord had no place here. He didn't get to ruin everything. He didn't get to be part of this.

"Love?" Tehl asked, nuzzling her cheek. "Are you all right?"

She forced herself to breathe normally and opened her eyes, guilt almost drowning her. Even now, the warlord invaded her mind. "I'm sorry," she croaked.

He gave her a tender look. "You have nothing to be sorry about."

Tehl began to pull away, but she seized his arms to keep him from escaping. The warlord would not ruin this. She wouldn't allow it.

"No."

"No?"

"No," she said pulling him close to kiss him. "This is about us."

Her lips curled into a smile as his glazed eyes met hers. His finger caught in the linen of her shirt, exposing her shoulder. She shivered from the touch of cool air and as his mouth moved across her bare shoulder, his fingers skating over her body. Her skin heated, and she blushed as she ran her own hands along his arms and shoulders.

This was how it was supposed to be. Mutual love and desire. The need for his skin on hers.

She dragged her fingers up his neck and through his dark hair, her teeth nipping at his lips. He rumbled his pleasure, which had her lips curling against his. There was something gratifying about pleasing the one you loved. Heat scorched her cheeks as she contemplated her next move and then followed through.

Sage reached between their bodies and slid her hands over the hard planes of his abdomen and up his chest. Stars above, he was perfect.

He stilled and then sat up. The firelight haloed his dark form, shadowing his expression from her. He reached for the hem of her shirt and paused, asking an unspoken question. Sage gathered her bravery around her and sat up, pulling the vest and shirt over her head. Goosebumps broke across her arms as her body was exposed to him.

"No corset?" he whispered, his voice rough.

Sage crossed her arms over her chest and glanced toward the balcony windows. She shrugged one shoulder. "They're uncomfortable and not practical when fighting."

She jumped when his hand circled her wrists and gently pulled her arms away from her body.

"Don't hide from me. You're stunning."

She peeked at him from beneath her lashes and was almost burned by the heat in his gaze. "Such beauty should *never* be hidden from your husband." His eyes drank her in as he leaned closer and placed a kiss over her heart. "Never."

He lowered himself onto her, and, again, his mouth found hers.

His fingers moved to the button of her trousers, no hesitation this time. She inhaled sharply as he slid the fabric down, and his fingertips grazed her thighs as he traced the lines of her body. Her breath hitched at his teasing touch. An unexpected giggle escaped her when his fingers explored the back of her knees.

He halted, and grinned. "You're ticklish, love?"

"Maybe." She wouldn't give him that information.

A dangerous glint entered his blue eyes. "We'll come back to this," he growled as his fingers began their journey again, running over her hips, the curve of her waist, her chest, and then back down. Each touch was deliberate, like he was trying to memorize every inch of her.

He kissed her again, his mouth hot and relentless. The world narrowed to just Tehl and her, and all she could do was hold onto him and remember to breathe.

All thoughts fled when the last vestige of her clothing disappeared along with his. Her breath hitched as Tehl stared at her, awe apparent on his face.

"I've never seen anything so precious and beautiful," he whispered. He nuzzled her neck, his tongue darting out to trace her throat.

Any nerves she had disappeared with his soft, honest words. Sage smiled as he pressed a tender kiss to her cheek.

"So perfect," he murmured.

She relaxed and brushed her fingers along her husband's sides, marveling at his strength. His breathing picked up and the world fell away when he pressed his body against hers, his touch growing wilder. She sank her fingers into his inky hair and yanked his mouth to hers, demanding more.

No doubts. No pain. Just love.

"I want you more than I've ever wanted anything," he panted against her lips. "This is everything."

"Everything," she echoed, when he guided her legs around his waist and they melded into one. Her fingers dug into his shoulders, and her eyes widened, breath completely leaving her.

He kissed her softly, cradling her in his arms. Tehl stroked her face, her lips, her eyebrows. He trembled and rested his forehead against hers, as if he was fighting to restrain himself. His dark lashes fluttered against her cheeks, and then deep blue eyes met hers.

"Only me," he whispered.

"Only you," she whispered.

His smile was blinding, and then, he *moved.* For a moment she wasn't sure if it was pleasure or pain, or a blend of both. All she knew was that it changed everything. Her awareness narrowed to nothing but him, his love, his touch, his kiss, and their bodies together.

Tonight was theirs.

CHAPTER THIRTY-NINE

Tehl

There was something wrong with him. Tehl couldn't look away from her.

Sage slept in his arms, her warm, naked body pressed to his. The fire burned low, and the light was muted, painting her pale skin a soft golden hue that he wanted to taste. Again.

He felt whole. Happy. And nowhere near sated. Even now, he wanted her again, to lounge in bed with her for days like they should have done at the beginning.

She sighed in his arms as he adjusted to her, and ran his hand along her spine, reveling in the silky skin. The differences between them intrigued him. Where he was calloused and rough, she was soft. His gaze flicked down the bed to the tangled sheets and discarded clothes. His lips twitched. She didn't wear a corset. That would prove to be distracting now that he knew.

He glanced back at his wife. Her whole being was distracting.

Sage snuggled into his chest, her long strands of hair a crazy mess around her head. He stifled his chuckle. Once her hair escaped its confines, it turned into an entity of itself.

"You're staring," she said, not opening her eyes.

Tehl pressed a kiss to her forehead, his gaze drifting to said hair. "It's alive."

She thumped his arm and opened her eyes, smiling. "It can't be helped."

He swallowed, emotion rocking him. Who knew his wild, rebel wife would bring so much joy into his life? She had her flaws, granted. She was stubborn and held a grudge. But he'd take the good with the bad. The good out-shadowed all the bad.

She blinked. "What are you thinking?"

He ran his hand along her shoulder and scanned her face. "Did I hurt you?" It had been on his mind since he'd woken. The first time was always painful for a woman, and he didn't want her to have any regrets.

A smile darted across her lips. "I dare say it was quite the opposite. Most enjoyable night I've ever had."

His body tightened as she ran her foot up his calf. "You aren't sore?"

She blushed at his blunt question. "Yes, and no." Her fingers brushed his chest. "I didn't expect it to be like that."

"Yes," he murmured. It could drive a man wild. No wonder Gav was so distracted after he married. Fingers brushed his thigh, causing his hands to press harder into her spine. Stars above. He was in so much trouble.

"I wouldn't mind if we..." Her cheeks heated again.

He grinned and traced the blush with a finger. She was brash most of the time, but, add sex into the mix, and now she was shy.

"I would love to touch you," he groaned. "But your body needs time to heal, and I would like to care for you before reality knocks at our door."

"Care for me?"

"Bathe with me." It wasn't really a question. "Let me care for my wife." It was something his father had beaten into him. He and Sam were to always care for their wives.

Sage shifted against him, watching him with lazy abandon. "I would love to bathe with you." She slapped a hand against her belly as it growled, and she gave him a silly smile. "Sorry."

He grinned and swiftly kissed her lips. "Food is on its way, love. I'll draw a bath." He popped from the bed, and Sage hissed. He spun with a raised eyebrow and followed her gaze to the red smear on the sheet. She jerked the blanket over it, hiding it from his view.

Tehl rounded the bed and sat next to his wife, who refused to look at him. "Don't be ashamed. This is not shameful. It's wonderful. Thank you for giving yourself to me. Your innocence is something I will always cherish."

She peeked at him over her shoulder. "You're so blunt and then, every once in a while, you say just the right thing."

He smiled and opened the drawer of the side table, pulling out a handkerchief. Corner by corner, he moved the fabric out of the way to reveal the treasure he had hidden there. Two silver cuffs sat in his hand. His heartbeat picked up as Sage leaned close and ran a finger along the decorative cuffs he'd made for her.

"I made them for you, since the other ones were lost."

"How long have you had these?" she whispered.

"I started working on them as soon as we returned."

"Why wait until now to give them to me?"

He cleared his throat and stared at his wife. "Because I wanted you to *want* to wear them. I wanted it to be truly your choice."

Sage smiled. "I want to wear them." She held out her wrists. "Will you put them on?"

The nervousness in her belly evaporated. She wanted this as much as he did. Sage gasped as he turned the cuff over, so she could see the inside.

"What's this?"

"I thought you'd like it." He touched the horse with wings engraved on the inside. "Peg makes you feel free. I wanted you to be able to carry her wherever you go. And know that even though we are bound, you will never be caged."

A fat, salty tear dripped down her cheek as he slid both cuffs into place.

"Thank you. I love them." She wiped the tear away and held her arms out to stare at her cuffs. "I'll wear them with pride." Sage threw an arm around him and kissed his left cheek. "Where are yours?"

He pulled his cuffs from the same drawer, eager to wear them. Sage plucked them from his hands and slid a cuff onto each of his biceps. They stared at each other for a moment, both grinning.

"Why are you so smiley?" she teased. "You happy to have your cuffs on me?"

"Beyond pleased." He kissed her shoulder, not able to help himself. "Maybe it's because my wife shared my bed," he tacked on, feeling lighter than he had in ages.

"My bed." Sage smiled impishly. "You should share my bed every day. It'll improve your diplomatic skills. Really, it would be best for our kingdom."

Apparently, she had no idea how appealing that was, and how

much he wanted to pounce on her. "You tease," he accused and forced himself to leave the bed. If he didn't, they'd stay there all day.

"Only for you," she called as he entered the bathing room.

***

He glared at all the clothing that hid her body from his view. It seemed like a travesty to cover such beauty.

"Stop pouting," she said, rolling her eyes. "You're the one who said we needed to be responsible."

"I'm regretting that decision now," he muttered. Her answering peal of laughter had him smiling.

She tossed her braid over her shoulder and winked at him. "Men, you all are always so predictable."

He growled and wrapped an arm around her waist, pulling her back into his chest. "I'm not the only one who enjoyed our time in the bath." Her skin pinked. He grinned wickedly. He knew she enjoyed teasing him and now he had the perfect weapon with which to tease her.

Sage opened her mouth to retort when there was a knock at their door. She scowled. "It was only a matter of time."

"Indeed."

He let her go, and she pulled open the door. "Sam."

His brother entered, and closed the door behind him as Sage moved back to Tehl's side to strap on the rest of her daggers. Sam eyed the two of them and then the bed. He froze and glanced away, a secret smile on his face as he met Tehl's eyes, his gaze dropping to the cuffs circling Tehl's biceps.

His brother arched a brow. All Tehl could do was smile. He had a wife in truth now. Everything was as it should be. His grin widened. Nothing compared to what he shared with his wife. It was as close to magic as he could imagine.

"So who's demanding our presence this morning?" Sage asked, buckling her last sheath around her thigh.

"Morning has come and gone. It's late in the afternoon."

Tehl's eyes widened as Sam grinned. Ah hell.

"What have you been doing all day?"

Sage blinked, and her mouth bobbed, at a loss for words.

"Enough," Tehl said, casting an apologetic glance at his wife. "What do you need?"

Sam's smile melted, his expression blank. "There's news."

"Has another village been attacked?" Sage asked.

"No, but Scythia's army has been spotted."

"How far from the Mort Wall?" Tehl demanded.

"A day's walk from the Potam River."

So close. "Our soldiers need to be moved there immediately."

"Gav has them moving already. A camp will be set up shortly."

Tehl snatched his sword from the side table and buckled the belt around his waist. "We depart within the hour."

"The men are assembling now." Sam stared at the floor. "There's more."

"What is it?"

"I married last night."

Tehl blinked. "That's not funny."

"Do you think I would joke of my marriage?" Sam asked seriously.

Why in the world would he get married? Then it occurred to him. His hands curled into fists, and he glared at his brother. "*Who* did you compromise?" He took a step forward, but a hand stopped him. Tehl glanced down at his wife. She wasn't looking at him, but her narrowed eyes were focused on Sam.

"It's done," she said. "There are much more pressing matters to deal with. His marriage hardly matters in the light of other things." She stepped closer to Sam and hugged the bastard. "My congratulations."

Sam stared over her shoulder at him as he hugged Sage. "Thank you," he said softly.

His brother didn't even look sorry. "Mum would be so disappointed."

Sam's face tightened, showing a flicker of hurt before he schooled his expression.

Sage released his brother and stepped back. "Who is the lucky woman?"

Sam focused on Sage. "Jasmine."

Tehl sucked in a sharp breath. "Out of all the women…" He broke off when Sage slapped Sam.

Sage poked Sam in the chest. "Shame on you! She's a good person." She heaved in a deep breath. "I know I'm missing other pieces to the puzzle, but I'm too angry to figure out what they are right now. Leave, before I get the feeling back in my hand and I'm tempted to slap you again."

Sam nodded, a red handprint on his left cheek. He strode to the door.

"Sam," Sage called. He paused by the door and glanced back at her. "I'm upset, but I still love you."

Sam glanced to Tehl and then back to Sage. "Love you too, sis."

Tehl rounded on Sage as soon as the door shut. "Why were you so easy on him? What he's done is deplorable. It's shameful."

"Your brother is a good man. Every decision he makes is calculated."

True. After all these years, his brother had been discreet enough that he never had to marry any of the girls he dallied with. Why now? "You think he compromised her on purpose?"

"It's a thought, but I don't know why."

"My brother is not one to be easily understood." He shook his head. "It matters not now. The deed is done." He drifted closer to Sage and stared down into her face. "I won't ask you not to go."

"If you did, I'd ignore you."

"This is your battle as much as mine. But I wish…" That they had more time. His gaze dropped farther, to her flat belly. His hands curled around her hips and pulled her close. "Last night could have resulted in a child."

"I'm sure that's not the case," she argued.

"But it's a possibility. War is never quick or easy. If you show signs, you will leave the battlefield, understood?"

She stared at her belly and then met his gaze. "If there is a child, I will leave."

He bent and kissed her lips, thankful she was being reasonable. "Prepare yourself, love. I'll be waiting for you with Peg."

Tehl pressed one more quick kiss to her lips and forced himself from their room. He couldn't think about how easily Sage could be hurt in the coming months. He would trust her and protect her to the best of his ability.

No one was taking her from him. Sage was finally his.

Together, they'd rid the world of the monsters.

CHAPTER FORTY

SAGE

Sage stared out at the ocean, her body slowly going numb. Scythia approached. He was coming for her. She knew it was only a matter of time before he hunted her down. Her gaze dropped to the waves crashing below, their siren call still there, but much less appealing.

She hissed and spun, storming inside. Even now she could feel the tell-tale panic trying to claw up her throat. Her reflection caught her attention, her steps pausing by the mirror. Every time she looked at herself, she saw the warlord. The product of his tampering.

Her hand wandered to her bare throat. He had no power over her anymore. She was free, and despite the changes to her physique, she was still herself. Cool, emerald eyes stared back at her, as cold as the light armor covering her arms and chest. If was ironic, really. The armor protected her body, but it was her mind that needed the protecting.

"Sage?"

She jumped and glanced at the door. Blaise stood in the doorway, watching with evident concern. The Scythian closed the door softly and leaned against it.

"He won't win," Blaise stated.

"Who are you trying to convince? Me or yourself? You and I both know we're not ready for war."

"Aermia is ready. You aren't."

She grimaced and turned back to the mirror, hating that Blaise was right. She wanted to pretend none of it ever happened. She wanted to forget.

"You can't pretend he's not out there. You can't wish him away. You need to fight, or he wins."

"I'm not strong enough." There. She'd said the words that had been haunting her for weeks. She was scared to be near the warlord. What if he messed with her mind again? Could she even trust herself?

Blaise moved to her side and stared at the mirror. Sage stared at her friend's reflection, eyeing the painted, swirling patterns that adorned the exposed part of Blaise's right arm. It was beautiful in a terrifying way. Blaise had always been stunning with her olive skin and dark hair, but the paint added a touch of danger.

Her friend pulled a small container from her pocket and plopped it down on the vanity. "Sit," she ordered. "And face me."

Sage turned and sat slowly, staring up at Blaise. "What now?"

"You sit still, and you listen."

Blaise leaned over her and opened the little container, pungent herbs filling the air. She dipped her thumb into the black sludge and pulled it back. She gave Sage an inscrutable look and lifted her chin up.

"Many years ago, my ancestors created the Tia paint. It was a rite of passage, if you will. Close your eyes."

Sage closed her eyes and shivered as Blaise smeared cold paint from her forehead to her eyes, and then down to her cheek.

"Keep them closed." Blaise shifted and began drawing on Sage's face again. "Birth is a miraculous thing. It's always been difficult for women as a whole. Only the strongest survive such a brutal experience. When the time came, the medicine women would paint an expectant mother's face. It was said to help her fight, to embolden her in the face of such pain and the possibility of death."

"I'm not with child."

"The tradition evolved. When war between clans erupted, as it always does, the men started to wear the face paint as a symbol of what they were fighting for: their women and children. It wasn't simply war paint, but a mark of their devotion and dedication to those they loved."

She spun Sage around. "Open your eyes."

Sage opened her eyes and stared at the painted woman in the mirror. Dark charcoal lined her eyes, causing the green to pop. Three bold lines slashed through her left brow and down to her cheek. Black dots followed the underside of her right brow and extended from her eye in three separate lines. Her gaze zeroed in on her obsidian lips. The creature in the mirror didn't look like her, and yet, when she smiled, so did her reflection.

Blaise placed her hands on Sage's shoulders and squeezed, pulling her attention from her reflection.

"You are not the woman he held in his cage. That Sage is dead and gone. He forged you into something else, not his pawn, but his demise." Blaise smiled, but it wasn't nice. "You are his greatest mistake. You are not his consort. *You* are his judgement, his enemy, and his ultimate destruction."

"I am not his consort," Sage whispered. "I am his destruction."

"You are his death."

"I am his death."

"My mother would have never risked her plans for you if you weren't important. She believed you would bring change. I believe that as well." Blaise hugged her from behind and rested her chin on Sage's shoulder. "We are sisters in arms, you and I."

"Sisters in arms," Sage murmured. "I will fight."

"And I will stand at your side. That monster will regret ever hurting those we love."

The ember of rage that always seemed to smolder in Sage's gut, ignited. She was his greatest weakness.

To eradicate the darkness, she had to become darkness.

He'd never see her coming.

CHAPTER FORTY-ONE

The Warlord

They thought they were so clever. They were children really, playing at being warriors. They had no idea what the future held.

Zane smiled as he watched the Aermian army scurry about like ants as they built their camps.

Ignorant.

They were ignorant of his spies. Ignorant that their greatest enemy walked among them. A leren among babes.

He stilled and glanced over his shoulder, as awareness tingled over his skin. A sixth sense that she was near. He narrowed his eyes on the approaching party. The crown prince lead the group, but Zane didn't care. He only had eyes for one person. The goddess in armor and war paint.

"Sage," he whispered, all covetousness and possession. His consort stole his breath away, her beauty so bright it felt like it burned him where he stood.

He kept his head bowed as the group passed him, his fingers brushed her cloak for one second before he receded into the bustling camp. He could steal her away now, but that would be too easy.

His consort has challenged him, and he loved a good fight. No, he wouldn't take her this day. He'd wait for her surrender, and it would be all the more sweet.

Zane adjusted his cloak, and grinned.

Soon enough she'd bow to him. All he needed was a little patience. His consort would grace him with her presence soon enough.

Then he'd destroy her world.

To be continued in Spy's Mask...

If you'd like more info on the next book, sign up for updates from Frost!
https://www.subscribepage.com/frostkayFREEebook_copy

Thank you for reading KING'S WARRIOR. I hope you enjoyed it! If you liked this book, please review it BECAUSE the review rating determines which series I prioritize. If you want the next book in this series soon, review this book♡ Thank you!

Read on for a sneak peek of Lilja and Hayjen's story!

Chapter One
Hayjen

Life was never simple. Months on the cursed ship taught him that.

Hayjen stared from his floating prison at the death trap surrounding him. The seductive black waves lapped below, beckoning, whispering to him to take the chance, to seize his freedom. Luminescent coral cast soft light below the obsidian waves offering a lie, a hope that one could survive the harsh sea if one stayed in the light, but Hayjen knew better. Just past the comforting glow of the coral, a beast hunted—so deadly that no one chanced the sea at night.

He shivered as a shiny, midnight fin sliced through the water, before silently disappearing into the inky waves.

A Leviathan.

He wouldn't make it two arms' lengths before it dragged him below and killed him. His lips lifted into a grim smile. It might not be such a bad way to go compared to what the Scythians had planned for him.

"Hayjen?" a small voice called.

Turning his head, he sought the unruly mop of white blond hair. Mer, a little girl who had been captured a couple weeks after he had, peeked at him over the top of a barrel. Her soft lilac eyes crinkled at the corners as she smiled at him, revealing a large gap where her tooth used to be. She scuttled from behind the barrel and slipped her small hand into his, their cuffs clinking together.

"What are you doing?"

What was he doing?

Hayjen stared at the tiny pale hand in his rough tan one. He could see her blue veins through her delicate skin. Mer was so fragile. His heart squeezed. This was why he couldn't escape. His gaze latched on to her sweet face, gazing at him with adoration. He couldn't leave Mer to the Scythians' cruelty. For some reason, they delighted in tormenting the little one. If he hadn't stepped in and given her some of his slop, she would've starved a long time ago. He also had his sister to think of. Where was she now? Was she okay?

"Hayjen?"

Hayjen blew out a breath and gave Mer his most brilliant smile. "I'm enjoying the view."

Her lilac eyes darted to the rolling black waves—they widened with excitement when a fin cut through the water. Mer stabbed a finger at the water, practically bouncing on her toes. "A Leviathan!"

"Only you would get excited over a Leviathan."

"They're nice. When I get bigger, I want one as a pet."

That made him snort. "I doubt that they would want to be kept as a pet." He tickled her neck. "I think they would probably want to snack on you."

Mer giggled. "No, they just like the way I smell. One sniffed me today."

Hayjen stiffened. What was she talking about? He knelt and placed his hands on her dainty shoulders. "How did they sniff you?" he questioned, attempting to keep his heart from beating out of his chest.

A little shrug. "I was hot, so I asked if I could go for a swim, and the mean man threw me in. The Leviathan were happy to have someone to play with."

Bile burned the back of his throat. They had thrown a little girl into Leviathan-infested waters? Unconsciously, his hands started to skim over her for injuries. "You swam with the Leviathan?" he croaked, trying to not throw up as he said the words.

Her innocent smile almost broke his heart. "Yep! We played tag. They darted in and bumped me with their noses before speeding off. I wish I was that fast in the water. When I got tired, one let me hold onto its fin. I got to ride one, Hayjen! Mama always said that one day I would be able to."

He sucked in a deep breath and considered Mer's unique lilac eyes. "You must not swim with the Leviathan again, Mer. It's dangerous."

"But they're my friends."

"I understand you had a wonderful time today, but they're not safe."

"They didn't hurt me."

"No more, Mer."

Her jaw jutted out stubbornly. "I like them."

If reason wasn't going to work, he had to scare her. "They like to eat people."

Her eyes bulged. "Eat people?" she squeaked.

"Yes." He nodded gravely. "Leviathan eat people, and I love you too much for you to be eaten, so please stay out of the water, for me." Hayjen watched her emotions flicker across her face until settling into resignation.

"I guess. I don't want to be eaten."

"Me neither." He pulled her into his arms and hugged her tightly. She could have died. Those bastards threw her in the water expecting her to be eaten. Fury boiled through his veins. She was just a little girl. Dropping a kiss onto the crown of her head, Hayjen pulled back and chucked her under the chin. "It's time for bed, little one."

"Awww…" she pouted.

"None of that. Let's go."

Mer skipped ahead, and bounded down the stairs leaving him behind. He took one last look at the sea, and put his fantasies of freedom behind him. There wouldn't be any escape for him tonight. Hayjen strode to the stairs and descended into the belly of the ship. He wove around hammocks swaying from the ceiling, filled with sleeping slaves. He was one of the few men captured. Hayjen hadn't believed the rumors that Scythians were stealing people. He was minding his own business fishing one day when he was stolen. His rigging was tied up, the ship approached and offered him help. They looked like a run of the mill merchant ship, right up until the moment they knocked him out. When he woke up, he was cuffed to the wall, bleeding with no idea where he was. He was alone at first, that is until Mer was captured a few weeks later. She looked so pitiful, sopping wet and shaking like a leaf. When she wouldn't stop crying, one of the men cuffed her so hard behind the ear, she flew forward into the mast unconscious. Hayjen made a decision then. He'd protect her.

She was a peculiar little girl, but she had wormed her way into his heart immediately. Even now, months later, he still didn't know much about her family. Mer couldn't remember much. He didn't know if it was due to the blow to her head, her age, or her mind protecting her from a traumatic event.

Hayjen spotted Mer swinging in her hammock. Carefully, he caught it, and gave her a stern look. "It's time for bed."

"Okay." She snuggled down and looked up at him expectantly. "A song?"

Her angelic face, so full of hope, ensnared him. How could he say no? "One song. Just one." He knelt down next to her and sang a song his mum used to sing to him as a child. Her eyes hooded as sleep tried to take her. At the end, she slipped her hand into his.

"Prayer?"

"Anything for you, baby girl." He didn't feel particularly thankful at the moment, but it calmed her. After uttering a few words of thanks, her little eyes closed and stayed closed. Hayjen brushed the blond fuzz from her cheek, admiring the planes of her face. She reminded him of his sister Gwen. After their parents died, he would tuck her into bed and say a prayer with her, even though he was only a handful of years older than she was.

Mer released a soft sigh and smiled in her sleep. He could have lost her today. Rage bubbled at the thought. They had thrown her into Leviathan-infested waters. How did she survive? Leviathan were known for being extremely aggressive and eating just about anything. It didn't make sense. He dropped a kiss on her forehead and wove through the swinging hammocks. He needed to have a word with the captain. He most likely would receive a whipping for saying anything. It wasn't the first time, nor would it be the last.

***

When Hayjen spotted Leth, it was all he could do not to tear his head off. Leth was an extremely tall, widely-built man with cheekbones so sharp you could cut yourself on them. The first mate had a particularly mean streak. He enjoyed causing suffering and pain. Hayjen had received lashes for just looking at the man the wrong way. He blew out a breath—he needed to execute this with care. Steeling himself, he strode toward Leth. The Scythian first mate spotted him and jerked his chin towards Hayjen, pulling the other Scythians' attention. He clenched his jaw at the slurs thrown his way and halted before the group. "I need to speak with the captain."

Leth pushed off his chair and moved to stand in front of him. "The slave demands to see the captain. What does a slave need with the captain?"

Hayjen tipped his chin up to meet the first mate's eyes. "One of his slaves almost died today."

Leth chuckled, his cronies joining in. "Why would the captain care about that?"

"Mer was thrown into the sea."

Leth's face screwed up in disgust. "She was unscathed the last time I saw the little brat, unfortunately."

Several men crossed themselves. Something about Mer unnerved them and stirred their hate something fierce. "You threw her to the Leviathan."

"What concern is it of yours? She's not your daughter."

He wasn't getting anywhere arguing with this lout. "I think our captain would be very concerned that his first mate threw one of his valuables overboard."

The laughter cut off, and Leth's eyes narrowed, taking on a menacing glint. "Are you threatening me, slave?" His tone took on a dangerous edge.

"No," Hayjen replied softly. "I am giving you my oath that if the little girl is harmed, I will make the Leviathan look tame."

Waves crashed against the ship as the air around them filled with tension. "You dare to speak to me this way?" hissed Leth. "You are nothing but a blight on this world. Tonight you will be taught a lesson you will never forget, boy."

"So be it. It will change nothing."

The first mate seemed to swell in size, towering over Hayjen. "Tie him to the mast."

He didn't fight as they roughly seized him and dragged him to the mast. It didn't matter if he resisted. In the beginning, he had fought, but quickly he had learned they were all unnaturally stronger than him. Every once in a while, he would land a blow, but the majority of the time it was he that sustained injury. Chain clipped into his metal manacle and bit into the abused flesh around his wrists. His hands were lifted above his head and his shirt cut from his back, exposing his healing lash marks to the cool air. This was going to hurt. He had calmed down for the sake of the girls on the ship to protect them as much as he could. One of the girls, Lera, had refused to sleep with a Scythian and was sentenced to forty lashes for disgracing her betters. He had stepped in and taken the punishment for her. She wouldn't have survived the lashing.

"Slave," Leth's voice leered. "Your very existence sickens me."

A sharp whistle, and then blinding pain. Hayjen choked back a cry as tears stung his eyes. It never got easier. He never became immune to the pain.

"You think you're better than us, but you're not."

More pain.

"You're worthless."

His flesh opened.

"When the time comes, taking your life will be a pleasure."

Another lash. The pain was so intense he couldn't help the bellow that escaped his lips.

"When you're gone, little Mer will be mine," Leth whispered in his ear.

Hayjen threw his head back, crashing it into the first mate's face. A satisfying crunch sounded. No one would hurt the little girl.

"You'll regret that," Leth spat. "And so will the little slave."

"I think not," a feminine voice purred.

Hayjen froze. He didn't recognize the voice. Slowly, he turned his neck and stared at the woman perched on the railing. Her shocking magenta eyes met his.

"Let's play a game, shall we?"

Chapter Two
Lilja

Scanning the deck, Lilja took pleasure in the way the crew of Scythian men gaped at her. She doubted they had ever encountered someone like her and lived to tell the tale. No sign of any of the slaves, other than the one tied to the mast. They had to be below. The tall warrior with the whip drew her attention as he turned towards her. His smile was sensual with a cruel edge. He was dangerous—she could see it in the way his body moved and the intelligent glint in his black eyes. She assumed he was one of the warlord's older creations, a warrior bred and altered to be perfect. She had to be careful with this one.

Cocking her head, she shifted so her naked thigh peeked out of her skirt, the moonlight highlighting her pale flesh. Would he take the bait? Most of the warlord's warriors had so much testosterone running through their bodies that they couldn't help themselves. The ringleader's eyes followed her movement and relaxed a fraction, his gaze running over her exposed skin.

Men. They were so easy to distract sometimes.

She held back her disgust when he licked his lips. "It's not safe for you to be wandering around at this time of night." His cronies laughed around him.

How unoriginal. Did they have a book that they all memorized? One with cliché lines to use on women? She shook her head, and allowed a smoky chuckle to emerge. Time to get down to business. "No, I assure you I am quite safe. It is your own health you should be worrying about."

"I highly doubt that." The ringleader glanced at his men before meeting her eyes with a challenge. "You are quite alone. I, on the other hand, am surrounded."

Surrounded. How appropriate. He was surrounded, he just didn't know it yet. Her crew was as silent as the night and just as deadly. Little did he know that they lurked in the shadows. There would be blood shed tonight, but it would not be hers. Her eyes sharpened, when he took a step towards her.

"I feel like I need to remind you that you are trespassing on my ship, Sirenidae whore." The Scythian leader spat.

So he knew what she was. Good. She wanted him to know it was a creature he deemed unworthy of life that had bested him. It would make her victory that much sweeter.

"Do you know what we do with your kind? We use them and then toss them back to the Leviathan where they belong."

The threat hardly registered. She'd heard worse over the years from indoctrinated Scythians. Their hate for her kind was legendary. Anything different was condemned. That was part of the reason the Sirenidae disappeared into the sea hundreds of years ago. Scythia was becoming too powerful, too dangerous, too radical. Lilja's eyes narrowed as he scanned her again, lingering on areas he had no business looking. His beastly nature was showing itself.

"But I'll make an exception for you. I like my women a little wild with some fight."

She slipped to the deck in a fluid movement and leaned against the rail, fighting to keep her disgust from her face. "When I spoke of games, that wasn't quite what I had in mind."

He shifted and Lilja tensed, knowing what would happen. In the space of a heartbeat he was pressed against her, his arms clasping the rail, caging her in. She wasn't a short woman, but he made her feel downright delicate. The warrior was uncommonly large. Her jaw tensed when he dipped, his lips by her ear. She hated this part.

"What kind of games would you like to play?" he hissed.

She ran her hands up his huge chest and ignored the flare of heat she saw in his eyes. Her fingers fluttered along his collarbone, drawing designs as his breathing became labored. Lilja met his eyes and tipped up onto her toes. He wrapped his hands around her waist and dipped his head so she could speak to him. She met the eyes of a burly man strapped to the mast as she whispered in the warrior's ear. "Lesson number one of hand-to-hand combat. Never let your opponent get too close." She pressed at the base of his skull, using the death touch. His body went slack and crashed to the deck.

There was a beat of silence before the other Scythians charged her. Lilja reached into the folds of her sarong and pulled her twin cutlasses from their sheaths. Her men exploded from the dark and scrambled up the sides of the ship, cutting Scythians down as she cleared a path to the slave. Several Scythians rushed into the fray from below deck, only to be mowed down, despite their biological advantages.

Lilja eyed the slave's back and grimaced. His flesh was laced with old scars and healing lashes that the new beating had ripped open—it was literally cut to ribbons. Would he survive such injuries? Lilja doubted it, but she wouldn't leave him there to die tied to the mast. She slipped to the side and jerked back as his ice blue eyes clashed with hers. Pain, hate, and rage simmered in them, just waiting to be released. She leaned forward until their noses almost touched. "I am going to release you. Don't attack me." Lilja gave him a warning look before straightening and slicing open the ropes.

"Behind you," his hoarse voice warned.

She ducked and slashed her cutlass across the calf of the Scythian attacking her. He bellowed and fell to his knees still viciously stabbing at her. Lilja deftly avoided his attacks and danced around him. She darted in and smashed her pommel against the back of his head. All fight went out of the giant as he crashed to the deck. Breathing hard, she pulled her eyes from the defeated Scythian to the carnage around her. Scythians littered the deck, moaning and cursing. Her gaze swept over her crew as they took care of any stragglers. Female shrieks, curses, and crying floated through the air announcing the arrival of the other slaves. Bedraggled women and girls poured out of the stairway led by her men. From the corner of her eye, she saw the male slave shuffle painfully over to the group.

"Hayjen!" a little girl with silvery blond hair cried.

Lilja's eyes zeroed in on the child. Mer. They had found her niece. She glanced at Lilja as she wrapped her arms around the male, causing him to cry out and fall to his knees. Lilja's heart pinched when there wasn't any recognition in Mer's eyes. This was the price of her ignorance and morals. Her family. Her niece should know her, but life wasn't always fair.

She cocked her head, intrigued as the group of girls surrounded the man, offering help. Curious. Every woman gazed at him with concern or adoration. She'd seen looks like those before. Hero worship.

"Are you okay, Hayjen?" One of the girls asked.

"I'm okay, Lera."

"Captain Femi?"

She pulled her attention from the spectacle and raised an eyebrow in question at her first mate Blair. "Yes?"

"Everyone on the ship is accounted for, Captain."

"Thank you."

"What would you have us do with all the slaves?"

"That's the question of the night, isn't it, Blair?" What would they do with the other slaves? Their priorities were to retrieve the little girl, return her to her parents, and ruin a Scythian ship. It wasn't until they had spotted the ship that they'd found out it was holding more kidnapped victims than just her niece. "I will deal with it."

Lilja strode to the group of slaves, halting five paces away. "Do you have a leader among you?" her voice cut through the dark night.

The man hefted himself up, a groan of pain slipping out. He wiped at the sweat beading across his forehead and pushed his shoulders back, the corner of his eyes pinching. "I am."

He must have been in an inordinate amount of pain, yet he stood before her like a warrior. Lilja was impressed. The little Sirenidae girl placed her little hand on his large, weathered one.

"I have a few questions," Lilja stated.

"I am sure you do, but how about you answer mine first?" His ice blue eyes narrowed. "What do you want with my people, pirate?"

"Nothing, actually." Pirate. She loved being called a pirate. "I hadn't planned on a bushel of slaves being on this ship when I attacked. We love to cause the Scythians grief when we can. I fully intended to burn the ship." The women gasped. "But rest assured, I don't plan on leaving you on this ship while it burns. While I may be in the business of thievery, mayhem, and vengeance, I am not in the business of murder. So if you'd be so kind as to board my ship, The Sirenidae, without carrying on, I would be much obliged to you." Lilja didn't think his eyes could get much colder, but they did.

"And what are you planning on doing with us once we board your ship? Do you have plans to sell us? Because I can tell you, we won't go down without a fight if that is the case."

Lilja eyed him. "A prideful one, aren't you? You're beaten and broken, yet you stand before me with dignity and demand answers. That takes courage." She dipped her chin. "I'll answer your questions. I despise slavery." Lilja jerked her thumb over her shoulder. "Just ask my crew, most of whom I have rescued from some form of slavery. It's a vile, evil practice that I have no aspirations to indulge in. I plan to drop you safely on Aermian soil, hopefully to never see you again."

He studied her, his eyes moving over her face like a physical touch. "What is your name?"

"Captain Lilja Femi at your service," she said as she dipped into a bow. "And to whom am I speaking?"

"Hayjen Fiori."

"Well, Hayjen Fiori, what say you?"

He looked at the women around him before turning back to her. "Do I have your solemn oath none of these women will be harmed in any way, and all will be returned to their families?"

"I promise to give them means to reach their families and that they will come to no harm, but getting to their families will be their responsibility."

Lilja placed her hand on the railing to watch the sea as Hayjen whispered to the women surrounding him. She turned back around when the whispering subsided. Hayjen dipped his chin, his mouth pulled tight by pain. "We accept your terms."

"Great!" She slapped her hands together, and smiled at the women warmly. "Blair!" Her second in command started moving in her direction. "Blair will organize you so that we can move you safely to our ship, The Sirenidae. If any of you need a healer, please let Blair know. May I speak with you for a moment in private, Hayjen?"

He nodded and moved towards her in jerky movements, eyeing her like she was a Leviathan circling him. "Are any of the children yours?" Her question surprised him. He jerked and glanced over his shoulder at Mer, who was sitting on a barrel watching them.

"Yes, the little one with the blond hair."

Lilja pursed her lips. He was lying. Why? Did he know Mer's worth? "I have to say, she looks nothing like you."

"She's adopted."

"I see."

Hayjen glared at her and leaned forward. "Your tone says otherwise. Unless you are going to accuse me of something, keep your questions and opinions to yourself. Mer is *mine.*"

"Now, now, I think you have the wrong impression of me." Lilja gave him her most sultry smile. "I've implied—" a whisper of a sound caught her attention. She turned just as the Scythian ringleader plowed into her, knocking all three of them over the balcony and into the black waters.

Lilja breathed a sigh of relief as the water caressed her skin.

Home.

She opened her eyes, seeing through the dark water clearly. The Scythian struggled to the surface but Hayjen sunk deeper, blood from his back swirling around in crimson streaks.

That wasn't good.

Leviathan could smell blood from hundreds of feet away.

She dove deeper, sucking in a painful breath of water as her lungs closed and her gills opened. Lilja pushed through the transition, reaching Hayjen as her skin began to tingle. The Leviathan were here. Lilja wrapped her arms around the male and lifted her head, her white hair floating in front of her, giving her glimpses of the sleek black bodies circling. Baring her teeth, she hummed a warning tone. One darted in, its sharp white teeth gleaming in the dark water. She snapped her teeth at the beast, causing it to retreat into the circle. Normally they wouldn't dare test a Sirenidae, but when a meal was in sight, they tended to get excited. The largest of the finned creatures faced her and swam until it was within arm's length. The alpha. She met its black eyes and stared it down until its nose dipped. Lilja reached her hand out, allowing the Leviathan the choice to make friends. It eyed her and then bumped its nose into her palm.

Relief washed through her. There wouldn't be a fight for dominance tonight.

The Leviathan turned its attention to the Scythian man fighting the waves above. A series of hums drifted through the water, making the hair on her arms stand up. Their hunting song always gave her chills. Lilja propelled herself and Hayjen to the surface. She braced herself for her first breath. Transitioning from sea breathing to air breathing hurt. Lilja choked and coughed as she expelled water from her lungs. Her chest burned and tears came to her eyes. She shuddered as she coughed more water and began hauling them to the side of the ship where a net swayed.

"Captain! You need to get out of the water now!" Blair shouted, fear tingeing his voice.

Lilja looked over her shoulder at what had caught his attention. The Leviathan were circling the Scythian, taking playful nips. They always liked to play with their food. It was the fins following her, however, that must have caused her first mate's panic. Lilja picked up her pace, ignoring the curious beasts following her. They were probably hoping she would give up her prey.

Not today, beasties.

A soul-shattering scream erupted behind her, making her wince. No one deserved to die like that. The scream cut off in abrupt silence. It was time to get out before a feeding frenzy started. Even she wasn't stupid enough to be in the water when they went crazy. Lilja latched onto the net, desperately holding on to Hayjen. "Pull us up!" she yelled.

Her arms screamed as she clung to the large man. His weight was almost too much to bear, but the sight of the dark creatures now directly below her was all she needed to help maintain her hold on him. Her crew heaved one last time and pulled them over the railing. She coughed up the rest of the sea water and pushed onto her hands and knees.

"Depths below, Captain. You smell so damn good."

Hell. The sea water activated her Lure. What was meant to be a protection for her kind, only caused her trouble. Her poor crew couldn't help but be drawn to her. It was chemistry.

"It's the Lure. Step back and the effect will lessen." She blinked the salt water out of her eyes and glanced over at Hayjen, eyes widening. "Get him off his back!"

Blair dropped to his knees and pressed on the man's chest. "We have to get the water from his lungs first or he won't survive."

Her first mate pushed on his chest over and over before Hayjen's lips sputtered and he spit up water. Blair quickly turned him to his side, blood and sea water pouring everywhere. Hayjen yelled and went limp.

"Is he okay?" she demanded, gaping at his back. It was a bloody mess.

"He's unconscious. We need to get him off this hunk of wood and onto our ship."

Lilja nodded, never taking her eyes off his back. The pain must have been excruciating. *Depths below*, the man had suffered, and all the open flesh had been subjected to the salty sea water. He was lucky he'd passed out. At least that way he'd feel no pain.

Chapter Three
Hayjen

Stars above, his body bloody hurt. He blinked at the colorful bedding beneath his cheek. Where was he? Hayjen moved to get up and yelped, falling back to the bed. He breathed hard as pain and nausea washed through him. That was stupid. He put his nose into the blankets and attempted to breathe through the pain assaulting him. Vaguely, he registered citrus and sea salt.

"What the hell did you do?" a smoky voice asked.

Hayjen jerked painfully, and turned his neck to spot pirate Captain Femi glaring at him.

"You opened your wounds back up," she scolded.

His nose twitched when her green silk dress brushed his nose. How cliché—a pirate wearing silk.

"I heard that, you ungrateful brute."

He had said that out loud? He must be addled. "Sorry."

"Hmmmm..."

Pain bit him. "Damn it, that hurt." What was she doing? Where was Mer?

"Stop being such a sissy, and hold still. You would think I was torturing you or something."

"Then stop poking me."

"I wouldn't be poking you if you hadn't ripped open your wounds."

"Where's Mer?"

"Behave, and I'll tell you. Hold still. I'm putting seaweed on your back."

"Seaweed?" She was talking in circles.

"Among other things."

"Mer?"

"She's fine."

"That's not an answer."

She remained silent as she worked.

Hayjen scowled, guessing that would be the only answer he received. Bloody pirates.

About the Author

If you'd like to know more about me, my books, or to connect with me online, you can visit my webpage https://www.frostkay.net/, check out my Facebook group Frost Fiends, or follow me on Bookbub to receive news about my new releases.

You've just read a book in my AERMIAN FEUDS series. Other books in this series include REBEL'S BLADE, CROWN'S SHIELD, ENEMY'S QUEEN, & SIREN'S LURE.

If you love SCI-FI, THE TWILIGHT ZONE, and ALIENS, check out my MIXOLOGISTS & PIRATES series!

Into DYSTOPIAN and POST APOCALYPTIC? I haves something for you too! Check my DOMINION OF ASH series!

Read More from Frost Kay

www.frostkay.net

Made in the USA
Coppell, TX
29 May 2020

26688804R00215